THE DAY HE STOPPED IN

HAWTHORNE HARBOR SECOND CHANCE
ROMANCE BOOK 2

ELANA JOHNSON

Copyright © 2020 by Elana Johnson

All rights reserved.

No part of this book may be reproduced in any form or by any electronic or mechanical means, including information storage and retrieval systems, without written permission from the author, except for the use of brief quotations in a book review.

ISBN-13: 979-8648250109

1

"I don't want to go," Adam Herrin said, but his best friend would not be deterred.

"Come on," Matt said, that perpetual smile still stuck to his face. "You like the Fall Festival." He nudged him, making Adam slop milk over the side of his cereal bowl. "Besides, you can pretend like you're already on the force. You know, scan for vandals and all that while I find the prettiest girl there and ask her to dance."

Adam grunted and wiped the spilled milk from the countertop of the apartment they shared. He'd been back in Hawthorne Harbor for just over a month, and he'd just finished his final round of police interviews.

"I'm starting work on Monday," he told Matt.

His friend whooped and sent his spoon clattering into his cereal. "You got on? They hired you?"

Adam let a smile spread across his face. "Yeah. I found out last night."

"And you're just now telling me?"

"You were out really late with Bea."

The joy on Matt's face disappeared as if Adam had flipped a switch. "Yeah, well, not tonight."

"You mean we won't be out late?" Adam's heart lifted, as he preferred the early-to-bed, early-to-rise method of living.

"Of course we'll be out late," Matt said. "I just meant not with Bea."

"You don't like her?"

"She's not my type."

Adam pictured the tall, beautiful blonde that he and Matt had grown up with. Both men had gone away to college and then returned to their hometown, and they were both settling back into the social scene of the small, beach-side town of Hawthorne Harbor. Bea Arnold had gone to college too, but only for a couple of years. Just long enough to get an accounting certificate so she could handle the finances of her father's hardware store.

"Well, if she's not, good luck finding someone here," Adam said, picking up his bowl and rinsing it out in the sink.

"There are lots of women here," Matt said, his blue eyes taking on that glint that said Adam wouldn't like was about to come out of his mouth. But he said nothing. Just re-focused on his breakfast.

Adam didn't need a lot of women; he had his eye on one: Janey Burns. He'd known her for as long as he could remember, as she was his younger brother's age. Just a couple of years younger than him, and still single. She'd been back in town for a few months, and she was already putting her Natural Resource Management degree to use at Olympic National Park, just a few minutes away from Hawthorne Harbor.

He'd had a crush on Janey since his junior year of high school. She was beautiful and kind and smart. But she'd had a boyfriend on the football team, and Adam had graduated before her and left town while she still had two years of high school to finish.

But tonight....

He banished the treacherous thought and said, "I'm going to go running."

"Again?" Matt lifted his eyebrows and Adam shook his head and started down the hall to his bedroom to change. "You already got the job!" Matt yelled after him, with a loud bit of laughter coming with it.

Sure, Adam had gotten the entry-level policeman job with the Hawthorne Harbor Police Department. But he wouldn't stay there for long. Oh, no. Adam had plans to climb that ladder until he stood at the top of the department, and that meant he had to maintain his top physical condition.

So he ran. His favored route took him right past Janey's house, which sat near the beach. He told himself it wasn't stalking, because she didn't even live there anymore. Her parents did though, and he waved to her mother as she worked in the rose garden to prepare it for the winter ahead. Though it didn't snow in Hawthorne Harbor, because the town sat right on the northwest edge of the North American continent, it got plenty cold.

Adam loved the cool sea spray in his face as he ran, the homes eventually fading behind him and the cliffs coming into view. High above the water sat the Magleby Mansion, where he'd worked mowing lawns and raking leaves as a teenager.

Without a job to fill his time, Adam spent the day working out and making plans for his first day on the job in just a couple of short days. When Matt knocked on his door and said, "Are you coming?" Adam couldn't wait to get out of the house.

They arrived at the Fall Festival, which took place in the square in downtown Hawthorne Harbor. The shops on Main Street seemed to glow among the twilight as dusk came quicker now that autumn was upon them.

He hunched his broad shoulders and stuck his hands in his pockets, his eyes constantly scanning for danger. Okay, fine. He wasn't looking for danger. Not tonight, at least. He let his mind have a brief fantasy of this time next year, and if he'd be on duty like the two officers he spotted hanging out near the face-painting booth.

The scent of freshly juiced apples hung in the air, along with a heavy dose of cinnamon. Matt brought him a cup of hot apple cider, and Adam wrapped both hands around it, back to searching the crowd for the one woman he wanted to see.

Janey Burns.

Tonight was the night. He was going to ask her to dance, and not just because they'd been old friends. His pulse picked up, and he couldn't make sense of what Matt had said. His friend handed him his plastic cup of cider and pressed through the crowd to an auburn-haired woman Adam couldn't quite remember.

Her name sat on the tip of his tongue, and he watched as Matt smiled and laughed and somehow knew exactly how to causally touch Nina—aha! Nina Goodwin—on the back as they walked out to the dance floor that had been laid over the grass in the park.

A band sat down on the other end, where a temporary stage had been erected. The slow warblings of a ballad filled the air, and Adam turned away from the blissful couples swaying together.

Carved pumpkins glittered with candlelight, and he smiled at their garish faces as he passed. Families were finishing up with the pony rides and petting zoo, and he leaned against a fence post as the day crowd thinned and the evening festivities took over.

A flash of brilliant brown hair the color of unroasted coffee beans caught his eye, and he finally saw Janey squeezing between two people as she headed toward the food booths. A jolt shot through Adam's bones and muscles, somehow kickstarting him into following her.

She was with one of her sisters, and he kept his eye on Anabelle's head, as she stood quite a bit taller than Janey. They stopped for funnel cakes, and he paused as if he were going to get a hot dog.

This is stupid, he told himself as the two women turned. Anabelle looked right at him and so did Janey.

"Hey, Adam," she said, a brilliant smile lighting up her whole face. Adam wanted to bask in the warmth of it for the rest of his life.

He managed to say, "Hey, Janey. Anabelle," but his voice sounded like he was suffering from a bad chest cold. He tried to clear the nerves from his throat and he almost ended up choking.

"Are you heading over to the dance?" he asked.

"Yes," Anabelle said, her eyes sliding down him in an appraising way. "Are you?"

He shrugged as if he wasn't really sure what his evening plans were.

"Why do you have two cups of cider?" Janey asked.

Adam looked dumbly at the red plastic cups he held. "Oh, one's for Matt."

"Matt Germaine?" Anabelle asked, her interest obviously piqued. "I didn't know Matt was back in town." She looked at Adam as if he'd deliberately kept the information from her.

"He's dancin' with...someone," he said.

Anabelle hooked her arm through Janey's and bent her head toward her sister's. They moved away, pressing back through the crowd to the dance floor.

Adam followed, because he didn't have much else to do and well, he wanted to dance with Janey. If he could get her sister off with Matt, Adam might have a chance at more than friendship with the girl he'd been thinking about for eight years.

"See? There he is." Adam gestured with Matt's apple cider toward where he stood on the dance floor, this time a blonde in his arms. Adam once again marveled at the easiness with which Matt did everything. He'd studied mechanical engineering at school while Adam had done a year in the police academy and then three years to get his criminal justice degree.

"What's he doing back?" Anabelle asked.

"He's working for the ferry system," Adam said. "He's their lead engineer. Started last week." He wanted to blurt out that he'd be starting with the police department on Monday, but neither Anabelle nor Janey asked.

They both couldn't seem to tear their eyes from Matt, and Adam frowned. He lifted his drink to his lips and in that brief flash of time, both women slipped away from him and out onto the dance floor.

Janey danced with a man named Clint that Adam recognized from the automotive shop on the edge of town. His mood darkened by the moment as she laughed and spun, her dark locks spraying out behind her when her fourth dance of the night twirled her.

He finished his cider and threw both cups in the trash. It was his turn.

No more sitting on the sidelines, watching.

He'd taken two steps onto the dance floor when the people parted to give him an unobstructed view of Janey. Her face was flushed and her smile captivated him.

A man stepped up to her and half-bowed to her, his hand extended as he asked her to dance. She ducked her head, the flush turning into a full-blown blush as she put her hand in his and they situated themselves for the next slow dance of the evening.

Adam stared, sure he'd be able to ask Janey to dance after Matt finished with her. After all, neither of them had danced more than one song with the same partner.

But the song ended, and Matt kept his hands on Janey's waist. They danced another song, and then one that wasn't even meant for couples as the beat took the music into the rock category.

Adam's feet seemed to have grown roots. He couldn't move them though he desperately wanted to. He couldn't look away either.

So he saw Matt lead Janey off the dance floor, her hand tucked securely into his, and watched them disappear into the night.

FOURTEEN YEARS LATER

Janey Germaine stood in front of her mirror, wondering when the lines around her eyes had gotten so deep. Or when the bags underneath had become some dark.

"Mom!" Her twelve-year-old son yelled from the kitchen, and Janey startled away from her reflection. So much had happened over the past decade and a half, and each line probably had a dozen stories to tell.

So don't be embarrassed by them, she told herself as she exited her bedroom and found Jess standing in the kitchen, the pantry door flung wide in front of him.

"Do we have any blueberry Pop-Tarts?"

"If we do, they'll be in there."

"I don't see them."

"Then we don't have any."

Jess grumbled and frowned and slammed the pantry

door, shaking the old house. She'd bought it the first summer she'd returned to Hawthorne Harbor, fresh out of college and with a job she'd been lucky to get.

She still had the job at Olympic National Park, something she was grateful for every day. She filled a coffee mug as she kept one eye on Jess. He'd started complaining that she watched him too much, so she'd been trying to do it on the sly these days.

"What are you doing after school today?" she asked.

"Don't know," he mumbled.

"I'm off today, and we can get Dixie when the elementary kids get out and go out to the lavender farm." She lifted her mug to her lips and took a sip of the bitter liquid. "I mean, if you want." She didn't want Jess to think she really cared about what he did or who he spent time with. She hoped he wouldn't veto the idea just because she'd suggested it, something that had been happening a lot since he started at the junior high a few weeks ago.

He picked up his backpack and threaded his arms through the straps. "Sure, whatever." He stomped on the end of his skateboard and caught the front of it as it popped up. "Bye."

"Bye," she called after him. "Have a good day!"

She used to drive him to school every day, or her best friend Gretchen would stop by. Both single moms, they'd been watching out for each other for years. But with Gretchen engaged now, and to be married by Christmas,

Janey stared out the window and wondered if she should get back into the dating pool.

Problem was, she didn't even own an appropriate swimming suit for such things. She had no idea who was available in town, or how Jess would take the news of her dating again, or why anyone would be interested in a thirty-seven-year-old woman with a twelve-year-old son and a husband who'd died thirteen years ago.

Everyone had loved Matt. It was always "Matt and Janey," never "Janey and Matt." He had a laugh that could fill the sky with fun, fill her heart with joy, fill anything that needed filling.

She saw so much of him in Jess and she stepped into the living room and ran her fingertips along the top edge of a gold frame. The picture inside showed Matt, with his trademark smile on his face. He sat with a very pregnant Janey at the Silver Lake Lodge, a commercial venue inside the National Park where she worked.

She got one free night at the lodge every year, and that year, she and Matt had used it for their anniversary getaway. Little did anyone know that he'd be dead within four months, drowned and presumed lost at sea after the ferry he'd been on had caught on fire and simultaneously gone up in flames and sank into the bay.

Janey turned away from the picture, wondering if it was time to purge the house of them. She'd lived in this space with Matt for exactly thirteen months before he'd left for work and never came home.

She hadn't been able to move, because the scent of his skin was still in some of his shirts. At least back then. She'd brought Jess home to this house. She loved the neighborhood, and everything about the small cottage spoke of home to her.

Carefully, so she wouldn't break the glass, she pushed the frame face-down. Matt's face no longer watched over the happenings in the house, and Janey paused, trying to find her feelings.

One breath in, and everything was okay. Just fine. Two breaths and a sense of...strangeness flowed over her. By the third breath, she could barely get her lungs to expand from the guilt crushing them.

She lifted the picture frame and stared into the handsome face of her husband, the man who had captivated her that night at the Fall Festival all those years ago. Boy, had her older sister been *maaad*.

Anabelle had apparently had a crush on Matt Germaine for a couple of years, and when he'd barely looked her way, Janey wanted to leave the dance with her sister. After all, she and Anabelle had always been close.

Matt had put a wedge between them for the first six months, and then Anabelle had come to terms with the relationship. Meeting her own husband had certainly helped, and she'd gotten married only two months before Matt's accident. Anabelle had been Janey's biggest support during that time, and then her life had moved on. She had three kids now, and while she stopped by often and called or texted Janey everyday, Janey had learned to rely more on Gretchen if she needed help with rides, homework, or babysitting for Jess.

She stared at the picture, the all-too familiar questions flowing through her mind. Do I have to grieve for him forever? Can I ever love someone else again? Should I start dating again?

Sometimes her life felt absolutely unfair. So unfair that it would be hard to breathe and she'd press her hand against her heart to feel it firing against her ribs. Other times, she existed in the world without a care. The taste of butterscotch in her mouth as she hiked, or the scent of pines as she helped junior rangers earn their badges, as easy as anything.

Most days, she oscillated between the two feelings, and the worst part was she never knew when one would strike or how long it would stay.

She listened to the analog clock in the kitchen tick, waiting waiting waiting for something to happen. What, she wasn't sure, and she turned away from the pictures neatly lined up on the mantle and returned to the kitchen.

Janey got a couple of days off each week, but it usually wasn't Saturday and Sunday. Wednesday seemed to be one of the slowest days at the park, so she had that day off. And usually Mondays as well. Jess didn't seem to mind going out to the Loveland's Lavender Farm, but he'd become surlier and surlier in the past couple of months.

On her days off, she usually went back to bed with her

cat, Princess, as she had a hard-to-break habit of staying up until all hours of the morning reading. With a bowl of chocolate chips and pretzels nearby, no less.

Surprisingly, it wasn't nighttime that haunted her, but the early morning hours just before the sun rose. She imagined the ferries getting prepped and ready for the day and wondered why her mechanical engineer husband had to be on the only ferry that had malfunctioned in the past two decades.

With a piece of toast and a banana in her hand, she retreated to her bedroom to eat and enjoy her second sleep. As she drifted from consciousness to unconsciousness, she wondered how she could meet a man in this town who didn't know everything about her.

Impossible, her hazy mind thought.

Might be easier anyway, she told herself. *Then you won't have to explain everything about Matt.*

∼

THAT AFTERNOON, FRESH FROM HER MORNING NAP, AND showered, and done with the yard work for the season, Janey sat on the front steps, waiting for her son to come home. When he didn't show up by three-ten—his usual arrival time—she started flipping her phone over and over.

Worry ate at her, first in small bites and then in huge, sweeping waves. But she didn't call. Jess didn't like it when she "babied him" by calling if he was ten seconds late. Sure, they'd had a talk about why it was important to be on time, and that he should send a text, even if it was only five minutes.

Five minutes could mean a lot. So many things could happen in five minutes.

Janey glanced both ways down the street, her heart catapulting to the back of her throat when the police cruiser eased around the corner and headed her way. She knew it was Adam Herrin—the Chief of Police himself—just by the way the car stayed right in the middle of the street and came to a simple stop at the end of her driveway.

With the tinted windows, Janey couldn't see into the backseat, and she didn't want to rush the car anyway. If it was an emergency, Adam wouldn't have driven four miles an hour down the street and he wouldn't have gotten out so slowly a moment ago and be stretching his back like he'd been driving for days now.

She'd known Adam Herrin for almost four decades. Her whole life. They'd been friends in elementary school, a relationship which had lasted all the way through high school and into adulthood. Matt had been his best friend, and Adam had been the best man at their wedding.

He opened the back door of the cruiser and Jess got out, his face set into an angry scowl. Adam said something to him and Jess nodded before he marched up the driveway to where Janey sat on the porch.

"What's going on?" she asked.

"He took my board," Jess said, taking the steps two at a time and disappearing into the house with a slam of the front door.

Janey flinched, a sigh leaking from her body as Adam popped the trunk on his cruiser and extracted Jess's skateboard. He came up the driveway and sidewalk too, his broad shoulders and mirrored sunglasses so police-like Janey stood and straightened her hair.

Don't be ridiculous, she thought. This was Adam. He'd seen her at her worst, all red-eyed and leaking from everywhere after Matt had died. It had been Adam who'd come to get her, to tell her about the fire. Adam who'd driven her to the dock. Adam who'd held her hand, and kept her close, and helped her stand when it was declared the ferry was a total loss.

Adam who'd stayed on her couch that night, listening to her sob and then dealing with a three-month-old Jess when he screamed and fussed in the middle of the night.

"Afternoon, Janey," he said in that deep, delicious voice of his. He'd sang in the high school choir, and now she imagined that no one dared to disobey a voice as powerful as his.

She sighed as she looked at him, something...odd firing in her. *What was that?* Her stomach felt like it had been flipped over and she had the strangest urge to reach up and trace her fingers along Adam's three-thirty shadow. He'd no doubt shaved that morning, but he'd started shaving when he was fourteen and it was a constant battle to have smooth skin.

She marveled at the maturity of him and a realization hit her square in the chest. *He's your age. And single.*

Her heart started beating irregularly, and she wasn't sure if it was because of the attractive silver she saw in his beard and hair, or if the sunglasses he wore made him so attractive, or if she was losing her mind.

Because Adam Herrin?

He'd never been on her romantic radar.

But it sure was screaming a warning at her right now.

"You okay, Janey?" he asked.

She pressed one hand over her heart, willing it to calm down, while she shoved her phone in her back pocket. "Yeah, fine." She took the skateboard from him and sank back to the steps. "Why'd you bring Jess home?"

"Oh, there was a little trouble at the skate park." He exhaled like he carried the weight of the world and Janey glanced at him, the word *trouble* bouncing around between her eardrums.

"Sit down," she said. "Rough day?"

"Sort of." He positioned himself next to her, and she got blasted with the scent of his cologne. Fresh, and beachy, and minty, she wondered if she could sprinkle some on her sheets and fall asleep with such a delectable smell in her nose.

"Is Jess in trouble?" She focused on her son, trying to figure out where all these traitorous thoughts about Adam were coming from. Jess was who mattered. Jess who'd been brought home by the Chief of Police himself.

"I know he didn't do it, but he's not sayin' who did." Adam gazed out across the front yard she'd just finished mowing and getting ready for the winter. She hoped she wouldn't have to do much more before the spring. Though she loved being and working outdoors, sometimes shouldering everything alone took its toll.

"What happened?" she asked, wishing she were as even and calm as Adam always was. She'd literally never seen the man get upset.

"There was some vandalism on the back of the building that borders the skate park," Adam said, finally swinging his attention to her. He took off his sunglasses, and wow, had his eyes always been that particular shade of brown? One step above black, liquid, and deep. Janey lost herself for a moment, quickly coming back to attention when he continued with, "And Jess was there, a spray paint can only a few feet from his backpack."

"He—he didn't say he wasn't going to skate park today." She wondered who he'd been with. "I was going to take him and Dix out to your brother's farm."

Adam looked at her steadily, and dang if that didn't make her pulse riot a little harder. "It looked like they'd been there a while, Janey."

"But school just got out, and—oh." She let her hands fall between her knees. "You think he skipped school."

"At least fourth period," Adam said. "He wouldn't say

anything to me." He cast a glance over his shoulder. "Which isn't normal for him. Everything okay here, at home? You're not...." He cleared his throat and for the first time, Janey saw a blip of discomfort steal across his face. "Datin' anyone new or switching jobs or anything that could disrupt his normal schedule?"

Dating anyone new. Dating anyone new?

Janey threw her head back and laughed.

2

Adam had no idea what he'd said that was so darn funny. But Janey couldn't stop laughing. Just when she started to quiet, she'd look at him again and dissolve into more giggles. After several seconds, Adam smiled, the infectious nature of her laughter too much to ignore.

Oh, how he loved the sound of her voice. He wished he could erase the stiffness in her shoulders and the worry from her eyes. If she'd ever given him any indication that his presence in her life as more than a friend would be welcome, he'd do it. But she'd been as closed off to men since Matt died as anyone he'd ever known.

"Nothing's changed," she finally said when she could stop laughing. "I have the same schedule I've had for five years, since I was promoted." She added a smile to the statement that left Adam concentrating on what should be an involuntary function: breathing.

"And I'm not dating anyone."

Do you want to start dating? He swallowed the thought and said, "Maybe it's just the hormones," instead.

Janey moaned and swatted his bicep. Was that flirting? The sign he'd been hoping for? The touch was so light and so quick, he had no idea.

"Don't tell me I have to deal with that already," she said.

"He's in seventh grade," Adam said. "I guarantee his brain's already fallen out of his head. It's probably rollin' around under his bed."

She laughed again, and this time Adam joined his chuckle to hers. "He's a good kid," he said. "I told him he needs to be careful who he chooses to hang around with. Even if he's not the one doin' anything, people can get the wrong idea about him just by who he's with."

Janey cut him a nervous look. "Who was he with?"

"A couple of older boys I couldn't see as they ran off. The Fenniman twins, who are also in seventh grade and not bad kids." Adam shrugged, not wanting to alarm Janey too badly. He knew she was a huge worrywart already, and while he would like to thump Jess on the noggin for causing worry for his mom, the boy hadn't actually done anything yet.

"Will you keep an eye on him?" Janey asked, peering at him now with those intoxicating eyes. He was a sucker for those big brown eyes of hers, and he found himself nodding. While technically, it was his job to keep an eye on everything, he could spare a few minutes every day for Jess. For Janey.

"So are you excited about the planning weekend?" she asked.

Adam blinked at her. "The what?"

She gazed right back at him. "You're the best man for Drew and Gretchen's wedding, right?"

Adam's mind whirred, trying to find the missing piece of the puzzle for this line of questioning. "Yes," he said slowly.

"I'm the matron of honor. Gretchen and Drew are taking everyone in the wedding party for a weekend at the beach, but we all know it's just to help them plan." She flashed one of her brilliant smiles. In her tan face, the contrast of her white teeth really stood out. "I'm thinking I won't even bring my bathing suit. Gretchen will have me poring over magazines and then patterns to find her perfect dress."

Adam got stuck on "bathing suit" and what that might entail for Janey. "When is this weekend?"

"End of September. Cutting it really close, if you ask me." She stood like she'd go inside and see what Jess had gotten up to. "I mean, if they want a Christmas wedding, that only leaves three months for all the preparations."

"As I recall, you and Matt got married after a short engagement." He stood too, not quite sure why he'd said anything about Matt. Though it had been almost twelve years since his death, the way Janey's face blanked, and the way she swallowed, meant his fantasies of asking her out would remain exactly that: a figment of his imagination.

"Just three months from him asking to you saying 'I do', same as Gretchen, right?" Why was he still talking? And who would remember that? He cleared his throat. "I'll keep an eye out for Jess." He started to walk away, unable to look at Janey's beautiful, horrified face for another moment.

He flipped his sunglasses back into place, a shield between him and the rest of the world. Once behind the safety of his tinted windows, and with the air conditioner running, he dared to glance back to Janey's porch. She still stood there, watching him, a peculiar look on her face. He couldn't place what it was, but he stared at her too, memorizing the confusion and the...hope? Was that hope?

She turned and climbed the stairs, and Adam headed back to his office at the police station. He pulled down the current Rubix cube he worked whenever his thoughts got too wrinkled and he needed to iron them flat.

While his fingers worked the rows and columns, and his mind sorted through the colors and what needed to go where, he freed up other important brain waves that could focus on the things that eluded him.

He had nineteen solved Rubix cubes in a variety of sizes and colorations, all in a row on the shelf behind his desk. Ten of them had been solved while he worked on particularly difficult cases as a beat cop and then a detective. A few while he debated whether he should leave Hawthorne Harbor and complete the FBI training—which he'd ultimately done. And a few more over the four years he'd been Chief of Police.

One after Anita had left him and he didn't leave the office for days on end. This one, he suspected, would be devoted to Janey and his rotating thoughts as he tried to figure out what to do about her.

And a beach weekend? How in the world had he missed that?

All the green squares lined up and he turned the Rubix cube over to find the other side a complete array of colors. He set the puzzle down and picked up his phone to call his brother.

"Drew," he said when he answered. "I just talked to Janey and she mentioned something about a beach weekend? How come I don't know anything about this?"

His brother started laughing, and Adam didn't appreciate the gesture for the second time that day. "I told you about this weeks ago," Drew said. "You said you'd clear your schedule."

Adam looked down at his desk calendar. He flipped the calendar from August to September, and sure enough, he'd reserved the third weekend in September for "personal vacation."

He sighed. "I swear I don't remember talking about it."

"That's because I brought over a half dozen of those cookies you like. You'd have agreed to anything."

Adam scoffed while Drew chuckled. "I do remember the cookies." And the four miles he'd put on the beach the next morning to get rid of the cookies. At least he still enjoyed running to the sound of the ocean waves coming ashore.

"Has something come up?" Drew asked. "You can make it, can't you?"

"Janey made it sound like you guys had disguised a weekend of work by taking us to the beach."

The silence on the other end of the line confirmed it, and Adam glanced up as his lieutenant poked his head into the office. "I have to go." He hung up before Drew could say anything else and asked, "What's up, Jason?"

Lieutenant Zimmerman came in and sat on the couch in front of Adam's windows. "Kristin wants you to come for dinner on Friday night." He wore a placid look, but Adam knew what a dinner invitation at the Zimmerman's house meant. On the weekend, no less.

"Who else did she invite?" he asked.

"She wouldn't say."

Adam swiped the Rubix cube from his desk and started twisting like he could wring Jason's neck the same way. "I don't need to be set up."

"It's been months since Anita."

He gave Jason a dark look. "I know how long it's been."

"You're grouchy when you're not dating."

Adam didn't know what to say to that, especially since Jason probably took the most flack from Adam's bad moods. He minded the least though, if the twinkle in his eyes was any indication.

"So just come." He stood and knocked twice on the doorjamb. "She's making that Brazilian steak you like." He walked out of the office, and Adam decided he couldn't spend the next hour doing paperwork or sitting at his desk. He rarely could contain himself behind walls if it wasn't absolutely necessary, which was why he'd been driving by the skate park at the exact right moment that afternoon.

He stopped at his secretary's desk when she lifted her hand to get his attention. Sarah held the phone receiver to her ear and said, "Yes, thank you, Beth."

Adam's heart skipped a beat. Beth Yardley was the director of the Fall Festival, and he'd been after her to find out the topic for this year's cook-off. "It better not be chili again," he said, the anticipation of what the culinary topic would be making his muscles tight.

Sarah sighed as she replaced the receiver and met Adam's glare head-on. She'd been a familiar face at the station for two decades—longer than him—and he appreciated her candor when he needed it, the fresh flowers on her desk in the summer, and the poinsettias at Christmastime.

She brought pastries for birthdays, and kept everything in the department running.

"Soups," she finally said.

Adam growled and smashed his hat on his head. "I'm

going to patrol something." He stalked out, his mind ping-ponging from Janey and the upcoming beach weekend and the half-dozen soup recipes he could try before entering the Fall Festival with something that could win.

After last year's chili debacle, he needed something to re-establish his street cred as the tough, no-nonsense Chief of Police—who also happened to be a genius in the kitchen.

3

Janey found Jess in his bedroom, earbuds in, staring at his phone. All she had to do was hold out her hand, and he turned over his device. She stuck it in her back pocket without looking at it.

"What happened?" she asked.

"Nothing," he said, sitting on the bed.

"Did you skip school?"

"Just last period, and it's dumb anyway."

"What's last period?" Janey wanted to tell him that he had to go to school whether he thought it was dumb or not. She'd attended many college classes she found little value in. Matt had too.

"PE. He lets the kids do whatever after we run if we stay on the field, and the skate park is right by the school."

In fact, the junior high fields were just through a chain

link fence to the skate park. It was practically the same lot. "Did you do the running?"

"Yes."

She sighed. "Why did Chief Herrin have to bring you home then?"

Jess's dark eyes stormed, and Janey hardly recognized her son. "There were some guys spray painting on the building. But it wasn't me, Mom. I swear."

At least he'd told her. Adam had said he couldn't get anything out of Jess. "I believe you." She stood. "Come on. Do you still want to go get Dixie and go out to the farm?"

He got up and Janey noticed how tall he'd gotten. How gangly. How skinny. She brushed his hair off his forehead and for a moment, she saw the hint of her little boy. This almost-teenager was still her Jess. Her son. Almost a clone of Matt if not for Janey's softer jaw and lighter eyes.

"Sorry, Mom." He hugged her, and Janey held on tight-tight, hoping he'd always come to her when he had problems.

"You can talk to me, you know." She pulled back and looked into his eyes. "About stuff."

"I know."

"I'm going to look at everything on your phone."

"I know."

"Nothing going on there? You're being responsible with what you say and what you're looking at?"

"Yes, Mom." His tone suggested an eye-roll, so Janey just nodded. She'd look and then she'd know anyway.

"All right. Let's go."

Forty minutes later, Dixie spilled from the backseat of Janey's Jeep, still jabbering about her day. Jess went with her, and after Dixie unceremoniously dumped her backpack on the front porch of the white farmhouse, they ran off into the lavender fields behind it.

Janey smiled, a thought flashing through her mind. She pulled out her phone and sent Adam a text. *He said he did see those kids spray painting, but that it wasn't him.*

I'm glad he told you. Adam's text came back quickly, and she wondered where he was, what he was doing, if maybe he'd like to come out to the lavender farm and talk face-to-face with her. But she wasn't going to ask him that.

Thank you for brining him home. She bit her bottom lip, wondering what to do with the weird, skippy pulse in her chest. She'd already asked Adam to keep an eye on Jess. That should've been enough. But strangely, Janey wanted to see Adam again. Hear his voice. He exuded comfort to her, like wrapping herself in a warm blanket.

She searched her mind for something she could ask him, anything to keep this conversation going. *Are you getting ready for the Fall Festival?*

Gretchen appeared on the porch, her gaze clearly asking when Janey would be coming in. She lifted her hand to say *Just a sec* and stared at her phone.

Getting the department ready, yes. Have you heard what the topic is for the cook-off?

Nope. She smiled just thinking about what he'd make

this year. Adam entered the Fall Festival cook-off every year, and he'd won five times in the past decade alone. Last year he'd lost by less than half a point, and Janey had never seen him so crestfallen.

Soups.

Oh, I bet you're good at that.

Not really. But I guess it's better than chili. What's your favorite soup?

French onion.

French onion? Really? Fascinating.

She giggled as if she were flirting with him. Which was ridiculous. She hadn't flirted with a man in ages. And this was *Adam.*

What's fascinating about that? She got out of the Jeep and started toward the porch, determined not to text away the whole afternoon with Adam. After all, he wasn't her boyfriend.

Her phone buzzed in her hand, but she ignored it as she hugged Gretchen. "Hey," she said. "Not working today?"

"I've got Suzie in the shop two afternoons a week now." She turned and went in the farmhouse. "It's nice to have a few hours to get things done."

Her fiancé, Drew, sat on the couch, his phone a few inches from his face.

"Do you need glasses?" she asked, about a dozen other questions piling up in her mind. He looked like a lighter version of Adam, and she realized she had access to a source about the man she hadn't been able to stop thinking about for an hour now. Was he dating anyone? Would he be interested in her? Why hadn't he ever gotten married? He was successful in his career, smart, kind, a good cook, extremely good-looking.... So what was wrong with him?

"Yeah, I might." Drew dropped his phone and looked at her. "Jess out back?"

"Yeah, I sent him with Dixie."

"I'll go see if they want to go out to the wishing well." He stood, and Janey lifted her hand.

"Adam brought him home today."

Drew paused, his eyes searching Janey's. Gretchen joined him, a united front against Janey. "Why'd he do that?" she asked.

"I guess he was with some kids at the skate park that were vandalizing a building. It wasn't Jess, but...." Janey sighed. "Maybe just see if Jess says anything about it and let me know?"

Drew's surprise melted away. "Sure thing. He's a great kid, Janey."

She nodded and Drew left, and Gretchen moved into the kitchen. "You want some lemonade?" She pulled out the pitcher and got down two glasses.

Janey sat at the bar and accepted the glass of lemonade Gretchen pushed her away. She picked a pink straw from the assortment presented to her and looked at Gretchen.

"What if I was interested in dating again?"

Gretchen choked and slopped lemonade over the side of her glass. She wiped her mouth and goggled at Janey. "You've got to give me some warning."

Janey smiled and shook her head as Gretchen turned to get a towel to wipe up the mess. She took a peek at her phone and found Adam's response. It's so sophisticated. I mean, not that you're not sophisticated. I guess I just figured you'd like something more rustic. Like what they serve at the lodge. Beef stew. Or clam chowder.

I do like clam chowder, she typed out as Gretchen sat beside her.

"You're texting him?"

Janey didn't look up as she finished her text. And they serve French onion at the lodge. That's where I first fell in love with it.

"What are you talking about?"

Janey waited to send the message. "Soup. It's the theme for the Fall Festival cook-off."

Gretchen sipped her lemonade, one eye still on the text. "Soups, huh? Seems like Adam could win that pretty easily."

Janey's stomach tossed and turned. "Am I crazy if I want to go out with Adam?" By the time she finished speaking, her voice had dropped to a whisper. She tilted the phone so Gretchen could easily read the texts. "Should I ask him if he wants to come up to the lodge and try the French onion soup?"

Her whole face heated in the few seconds it took for Gretchen to read the brief text exchange. She lifted her lemonade and gulped it, trying to cool off.

"You both grew up here," Gretchen said. "It would be easy to invite him up to the lodge without making it sound like a date. Then you can feel him out."

Nothing Adam had ever said or done had ever sent Janey the message that he was interested in her. In anyone, really. Not that she'd really paid that much attention to him and his dating habits, who he went out with, or anything to do with his love life.

She sent what she'd already typed out and continued with *You should come up to the lodge and try it. It's good.*

She showed it to Gretchen. "Good?"

"Totally good. It's not an invitation to eat it with you."

"I work at the lodge."

"No, you work as a ranger at the lodge."

Janey rolled her eyes. "Same thing. I'm on the premises." Janey worked with guests at the lodge one day a week, giving tours of the nearby forests and the lake. She taught environmental classes and took groups out to the tallest trees in the Olympic National Forest.

As part of her job, she also collected samples, both water and organic, kept track of the wildlife in the park, and wrote reports on the impact of humans on the environment. She loved her work at the lodge, and she'd put in many years working information desks before she'd been promoted to more of a environmentalist and researcher than a ranger who worked with the public.

When's a good time?

She read Adam's text out loud and looked at Gretchen with wide eyes. "What—? How do I respond to that?"

Gretchen laughed and swiped Janey's phone from her. "You've been out of the dating game for a while. Let me." Her fingers flew over the screen, and Janey thought she'd at least get to preview the message before Gretchen sent it. But nope. She touched her thumb down in the bottom right corner of the screen, and said, "There," before handing the phone back.

Janey's heart bumped and thumped as she read. The lodge is open seven days a week for lunch and dinner. If you wanted to eat with me, I'll have to consult my schedule.

She blinked, sure the words hadn't been ordered properly. "Gretchen," she said, a slight whine in her voice as her phone buzzed again.

I want to eat with you. When's a good time to do that?

The breath left her body. Her fingers didn't seem capable of holding her phone any longer, because they dropped it. "He's just being friendly," she said. "It doesn't mean anything."

Gretchen picked up the phone and read the message. "It is hard to get the true feeling in a text. If you could see him, see his eyes, hear his voice, then you'd know."

"Know what?"

"If he was interested in going out with you as friends, or as more."

More.

The word haunted Janey for the rest of the afternoon and well into the evening. She still hadn't answered Adam by the time she sent Jess to bed and then changed into her pajamas. Her book called to her, as did the snack mix she kept concealed in the top drawer of her nightstand. Her nightly ritual of reading and snacking on pretzels and chocolate chips had been disrupted by her churning thoughts.

"Just tell him," she said. "Get it over with. Silence the phone. Read until you fall asleep." Her usual routine anyway, minus the texting with a handsome man she'd been friends with her whole life.

I don't work Wednesdays or Mondays, she typed out. *I'm not usually at the lodge during dinner either, but we can go back up one night if you want.*

Surely he didn't want to. He worked long hours, and she imagined him to be the kind of man who went home to his dogs and his kitchen, happy to have a couple of hours to himself before falling asleep.

How about Friday night?

Her heart fell right to the bottom of her feet.

Friday night was date night. So he must not have a girlfriend. But what about Jess? She couldn't just leave her son home alone at night. Completely out of her league as to what to do, Janey fired off a text to Gretchen to find out what she should do.

It seemed to take forever for her friend to answer, but when she did, Gretchen had said *Call him. You'll know then.*

"Call him?" Janey's voice sounded like she'd inhaled helium.

Taking a deep breath, she navigated back to Adam's text chain and pressed the phone icon at the top of the screen.

4

Adam stared at his phone as it rang once, then twice. Then reason took over and he swiped on the call from Janey. "Hey," he said, his voice gruffer than he meant it to be. He cleared his throat, wishing he'd thought further ahead than a greeting. The texting had been going well. He could ask her out easily that way. But talking to her? His heart danced in his chest like it was trying to tango it's way out. And his brain seemed to have decided a vacation was in order.

"Hey," she said. "So I thought it might be easier to just call."

"All right." How that was easier, he wasn't sure. He reminded himself he was nearly forty years old and could certainly talk to a woman.

"So when you say Friday night, you mean like a date? And do you want me to bring Jess, or should I get someone to stay with him?" The words poured out of her in a rush, and he couldn't tell from the tone of her voice if a date with him was desirable or disgusting.

"Jess can come." He pressed his eyes closed, wishing he hadn't said that. He liked Jess a lot. Just looking at him was like looking at Matt. Was Adam selfish to want some time alone with Janey? Without a reminder of her late husband and his best friend?

"Or we can just go. It's up to you." He didn't want to make things hard for her. He'd spent the last twelve years since Matt's death trying to make everything in her life easier.

Is that why you've never acted on your decades-old feelings? The thought had just enough time to flood his mind before she said, "Oh, Jess hates the food at the lodge. He loves the lake and the forest, but I can't get him to eat there."

"So just me and you." Adam's hopes pinged around the living room like he'd just won the lottery.

"On Friday night." The way she drew out the words made them seem like a question.

Adam took a deep breath and decided to lay a card or two on the table. "You can call it a date if you want," he said. "Or not. I'll follow your lead on that."

Several long beats of silence filled his ears. Then her musical voice said, "I'll let you know on Friday night."

He chuckled, not really caring what label she put on the

meal. The fact was, he had a scheduled activity with a woman —*not just any woman*, his mind screamed—on Friday night. No more frozen pizzas because he was too tired to cook by the end of the week. No more sitting on the couch while whatever sport happened to be in season played on the television.

They said good-bye, and Adam relaxed into the couch, a smile on his face that he couldn't wipe away.

The next day found him directing traffic while the public works department repaired a stop light near the junior high. He wore the neon green vest and waved his arms like he was bringing in military airplanes, not making sure men and women could get to work and the grocery store.

With such a mundane chore, he was free to think through some things. As if he hadn't spent most of the night doing that as well. He'd promised Matt he'd look after Janey and Jess if anything happened to him.

Adam could remember the conversation as clearly as if it had happened yesterday. Matt and Janey were three days away from saying "I do" and Matt and Adam had gone to Seattle with a few other friends. Not really a bachelor party, as Matt liked to have a good time, but not with women and alcohol.

They'd gone bowling and seen three science fiction action movies and headed out on a friend's sailboat.

Before anyone else had arrived, Matt and Adam had gone to dinner, and Matt had made Adam promise to take care of Janey and any family he might have if he should pass away.

Adam felt the same confusion now, waving a blue minivan through the intersection, as he had then.

"What makes you think something's going to happen?" he'd asked.

"I don't think that." Matt had eaten an entire order of fried cheese by himself. The man loved junk food, and Adam made the fried cheese sticks every year on the anniversary of his friend's death.

"Then where is this coming from?"

"You know Janey," Matt said. "I just want to make sure someone's there, taking care of things if something happens to me."

So Adam had promised. The other men had shown up soon after that, and the weekend had continued as normal.

But when Matt died only a year later, Adam couldn't help wondering if Matt really had known something. Felt something. A premonition, perhaps. It didn't matter. Adam had promised him he'd take care of Janey, and he had.

Every time he asked if she needed something, she said no. So he'd stopped asking in the first six months. After that, he simply took a meal, a package of diapers, or a gift card to the superstore over to her house and left it on the front porch.

As Jess grew, the offerings Adam had left changed too.

A scooter on the boy's fifth birthday. A baseball bat and mitt and ball on his eighth. He thought he'd done a decent job acting surprised whenever Jess or Janey told him about the gifts left by their "anonymous angel," as Janey had been calling him for a decade.

His chest tightened. If he was going to have a real relationship with her, he'd have to tell her he was the angel. Tell her about the promise he'd made to Matt. Tell her about his crush on her in high school—and beyond.

Are you ready to do that?

He wasn't sure, but he knew one thing: He was ready to do something different. He preached to his men about not passing judgment on those they came in contact with. That everyone had bad days and everyone made stupid decisions sometimes. That there was always the chance to fix things, do better the next day, try something new.

His phone buzzed in his front pocket, and he finished motioning a stream of cars through the intersection before checking it.

Trent, one of his officers, had said, Sarah wants to know what you want for lunch from the Anchor.

His stomach growled, and he wondered how much longer the public works guys needed to get this stoplight working.

"The whole ham," he dictated into his phone while waving one arm to get a red sedan to keep moving. "With those vinegar chips." He could put in an extra ten minutes on the beach tomorrow morning. The dogs never minded, and Adam sure did love a bag of vinegar chips.

He didn't really care if he gained weight or not. It was public perception that mattered. And the people of Hawthorne Harbor wanted a Chief of Police that was big, brawny, and bold. Adam was determined to be the man the citizens wanted him to be; he would not let them down if there ever came a time when he needed to use his physicality to keep someone safe.

"Twenty more minutes," one of the public works men yelled from his position next to the utility truck.

Adam nodded to show he'd heard, deciding all this arm-waving counted as the additional exercise he needed to eat vinegar chips.

~

"Come on, guys," he said the following morning. Friday morning. Which meant Friday night was only a few short hours away. He cleared the smile from his face. "Trent wants you with the crew today." The dogs jumped into the cruiser, filling the entire back seat.

Gypsy, the golden retriever, tried to stick her nose through the metal mesh while Fable, the husky, sat on the seat and stared at Adam with his keen, blue eyes.

Trent had secured the funding to start a K9 unit in Hawthorne Harbor, and he sometimes wanted the four German Shepherds he was training to have other dogs in the pack. Gypsy loved the added social time with the canines. Fable...not so much. He whined as Adam navigated toward the police station and parked around the block so he could take the dogs into the fenced yard.

Gypsy paced at the gate while Adam tugged on Fable's leash. "You'll like it," he told the husky. "Just don't be so standoffish." But it was in the husky's nature to stare down other dogs and then snap if one got too close.

Adam had explained all this to Trent, but he still wanted Fable to come socialize with the other dogs. It was definitely more for them than Fable, though Adam thought it was good for his husky to realize he wasn't the only dog on the planet. Maybe the most handsome, but definitely not the only canine worth having around.

Unlatching the gate, Adam waited while Gypsy streaked inside, her tail wagging her whole body. He took Fable in too and unlatched the leash. "Go on." The husky started forward, almost like he wanted to see the other dogs. Adam lifted his hand to wave to Trent, who returned the gesture. The gate slammed closed, and Fable jumped and barked.

Gypsy ran in circles around the four German shepherds, who all sat. Two of them had their tongues hanging out, and the other two had tails going *bang bang bang!* against the ground.

Trent made a noise and the shepherds released from their poised position. Gypsy barked and all but one of the shepherds herded around her. The other one—the largest

—came over to Fable and started sniffing him. A low growl started in Fable's throat, and Adam snapped his fingers.

Trent came over, and Adam said, "Maybe you can train him up."

"Huskies are a little finicky." Trent shook Adam's hand. "But look at the shepherds. They all sat there and waited. And they like other dogs."

Adam had not been trained in training dogs as part of his education. They didn't have a huge drug problem in Hawthorne Harbor, or other reasons to have a fully trained police dog. "So show me something they can do."

Trent looked at him, an eagerness in his face Adam appreciated. "Wilson's the best one," he said.

"Which one's that?"

"He's the pack leader." Trent pointed. "The one who went straight to Fable." The German shepherd still hovered near Fable, his happy face inviting Fable to just relax and start to play.

"So I'll put on the suit." Trent walked away before Adam could inquire further about the suit and what that might mean. Trent returned wearing a canvas-colored suit that made him look three times as big as usual.

He whistled through his teeth and all four dogs came over to him, their desire to work obvious in their sharp eyes. "Wilson," he said. He lifted his arm until it was level with his shoulder and continued with a sharp command in another language Adam didn't understand, and the dog ran and leapt at Trent. The dog's teeth landed right in the middle of Trent's forearm, causing the man to stumble backward.

He stayed upright, but the other dogs started to bark. He said something else and Wilson released, falling back into line with the other dogs. Another one inched forward, a whine in the back of his throat.

"Wow," Adam said. "That was amazing."

"They can find things too," Trent said. "We're still working on all of it."

"What language are you using?"

"Danish." He shook his arm, though there was no way the dog's teeth could've penetrated it. "Hey, what are you doin' tonight? A few of us are going down to the beach for a little barbeque before it gets too cold."

Sounded like just something Adam would do. At least his friends didn't seem too worried about his position as Chief of Police—the reason he'd finally gotten from Anita about why she'd broken up with him.

"The relationship was too public," she'd said. Adam mentally scoffed just thinking about it. Yes, he was a public figure. Sat on the City Council. Everyone knew his face. And she didn't want to be held to the same standard.

Adam didn't quite believe her. There was something else about him she didn't like, and she was using his job as an excuse.

"Adam?" Trent asked. "Tonight?"

"Oh, right." He shook his head. "I can't. I have a...a

date." He wasn't sure how Janey was quantifying their dinner tonight, but in Adam's mind, it was a date.

"Oh, yeah?" Trent grinned at him. "Who are you goin' out with?"

Adam balked, his voice suddenly mute.

"I see how it is." Trent shook his head. "You don't have to say."

"It's just a little early," Adam said. Especially because he wasn't even sure how Janey was classifying their dinner that evening. He realized now he shouldn't have said anything. He should've just said he couldn't make it to the beach and left it alone.

The door slammed, and Adam looked up to find himself alone in the yard with six dogs, one of which was a husky whose growl indicated he really didn't want to be there.

5

Janey could barely focus at work. Luckily, she wasn't working with any groups today—those usually happened on the weekends, when the lodge was fully booked. She worked in her office on the main floor of the lodge, tucked behind the reception desk.

Music filtered into the room from the speakers set into the ceiling, and the whole place smelled like pine trees. But she couldn't focus on the report she was supposed to be reading about the reintroduction of the char that had once been native to the lake just a few hundred yards from the lodge.

"Heya."

Janey yelped and spun from her desk to find Maya standing in the doorway. "Oh." She pressed her palm against her heartbeat. "You scared me."

Maya giggled and bounced into the office. She sat

down in the chair opposite of Janey, her black, curly hair still springing once she'd settled. "You're still reading that memo about the char?"

Janey slapped her hand over it. "Yes. No. I'm...." She didn't know how to finish, and she exhaled with a small laugh. "Distracted today." She'd wanted to text Gretchen until she figured everything out, but Gretchen was way too close to Adam for Janey's comfort. She'd asked her friend not to say anything to Drew, but the man was Gretchen's fiancé. Neither of them should be caught inside Janey's insanity, so she'd been on her own.

And she'd obsessed all day yesterday about texting Adam. Should she? Was that too eager? But if she didn't, was that being rude? Was it conveying some silent message to him that she wasn't excited about their dinner that evening?

It wasn't even dinner. More of a soup tasting.

"Why so distracted?" Maya asked, reaching for the package of gum on Janey's desk. "Can I?"

"Sure, yeah." Janey looked at Maya, oscillating between spilling everything and keeping her mouth shut. She'd worked with Maya for about six years, and the two were good friends. "Can I ask you something?"

Maya leaned forward and nodded, her mouth full of gum.

"So if you were coming up to the lodge with a man tonight, would you consider that a date?"

Maya blinked and glanced over her shoulder to the open doorway. "Depends on who the man is."

That was what Janey had thought too. When she'd come to the lodge with Matt, it was a date. She didn't have anyone else to reference, and part of Janey liked that and part of her surely didn't.

"So who is it?" Maya asked.

"Adam Herrin." Janey's heart skipped a beat just thinking about the man.

Maya sucked in a breath and her eyes rounded. She started nodding, her curls bouncing with the movement. "If a woman goes to dinner with Adam Herrin, it's a date."

"I've known him my whole life. Like, my *entire* life."

"So what?" Maya cocked her head like she really didn't understand.

"He's my friend."

"So how did the dinner come about?"

Janey told Maya about it, and then said, "And I can't decide if this is a date or not."

"So the real question is, do you *want* this to be a date?"

Before Janey could answer, Maya's phone rang and she squealed as she saw who was calling. "It's Aaron. I'll catch you later." She answered as she left Janey to decide if she wanted her soup tasting with Adam to be a date.

She hadn't decided when it was time to go home. Nor when she took Jess out to the Loveland's where he'd spend the night with Joel and Donna, Adam's parents. If that wasn't ironic, Janey wasn't sure was.

His mother worked in the kitchen when they arrived, and she turned as Jess entered. "There he is." She beamed at him. "I hope you're ready for this." She gestured to the recipe book sitting on the counter.

"What are you guys making today?" Janey asked, hoping to keep the conversation away from her and why she needed a babysitter. When she'd called Donna yesterday morning, all she'd said was she needed someone to watch Jess tonight, and Donna had offered for Jess to sleep over.

Janey had taken it, because she had no idea how long her...outing with Adam would last, and this way, she didn't have to explain anything to Jess.

"Pumpkin pancakes," Donna said, beaming at Jess. "Did you know your son loves anything with pumpkin in it?"

Janey tousled Jess's head as he grinned. "Yeah, he gets that from his dad." She sucked in a breath, wishing not every single thing about her life reminded her of her husband.

"We need three eggs from the coops." Donna smiled at Jess, and he practically ran from the back door. She chuckled after him and asked, "So where are you going tonight?"

"Oh, uh, just up to the lodge," Janey said, swallowing past the hitch in her voice.

Donna turned back to the fridge. "Adam said he was going up there too."

Janey almost choked, but she managed to turn the noise into a cough. "What did Adam say?"

Donna barely glanced over her shoulder. "Said he was meeting a friend."

"Oh, that sounds fun. That's what I'm doing too." A nervous giggle escaped her lips and she wiped her hands down her thighs. "I better go." She made a hasty escape, sighing once she made it out of the farmhouse.

Then her anxiety turned to getting home before Adam arrived to pick her up. Turned out, he was already sitting in the driveway when Janey pulled her Jeep in beside him. She was glad she'd done her hair before taking Jess out to the lavender farm.

Adam straightened from his police cruiser and gave her a long look, a smile pulling at the corners of his mouth. "You look great."

Janey could barely remember how to breathe. Adam Herrin had never told her she looked nice. He'd been friendly, sure. But this felt...that statement...everything was like this was a date.

He wore a dark pair of slacks and a dark green shirt, not his usual police uniform. He was stunning and magnificent, and Janey's mouth felt like someone had stuffed it with cotton balls.

She'd felt like this with Matt, that night at the Fall Festival. Could she have similar feelings for Adam, now, all these years later? How had she never seen him before?

"So compliments are bad," he said, the smile slipping from his face.

"What?"

"I said you looked great and you're just staring at me." A blush crawled up his neck as he gestured to her front steps. "There's something there for you."

Her eyes flew to the porch, where sure enough, a pastry box sat. It wasn't the first time she'd found exactly what she needed sitting on her porch. Her anonymous angel had been leaving food, diapers, clothes, and gifts since Matt's death. She'd asked her neighbors, and they all denied it. No one had ever seen someone dropping things off at the house.

Janey took a step toward the box, knowing that there were fruit tarts inside. Her mouth watered, but she paused. Looking up into Adam's penetrating eyes, she touched his collar. "Compliments are always good. Thank you. I think you look great too."

His smile returned and he lifted his hand as if he'd touch his hat—if he were wearing one. "You want to run that box inside before we go?"

"Yes, I'll throw it in the fridge." She swiped the box off the top step and hurried into the house. She resisted the urge to stuff something in her mouth so she wouldn't be so hungry at dinner. Taking just a moment to center herself, she drew in a deep breath. So her stomach felt like she'd swallowed jumping beans. And her hand itched to hold Adam's.

So what?

She was allowed. He was only a couple of years older than her, and he was single. A tremor shook her fingers at the thought of really becoming involved with him. Matt hadn't had a dangerous job at all, but Adam's job required him to carry a weapon and wear protective gear. What if he passed away too?

Janey swallowed, her fear irrational. She knew that much. And still it tumbled through her with the power of water falling over a cliff.

She turned when she heard the door creak. "I'm coming," she said.

"If this is too...weird, I get it," he said, filling the doorway with his height and his broad shoulders. Matt had been tall and skinny, and Janey wished she wasn't comparing the two of them.

"It's not weird," she said. "I was just putting the tarts in the fridge."

"Tarts?"

"Fruit tarts. They're my favorite."

"Oh, right. I think I've heard you say that. Who brought them over?" He fell back to the porch as she approached.

"I don't know. Someone just drops things off from time to time."

His right eyebrow quirked, which elicited a giggle from her. "Oh, yeah? A secret admirer, maybe?"

"I doubt it," she said. "I think it's Nana Sophie on the corner, but she keeps denying it."

Adam waved for her to go down the steps first. "I hope it's not lame that I brought the cruiser. It's either that or an old truck that smells like dogs and doesn't have heat."

Janey laughed, glad some of her earlier tension had fled. "It's fine." She slipped into the passenger seat, all of his police equipment between them. He closed her door behind her and sauntered around the front of the car with all the confidence of the police chief.

He exhaled as he got behind the wheel. "So, I'm dyin' to know how we're classifying this."

The moment had come, and Janey had to define the thrumming of her pulse and the way he smelled like a musky version of heaven. She looked at him, and he met her gaze with something sharp and heated in his.

Something zinged along her skin, and she couldn't believe that this attraction between them was one-sided. "It's a date," she said, her voice hardly her own. She cleared the frog from her throat. "Is that okay with you?"

Adam grinned and flipped the car into reverse. "I was hoping you'd say so."

Janey relaxed into the seat after that, the conversation between them as easy as it ever had been. Everything about Adam was the same as it always had been. He was strong, and kind, and while he spoke, he didn't use words he didn't need to. When things fell silent between them, that was okay too.

He pulled into the parking lot at the lodge, and Janey got out to the dusky sight of pine trees, the sound of water lapping the shore in the distance, and the scent of cooking meat. She ran her hands up her arms and said, "Mm. I love this place."

Adam glanced left and right as he came around the car to join her. "I don't get up here much. It's beautiful." His movement was sure, and his fingers warm, as he drew her hand into his. "You work here, right?"

"My office is just behind reception," she said. "We could stop by and I'll show you around after we eat."

He flashed her another grin as he opened the door to the restaurant. "Sure."

The restaurant seemed filled to capacity, but Adam stepped up to the hostess and took her hand again as they were led to a booth in the back corner. The noise wasn't quite as intense here, and Janey ordered a soda and a water when the waiter appeared mere moments after she'd sat down. She mourned the loss of Adam's hand in hers as he settled across from her, and new fantasies swam to the front of her mind.

But she would not be kissing him that night. She'd never kissed on the first date, and she wasn't going to start now. She had to be careful. Cautious. Go slow. Be sure. After all, this wasn't just her life anymore.

"So you didn't tell your mother about us going to dinner together," she said.

Adam's eyes flew to hers, a fair bit of panic in them. "I

didn't know what to tell her." He lifted one shoulder into a shrug, the surprise fading from his expression. "Plus, I keep things pretty close to the vest until I have all the facts I need to start talking about them."

"She's watching Jess tonight."

"She and Joel love Jess."

Janey nodded, a ball of emotion forming in her throat as quickly as it took to blink. "They do, yes."

"Good thing my brother got that started for me." Adam graced her with another smile. "My mom says Jess likes to cook with her. Maybe he'd like to come help me with the soup recipes for the Fall Festival."

"And you can keep an eye on him that way," Janey said.

A flicker of emotion ran across his face, but he erased it quickly. "Yeah, that too."

Janey had said something wrong, but she wasn't sure what. Maybe she shouldn't have brought up her son. Or Adam's parents. Or something.

The waiter arrived with their drinks, and Janey attacked her diet cola so she could give herself a few seconds to cool down and think things through before she said something else to make Adam's handsome features furrow in confusion.

6

Adam studied the menu, though he already knew he wanted to order all the soups. Janey had talked a lot on the way into the National Park. Adam liked listening to her talk, and for the most part, he'd liked what she had to say.

But with the few things she'd said about her son and the lodge indicated that she wasn't anywhere ready to be dating again.

But she said it was a date, he told himself. And she didn't have to do that. He'd made his position vibrantly clear, what with saying their dinner was weird, and then asking her point-blank what the label was. And the hand-holding.... If she hadn't known his intentions by then, that gesture was a dead giveaway.

But oh, how wonderful her fingers had felt between his. Just as magical as he'd imagined for all these years.

Her skin was just as soft, and he wondered if he could just ask her to go for a walk with him after dinner so he could hold her hand again.

It was probably overly hopeful to think she could ever love him the way she'd loved Matt. To his knowledge, she hadn't gone out with another man since the accident, and he had a lot of people around town he could ask.

But his hopes wouldn't be dashed, especially because Janey's eyes glittered when she met his gaze across the table. "What are you gonna get?"

"The soup, of course." He closed the menu and set it aside. "How's your mom?"

The waiter appeared, and Adam ordered a bowl of every soup on the menu. When he said, "Every soup?" Adam nodded like he took soup incredibly seriously.

He made a note and looked at Janey. "And I'll have the French onion soup and the surf and turf." She handed him her menu, confirmed she wanted a medium cook on her steak, and folded her hands in front of her on the table when he walked away.

"My mom's deaf, but she won't get a hearing aid. Annabelle's tried. JoJo's tried. Even Sami called from Florida and yelled at her to get something so she could hear her kids when they call." She shook her head and laughed.

Everything in Adam tightened, his craving for her in his life so strong, he couldn't contain his desperation to see things through to the end this time.

"So, tell me about you," she said.

"You know all about me." He took a drink of his water, the lemon a bit too tart for him.

"I used to know all about you. You're...different. You're the—"

"Excuse me, Chief?"

They both turned toward a woman standing at the end of their booth with her little boy.

"See, Mom! It *is* him." The boy bounced on the balls of his feet and grinned at Adam like he was Santa Claus.

The woman smiled, clearly uncomfortable but willing to interrupt his dinner nonetheless. "My son is obsessed with being a cop. He insisted it was you, even though you're not wearing your uniform."

Adam smiled at the boy, who couldn't be older than five. "Hey, there, bud. Being a cop is a great thing."

"He came to my school!" The boy's whole face was lit up, and Adam couldn't help getting infected by his enthusiasm.

"Let me guess...." Adam cocked his head and pretended to think. But he didn't really need to. He visited all the schools in Hawthorne Harbor each year, and there were only two elementary schools. Only one of those had a preschool.

"Lower Lincoln?" Adam said.

The boy clapped and said, "Yes!"

Adam laughed and reached for the child. He brought him close so he could look right into his eyes. "So you work hard in school and stay out of trouble. Then you could be a cop too."

"Like you," the boy said with wonder in his voice.

"Sure, like me." Adam didn't want to tell him how many years he'd put in doing anything but fun police work. Or about the dozens of trainings and classes he'd taken to qualify to become Chief of Police. Or how the timing had to be exactly right to get the job he wanted, where he wanted it.

"Take my picture, Mom." The boy turned back to his mom, who snapped a picture and scurried her son away.

"Wow," Janey said once they'd gone. "I didn't know I'd be out with a real celebrity."

Adam scoffed and waved his hand. "Everyone recognizes me. It comes with the job." He watched her carefully, hoping that wouldn't be a deal-breaker for her.

She lifted her water to her lips and sipped. Adam had never been jealous of a glass before, but he was in that moment. "And how do you feel about that? As I recall, seventeen-year-old Adam Herrin wouldn't even get on the stage for the choir concert."

He blinked, his thoughts completely vacating his brain for a moment. Then a laugh bubbled out of his chest and he wondered if now would be a good time to admit to her that he'd had a crush on her since his seventeen-year-old days.

"Not much of a singer, that's all," he said.

"Mm hm." She watched him with those gorgeous eyes,

and Adam—who had studied for twelve weeks in Washington D.C. to learn how to read people, their body language, their emotions—saw mirrored in her gaze what he had rioting inside his chest.

Hope. Desire. Wonder.

Fear.

Their meal arrived, and Adam stared at the five bowls of soup the waiter and a helper placed before him. "All right." He grinned at Janey, wishing he'd gotten a steak and lobster too. "French onion, you say?"

The bowl was beautiful, with gooey, browned cheese covering the bowl, hiding what was underneath. She had a bowl of it too, and she smiled as she broke through a corner of the cheese and said, "Oh, yeah. This stuff is like gold." She took a sip and moaned, her eyes closing in bliss.

Adam copied her, getting some cheese with his beef broth and caramelized onions. The taste was delicious—salty and oniony, rich and deep. "These are definitely the best onions I've ever had in French onion soup," he admitted. Usually he disliked the texture of the onions, but the lodge had really perfected this soup.

The real question was: Could Adam do the same?

～

ADAM WOKE TO A SLOPPY, WARM TONGUE ON HIS FACE. "No," he moaned, shoving Gypsy back. The dog was relentless though, and finally Adam chuckled and sat up. "Fine. I'm up." He pushed her away again. "I'm up."

She barked and trotted out of the bedroom, her claws clicking on the hard floor once she left the carpet. Adam yawned and stretched and looked up to make sure there was a ceiling above him. Because he felt like he was floating, on a high from the walk along the lake with Janey's hand in his.

There had been no kiss, and Adam was actually glad about that. He didn't want to push Janey past where she was comfortable, and while she hadn't said Matt's name, there was a spot near the curve of the lake where she'd paused, started to tell a memory, and then sort of...stalled. Got lost.

Adam was sure it had something to do with Matt, but he hadn't asked. The fact was, Janey's past was filled with Matt, and he'd have to deal with it one piece at a time.

Gypsy barked again, and Adam padded down the hall and around the corner into the kitchen to let her into the backyard. Fable followed, and Adam turned to make his weekend coffee. He didn't typically work weekends, and his plans for the day included grocery shopping and experimenting with French onion soup recipes.

His phone dinged from in the bedroom, and he practically sprinted toward it. Janey had mentioned dropping Jess off before she went to work, and Adam had agreed that the boy could come help him cook that day.

Janey had classes and tours going on today, and part of

Adam wanted to sneak into the back of the theater just to hear her talk about the trees and wildlife in the Olympic National Park.

The message wasn't from Janey, unfortunately, but his mother. Jess is staying here for the day. Hope that's okay. Janey said she was going to bring him to you, but he's out with Drew in the fields and it seems silly to drive him back to your place.

Adam read and re-read the message, his frown growing. He didn't like that his brother was the one bonding with Janey's son. Sure, it made sense, as Jess and Dixie were good friends, and Dixie's mother was Drew's fiancée.

Still, Adam wanted to spend time with Jess. Learn more about the boy. Develop a friendship there beyond that which they currently had, if he could. He'd tried not to be over-eager to do such a thing in the past. Janey was very protective of her son, and Adam understood why.

He had a grandfather and three uncles and now Drew and Joel, Adam's stepfather.

Adam didn't know how to respond, at least not to his mother. He typed out a message to Janey instead, hoping he wasn't being too forward but also tired of keeping his feelings for the woman secret. Dormant. Bottled up.

So no Jess today? It's fine, really. Maybe when you get off work, you'll bring him to taste my soup attempts.

Before he could second-guess himself, he sent the text and stepped into the shower. When he got out, she'd said, *Yeah, sure. Around 4?*

He confirmed and went to the grocery store to get the

ingredients he needed to try to replicate the French onion soup at the lodge, as well as a chicken and wild rice soup that might be a hit.

It seemed like every eye gravitated to his as he parked and strolled into the grocery store. He was used to it. So used to it that sometimes he didn't notice as he went about being a human being in the town of Hawthorne Harbor. Sometimes, like today, he felt the weight of each glance, each look, each blip of recognition.

He felt like an outsider in his own town, where he'd grown up. But he pushed his cart through the aisles, collecting the whole chicken he'd need to make broth, and cheesecloth for the spices and herbs he'd use to flavor the rice.

"Hey, Chief," someone said as they passed, and Adam caught a fleeting look at a man he probably should recognize. But he turned the corner before Adam could fully identify him.

"Hey," he said, way too late. He sighed as he turned back to his cart and ran smack dab into his groceries, which had been nudged closer to him.

He grunted and a truckload of embarrassment flowed through him, especially when he heard a woman say, "I'm so sorry. I was just moving it to get to the—"

His eyes met hers, and horror replaced the humiliation. "Anita," he managed to say.

"Adam." Her surprise was only matched by his. She giggled and lifted the peanut butter jar his cart had obviously been blocking. "Just getting the all-natural stuff I like off the bottom shelf." She tucked her auburn hair behind her ear and ducked her head.

Adam had once found the gesture so sweet, so adorable. Now, he didn't know what to make of it. They'd broken up a few months ago, and he'd texted her to find out the reason she'd broken up with him, but this was the first time he'd come face-to-face with her.

She surveyed his cart while he tried to find something to say. "Looks like you're making soup."

He nodded, some thoughts finally coming together. "Yes. The theme for the Fall Festival is soup this year."

"What are you making?" She tucked her peanut butter jar into the basket hanging on her elbow.

"Oh, just this new chicken noodle recipe." He didn't want his ideas out in the open, and two women walked by, noting the exchange.

"You have no pasta."

"Not there yet," he said, his annoyance starting to drive his need to get away from Anita. He had, in fact, been down the pasta aisle, but he wasn't making chicken noodle soup. So he'd told half the truth. He wasn't going to have one of his officers arrest him over it.

Anita tucked that same lock of hair that hadn't come loose yet and stepped almost past him. "Well, it was good to see you, Adam." She touched his bicep, a feather-light touch that was there, then gone. "Call me." She walked away.

Adam stared at his arm where she'd touched him, wondering why it felt like ice, and then spun, sure he'd just hallucinated. "Call me?" he whispered to himself upon finding himself alone in the aisle.

There was no way that was happening. He turned back to his cart for a second time and gripped the handle, angry at Anita's toying ways. She wasn't hard to clear from his head, and he finished his shopping and got on home to start the French onion soup—which reminded him of Janey, the woman he really wanted to focus on.

7

Janey pulled into Adam's driveway, Jess still chattering about the triple chocolate chip cookies from last night, and the day on the farm. She loved that Jess had this place where he could go, where he could experience such different things than she could provide for him.

At the same time, the burden of guilt that came with his excitement always stuck with her for days and was hard to shake. And every time she took him out to the lavender farm and let him have any experiences there, it took a little longer and was a little harder to purge herself from that negative emotion.

She simply couldn't give him the life he was meant to lead. Without Matt, she'd had to work since the time Jess could roll over. She'd taken him up to the National Park as often as she could, and she knew of his love for the outdoors, for animals, for hiking, and fishing, and canoeing.

But she didn't have eighty acres of lavender, or goats, or a wishing well. She flashed her son a smile as she put the Jeep in park.

"What are we doin' here again?" Jess asked, peering out the windshield to Adam's house.

"He made a bunch of soup for the upcoming Fall Festival." Janey tried to make her voice light, easy, conversational. "He wants to win again this year, and he wanted you to taste it and tell him what you thought."

Jess turned toward her, a dubious look in his dark eyes. "I don't believe that."

"No? He wanted you to come cook with him today. Seems Donna has been talking you up."

A glimmer of light stole through Jess's expression, and he turned back to the house. "All right."

"What?" Janey laughed as she reached over to tousle his hair. "You're too cool to be a soup taster?"

"No, it's...." Jess shook his head. "It's nothing."

But Janey noticed how he looked up and down the street before practically sprinting to Adam's front door, which was more protected by the awning and deep porch.

"Heya, Jess," Adam said when he opened the door. "You made it." He searched for Janey as she came up the steps, and she gave him a small smile she hoped would convey to him not to indicate anything about their date the previous evening.

Jess ducked inside, leaving the two of them on the porch, and Adam glanced at the boy's retreating back and then to Janey. "So...what's goin' on?"

"He didn't really say," she said. "But I get the feeling he doesn't want anyone to see him here."

A cloud overtook Adam's face, and he practically growled, "Well, come on in," before striding back into the house. No sly touch while they were alone. No, "You look great, Janey," whispered so Jess couldn't overhear.

She sighed. What did she expect? Bringing her son here without properly telling him where she'd been last night, who she'd been with, and what they'd done.

Not that they'd done anything wrong. She wasn't married anymore. Adam was available. She'd liked holding his hand, and listening to him laugh, and hoping he'd kiss her later.

He hadn't, and she hadn't really quantified "later" anyway. He could kiss her now and it would be "later."

The scent of something salty and savory filled Adam's house, along with the tell-tale smell of freshly baked bread. Janey had never been so happy in her life to have been so busy, she'd worked through lunch.

A golden retriever trotted toward her as she shut the door, and she paused to give the dog a pat. "Oh, she looks so happy," she called toward the kitchen, really burying her hands in the dog's fur now.

"You pet her, she won't leave you alone," Adam called to her, adding a laugh to the end of the statement. So maybe tonight's tasting would go just fine. Janey entered the kitchen to find Jess at the stove, stirring a pot of soup.

"Oh, well, you've put him to work already."

"He just added the cream to the chicken and wild rice soup," Adam said. An alarm sounded, and he added, "Oh, that's the bread. Look out, Jess."

Jess stood back while Adam pulled a round loaf of bread out of the oven and set it on the counter beside the stove. "So there's three kinds," he said with a sigh. "That chicken and wild rice Jess is finishing up. The French onion, which I will cheese up in just a minute, and a more traditional beef stew."

"I'll take one of each," Janey said, a secret nod to their date last night she hoped he understood.

Adam held her gaze for an extra heartbeat and said, "Right, well, you heard your mom, Jess. Let's get the bowls out. What do you want?" He pulled bowls from the cupboard and told Jess where to get the spoons.

Janey stood back and watched them work in the kitchen, marveling at how Jess looked like he could easily belong to Adam. Her pulse stuttered, and she blinked to try to put Matt in Adam's place. But her husband had been a horrible cook, unable to even scramble eggs.

Adam had the same dark hair as Jess, the same brooding jawline. Adam's had a couple day's worth of scruff on it, and she wanted to feel his face with her fingertips. Startled, she turned away from the kitchen and looked out the French doors that led to the backyard. Of course, it was trimmed and neat—everything about Adam seemed to be in order. Nothing out of place, which made her wonder what in the world she was doing there.

"French onion," Adam said, and Janey turned back to the bar, where nine bowls of soup now sat. How long had she been staring out the window? Neither Jess nor Adam seemed like they'd tried to get her attention, so she moved to sit on the middle barstool, the Swiss cheese perfectly melty and browned on top of the French onion soup.

"This smells divine," she said as Adam put a butter dish on the counter in front of her.

"Mom, can I invite Thayne to the beach next weekend?" Jess sat on the stool next to her, his spoon already poised to dive into the chicken and wild rice soup.

Frustration expanded her chest, and she took an extra moment to school the emotion out of her voice. "I don't know if it's a friend weekend, Jess," she said. She hated it when he asked her things like this in front of other people, which was exactly why he'd done it.

"You're going with your friend."

"To plan her wedding. Dixie will be there. If you bring a friend, what's she to do?"

Jess slurped up a spoonful of soup, but Janey knew the conversation wasn't over. She dug into her cheese and soup, the scent of beef broth making her mouth water. "This smells great, Adam."

"Mine's good too," Jess said.

Adam had a spoonful of beef stew poised, but he stuck

a piece of bread into the broth first and took a bite. He nodded, still chewing.

"Dixie's a girl," Jess said as if Janey didn't know.

"And she's only a year younger than you, and you've always been best friends."

Jess's spoon clinked against the bowl. "Well, me and Thayne are best friends now."

Adam's elbow bumped Janey's, and she cut him a glance. But he didn't look up at her, didn't say anything.

"I'll need to talk to Gretchen and make sure it's okay with her."

"Mom—"

"There are only a certain number of beds, Jess. Food to be bought and meals planned. Activities for a certain number of guests. It's in a week. We can't just bring extra people without talking to the host. It would be rude." She gave him a look that said, *So drop it*, and Jess focused back on his soup, a disgruntled look on his face.

Janey took a deep breath, trying to surface through the awkward tension that now existed in the kitchen. She tried to think of something to say, but nothing came to mind. So she scooped another bite of the delicious soup into her mouth.

"Maybe you two would like to go see my latest project."

Janey twisted toward him. "A secret project, huh?"

"What is it?" Jess asked.

"Finish up and I'll show you." He threw a smile to the

both of them before taking another bite of his stew. Adam asked Jess something about skateboarding, and Jess said, "Yeah, my trucks are pretty stiff."

Janey had no idea what that meant, but Adam seemed to, and they talked for a minute or two about Jess's preferred method of travel. Even though she'd bought him a bike for his birthday, he usually only rode it down to the beach and back, preferring the skateboard for going to school or Main Street.

Adam finished first and got up to clear his bowls. Jess helped, saying, "The best one was that chicken one."

"Even with the rice?" Adam asked, peering down at the boy.

"I like that wild rice." He made a face. "I don't like the onions. My mom always makes me eat them too."

"Oh, come on," Janey said. "When's the last time I made you eat anything?"

"You put them in the meatballs," he said. "They're actually the best thing she cooks." He looked at Adam now. "When she makes anything."

"Hey." Janey stood, though she'd only had a few bites of the other soups. Her French onion bowl was empty, and she handed it to her son. "I work all day. If I don't want to cook, it's okay. We're still alive, aren't we?" She put her hands on her hips and gave Jess a smile that didn't reach further than her lips.

She couldn't believe he was bringing up her lack of cooking in front of Adam. She couldn't believe she cared to hide all her flaws until later in her relationship with him, because that indicated that she wanted a relationship.

"Only because I know how to open cans." Jess smirked at her, because he knew she wouldn't reprimand him in front of Adam.

"Well, then maybe you should start cooking for her," Adam said, one eyebrow cocked. "Pretty much all I did here was open some cans and mix some stuff together."

"She won't let me use a knife," Jess said as if Janey wasn't standing right there.

"Really?" Adam tossed her a glance. "Well, you come over any time, Jess. I'll teach you how to use a knife."

"Your mom won't let me either."

Adam chuckled and started for the back door. "We can't really blame them," he said as he opened the door and the dogs streaked out ahead of him. "Knives are dangerous." He walked onto the back deck and down the steps, Jess practically tripping over his feet as he hastened to follow.

He started peppering Adam with questions like, "Do you have any horses? This yard is huge, so you could totally have some horses," and "Do you ever go out to the wishing well anymore? Drew said your dad built it for you when you wanted to make the football team."

Adam spoke to him, his voice too deep for Janey to understand discernable sounds and form them into words. Jess laughed as Adam led them toward a shed in the corner of his backyard. There wasn't anything too remarkable about it. Made of wood and roughly the size of a three-car garage, the shed had been painted blue in the distant past. Bits of the paint still clung to the wood, but she flicked one chip off with her fingernail.

"No way!" Jess's whoops from inside the shed made Janey increase her pace. "Mom, you gotta see this!" He appeared in the doorway and then ducked back inside.

Janey entered the shed too and found it filled with sunlight. A light had also been turned on, but Janey didn't need it to see the huge motorcycle sitting in the front third of the shed. Jess jumped around it, exclaiming about horsepower and brand names Janey had at least heard of.

"What is all this?" she asked, tucking her hands into her back pockets and trying to take in the beast before her. There were lots of little parts on the dropcloth that had been spread over the ground.

"I'm rebuilding the engine," Adam said. "In my spare time."

Her gaze flew to his. "You have spare time?"

His dark-as-coal eyes glittered at her as he stared straight into hers. "Here and there." He waved her closer. "Come see."

Janey wasn't sure what there was to see, but she wanted to be closer to Adam, so she stepped over to him, the heat from his body brushing against her forearm as she pointed to a particularly large piece and asked, "What's that?"

Adam started telling her about a carburetor and while she didn't understand hardly a word he said, she loved listening to the rumbly sound of his voice as he talked, as he pointed out parts, as he shared with her something she hadn't known about him and that meant a great deal to him.

"I like solving puzzles and problems," he said. "Putting things together." He added a shrug that couldn't have been any sexier. "This satisfies part of that craving, I guess."

"Does it run?" Jess asked, at least the tenth question out of his mouth.

"Not yet." Adam smiled at him. "But you can come help me work on it any time you want."

"Yeah!" Jess pumped his fist in the air, and Janey felt like she'd just entered a deliciously warm hot tub as she watched Adam interact with her son. By the time she left in her Jeep, she was warm and woozy from head to toe and hoping the next weekend at the beach wouldn't leave her burned.

8

Adam had so much leftover soup that he took it into the crew working that Sunday. He didn't normally go in on weekends, but he stayed and talked with some of the boys, as well as his Deputy Lieutenant—the man in charge when Adam was gone.

"So you're good for this Friday, right?" he asked Milo.

"What's this weekend?" He paused in shoveling his mouth full of more beef stew.

"I have to go help my brother plan his wedding, remember?" Around and around the Rubix cube went. A new one, one with only black and white squares that needed to be lined up and squared off. He wasn't really trying to solve it at the moment, but his hands needed something to do, so the cube got twisted.

He supposed that was why he'd bought the black Harley Davidson from an older gentleman in Bell Hill and started trying to fix it up one weekend at a time. It was something to keep his idle hands busy. Between a mechanic manual and the Internet, Adam had made some real progress on the motorcycle.

"Oh, right," Milo said. "We'll be fine."

"I just need you to go over the procedures for public safety if a weapon is presented in the park."

Milo patted a stack of folders on the corner of his desk. "Right here."

Adam had no idea what was in the colorful assortment of folders. He didn't much care, as long as his officers got the training they needed before the Fall Festival in only five weeks.

Five weeks.

He drew in a deep breath. Drew's wedding planning weekend wasn't exactly convenient for Adam. He supposed no time would be, as Hawthorne Harbor seemed to have something going on every weekend. If it wasn't the biggest lavender festival in the world, it was a farmer's market. And if not the Fall Festival, then the Festival of Trees, which happened from the Friday following Thanksgiving and lasted all the way through Three King's Day in January.

"I'll do the tourist influx training on Wednesday," he said, more to himself than to Milo. The other man nodded anyway and turned toward the soups on Sarah's desk, where Adam had placed them. "Is there any more of that chicken and wild rice?"

Adam shook his head, a chuckle escaping his lips. He was glad he could provide lunch for the weekend crew, as he didn't get in to see them all that often. He was also surprised the chicken and wild rice soup had been such a hit. From twelve-year-old boys to fifty-year-old men, the soup seemed to be a winner.

He looked into the pot after Milo had ladled himself another bowl. Was it a winning recipe? Maybe he should try reducing the size of the carrots. He'd noticed that Janey had left most of hers in the bowl, but maybe she just didn't like cooked carrots.

Adam riddled through the recipe the same way he poured over puzzles and problems. He liked trying to put together flavors and increments of ingredients, the same way he twisted the Rubix cube until it was perfect.

He knocked on the desktop and said, "All right. I'm gonna head out. Help me with these pots?"

Milo slurped up one more bite of soup and stood to help Adam carry his dishes out to the cruiser. Adam tinkered in the shed before taking Gypsy and Fable down to the beach for an evening run.

He somehow made it through the day—and two more —before texting Janey. *Hey, what are you doing for lunch tomorrow?*

With Jess at school, maybe Adam could sneak a quick date with her midweek. He stared at the sportscasters on the TV as they went over the same two college football teams as that morning. How they could sit and talk about the same things over and over, he wasn't sure.

Working tomorrow, she texted back.

Adam abandoned his feigned interest in the TV and focused on his phone. *I thought you said you didn't work Wednesdays.* His heart bobbed around in his chest like it wasn't anchored properly.

I usually don't. But I'm taking the whole weekend off. Working this Wednesday and next.

His hopes of seeing her before the weekend withered.

What about tomorrow night for dinner? she messaged, bringing them right back to life.

Bringing Jess? I can cook and take him out to the shed.

He has a youth activity. They're going out to the apple orchards, so there should be time for dinner.

Adam grinned like he might take up a new career as a clown. "Sure," he said as he typed. "Dinner tomorrow."

With the date set, he relaxed back into the couch. With a jolt, he sat straight up again. If he went out with Janey here in town, everyone would know about it. The very walls of every restaurant in Hawthorne Harbor had eyes, and it wouldn't take long for the news of him dining with Janey Germaine to get around the gossip circles in town.

So what? He didn't care if people knew they'd gone out. But she might. And he usually waited until a relationship was well-seated before taking it public. Because he was a public figure, whether he—or Janey—liked it.

Worry pulled his eyebrows into a frown, and he did the only thing he could think of: He called Janey.

"Hey," she said, adding a giggle to the word that made him breathless.

"Hey." He cleared his throat. "This is going to sound weird, but hear me out, okay?"

Scuffling came through the line and she said, "Just a sec." He could hear her breathing and a few seconds later, she said, "Okay, I'm alone now."

So they were keeping their relationship on the down-low. He nodded though she couldn't see him. It made sense. She had a son. He had every eye in town on him.

"So it's about why you just made sure you were alone."

"I just—I've never dated anyone before. I don't know how Jess will take it."

Adam's eyebrows practically flew off his forehead. "We're dating?"

"Um." Her giggle had turned nervous. "We went to dinner, and now we're going again. I said it was a date. So yeah." Her voice took on some strength. "I'd say we're dating."

"But you don't want to tell Jess about it yet."

"Right."

"Then we can't go to dinner in town tomorrow." At least some of the pressure was off of him.

"Why not?"

"Why not?" He chuckled. "Janey, I realize that we grew up together and you might not see me the way everyone else does." Wow, he really hoped she didn't see him the way everyone else in Hawthorne Harbor did. "But I'm the Chief of Police, and I've been single forever, and who I go to dinner with can quickly become the topic of *a lot* of gossip."

"Ohhh." She drew the word out as she exhaled. "I see."

He wanted to offer to cook, but at the same time, he didn't. He wanted to go out with her. "What about if we drive over to Forks?" he asked.

"That's quite the drive."

"Forty-five minutes, tops."

She snorted and laughed. "Are you planning to use the siren to get us there in forty-five minutes? Because that's an hour-long drive, easy."

"Sure. I can use the siren if you'd like." He sifted through more possibilities in his mind. "We could go to this great place I know in Bell Hill."

"Bell Hill is more reasonable," she agreed.

"Great, so I'll come get you around six-thirty, and we'll head over to Bell Hill." It was only twenty minutes to the slightly bigger town, and Adam had spent some time there after his girlfriend two or three ago had broken up with him.

"Jess is leaving at six-thirty," Janey said. "So like, six-forty."

Adam agreed and got off the line before he said something too soft, that might reveal too much. He wasn't sure who he was hiding from. Himself? Janey? His feelings for her weren't secret anymore, something he was actually very happy about. But he still didn't want to come on too strong, too soon.

After all, he'd told her a little bit about himself and his love of puzzles and putting things together. He hadn't told her about his promise to Matt, or that he'd only had eyes for her for over two decades.

"And you don't need to," he told himself as he picked up the remote control and turned off the TV. "Not right now. Save it for when things are actually serious." He hoped with everything in him that he could continue the relationship with her until it reached serious status. Otherwise, the last twenty-one years of his life would've been a complete waste.

~

"Specialty macaroni and cheese?" Janey gazed at the trifold sign standing on the sidewalk outside of Cheese, the joint Adam had just parked in front of.

"They have everything cheese you can think of," he said. "Cheese and crackers. Cheesy dips with chips. And yes, mac and cheese." He beamed at her as he opened the door and ushered her in.

Just the salty, savory scent of the shop made his mouth water and his pulse calm. He'd waited at the end of her street until he saw Jess skateboard in the opposite direction. Then he'd eased into the driveway and collected Janey for their date.

The drive had happened in a blink, and he wasn't even sure what he'd said. She wore a simple T-shirt the color of plums and a pair of denim shorts that barely reached her knees, and he couldn't seem to get a proper breath because of her floral, fruity scent.

"Grilled cheese sandwiches," she said, her whole face lighting up.

"The one made with a waffle will change your world," he said. "It's so good."

"Three cheeses embedded inside a crispy, savory waffle." She scanned the menu. "Yeah, that's what I want."

"With soup or without?"

"Which soup? Oh. The tomato bisque? Is it good?"

"I mean, it's not as good as what I make, but it's decent."

She pushed against his bicep playfully, and Adam's whole body felt like he'd been hooked up to a live wire. "Not as good as what you make. Come on." She peered up at him. "Do you make tomato bisque?"

He laughed and slung his arm around her shoulders, claiming her as his in front of everyone in the shop. "Only once, and it wasn't that great."

"So no bisque for the festival."

"No way. It wouldn't win anyway."

"No?"

"No. The cook-off is too hoity-toity for mere bisque."

"Then why do you want to win so bad?"

He lifted one shoulder and stepped up to the counter to order. "Street cred." He rattled off what he wanted and added Janey's waffle grilled cheese and tomato bisque. Without thinking, he stepped back while the cashier ran his card, threading his fingers through Janey's again and sweeping a kiss across her temple.

She froze, and he stiffened too, cursing himself for doing something that felt so natural to him, but that he knew—*he knew*—would freak her out.

He stepped away from her in the pretense of taking his debit card and putting it back in his wallet. Maybe if he played the kiss off as nothing, she would too. He flashed her a smile and took the number the cashier handed him.

"Where do you want to sit?"

9

A thread of awkwardness still connected her and Adam while they waited for their food. He made small talk and didn't seem to care that she barely contributed to the conversation. She couldn't. Every internal organ was quaking, shaking, wondering what in the world she was doing.

Dating her late husband's best friend? Who did that?

But Maya hadn't seemed to have a problem with it, on any of the numerous occasions Janey had brought it up with her. She really needed to talk to Gretchen about it, but she didn't want to. Didn't want this weekend to be anything but perfect for her best friend. And besides, Adam wanted to keep their relationship in the shadows for now too.

Their number was called, and he got up to get their food. When he returned, she'd finally managed to quell the tremors in her stomach. Her pulse still rippled whenever Adam trained his handsome eyes in her direction.

He'd ordered a buffalo chicken wing mac-and-cheese as well as a cheesy chips and queso. She stared at the huge portion and asked, "Can you eat all that?"

"Sure." He picked up a chip and dunked it in the spicy cheese dip. "You can have some, though."

She picked up one half of her waffle grilled cheese, which had been cut into triangles, and bit into the corner. Salt, cream, and crispy, browned waffle met her tongue, and she moaned. "Oh, my gosh."

"Right?" He nudged his queso closer to her and she took a chip to try it.

"Also delicious," she said, grinning at him.

They ate in silence for a few minutes, and then he cleared his throat. "So, we should probably talk about Matt."

Janey's muscles seized and then seemed to melt, leaving her feeling discombobulated and out of sort. "Oh, uh...."

"Just something you said on the phone last night," he said.

"Oh, what did I say?" She searched her memory for what she could've said during their brief call the previous evening.

"You said you never dated, which I know isn't true." He took a drink of his soda. "You meant you haven't dated since Matt died."

Janey swallowed and nodded. "Yeah, that's what I meant." She dunked her waffle sandwich into her bisque and took a bite, the spiciness of the soup only enhancing the mellow cheese.

"Why's that?" he asked.

She paused, searching his face to see if he was joking. He didn't seem to be. "Are you asking me why I haven't dated since my husband died?"

He flinched as if she'd flicked water in his face. "Yes, that's what I'm asking. It's been twelve years. I mean, I didn't expect you to start dating the next day or anything." He stirred his mac and cheese. "But twelve years?" He shrugged, like that would punctuate it all perfectly.

She squinted at him. He'd never been vague like this before. What Adam Herrin thought, everyone knew, because he said it. Unapologetically, the way he had last year when he'd argued against increasing the budget to expand the library. He hadn't been popular with moms for a few months, but in the end, he'd been right. The old community center functioned brilliantly as the new library, and the smaller building now housed the public works city offices.

Tilting her head, she took another chip and dipped it. "What are you really asking me?"

He shrugged one of those powerful shoulders again, and while she'd found it cute before, she didn't now. "Come on," she said. "Tell me."

He exhaled and put his fork down. "I guess I'm just

wondering if I even have a shot here." He looked away. "I mean, I don't think how I feel is a secret anymore, and I'm not gettin' any younger. So."

Since he was the first man she'd even seen since Matt's death, Janey had no idea how to tell if he had a shot or not. They'd been friends for a lifetime. How could he not have a shot?

"Why haven't you gotten married?" she asked, dipping her sandwich again.

He cleared his throat and then put an overly-large bite of food into his mouth. She waited until he chewed and swallowed, admiring the slow flush that crawled across his cheeks.

"I'd rather not say," he said. "Right now. Maybe after—I mean—maybe in the future."

Janey liked that she could fluster the tough, tall chief. "I think you have a shot," she said, causing his gaze to fly to hers.

"Yeah?" He looked so boyish with all that hope shining in his eyes.

She laughed and reached across the table to squeeze his hand. "Yeah. Why are you so surprised?"

"I don't know."

But he did, Janey could tell. The Chief of Police wasn't a great liar. He just had another thing he didn't want to tell her. *Right now*, she thought. And she had time to get answers from him. She wanted to go slow, see if she could work out her knotted feelings before she made any big life changes.

Since he'd put something on the table between them, she leaned forward and said, "I'm interested in whatever you want to tell me in the future."

"Could be a while," he said, his voice taking on the gruff tone he used as a police officer.

"I've got time," she said. "I—I don't want to go too fast anyway."

He nodded, the sparkle in his eyes so darn attractive Janey could barely maintain eye contact. "Sounds like a plan."

She groaned. "No plans until the weekend. Then I'm sure Gretchen will have me running from dawn until dusk." Her phone chimed and she glanced at it to see she'd gotten a text from her best friend. "Speak of the devil...."

Janey swiped open the email and read quickly, a laugh starting in her chest. She turned it toward Adam. "I was so right. Look. An itinerary for this weekend."

He studied her phone and then picked up his. "Do you think I got one of those?" He swiped and tapped and scrolled. "Yep. I sure did." He shook his head but he was smiling. "She's detail-oriented, isn't she?"

"She's the best." Janey flipped her phone over and set it on the table, a wild idea occurring to her. "Have you ever been up to the bell tower this town is named after?"

"Oh, sure," he said. "I got to come when they rededicated it and stand in uniform behind the podium. You know how cops sometimes do." He rolled his shoulders as if to say *No big deal. I'm just a celebrity.*

Janey finished her soup and sandwich and said, "Well, I'd like to go see it. I've only been there once, and it was before the rededication."

"Oh, it's great," he said. "They built new bathrooms, and put down a huge field, and there's a nice plaque and monument now."

She stood and extended her hand toward him. "Care to take me there, Chief?" The moment his hand met hers, Janey's whole body sighed. She remembered feeling like this with Matt too, and she basked in the memories instead of pushing them away.

Adam had already brought him up; maybe Janey could too. "I miss him a lot, some days," she said as they left the cheese restaurant. "And other days, I don't think about him at all. It's strange, and there's no rhyme or reason to any of it."

She couldn't look at him, but the way his hand tightened on hers was enough of an indication that he'd heard. That he was okay talking about Matt.

"Sometimes I wonder what he'd be doing if he was still alive." Adam's voice was so quiet, Janey could barely hear him.

"He loved the ferries."

"But he was more than that," Adam said.

Janey scrunched up her face, trying to imagine Matt

now. She couldn't. "He's completely frozen in time for me," she said. "I can't even imagine what he might look like now, or what he'd be doing. He's still that twenty-four-year-old man I fell in love with."

"He was a great man," Adam said, his head down and his hand still tight in hers.

"He was." Janey lifted her head and put one foot in front of the other as Adam led her down the street and through a park. She'd only spoken to her mother and sisters about Matt, and it felt cleansing to add Adam to her very short list of trusted confidantes. It also reminded her to call her mom and talk to her about Adam.

Why hadn't she thought of that before? She didn't need Gretchen—she could call Annabelle after she put Jess to bed that night. Set on her plan, and hoping for some good advice about the upcoming beach weekend with Adam, she could focus on the beautiful bell towers that had been built on the rise of the hill and thus earned the town of Bell Hill it's name.

∼

"Oh, my gosh, I was just going to call you." Annabelle didn't even use "hello" to answer Janey's calls anymore. Janey swore her sister just picked up and continued a previous conversation whenever she called.

"What? Why?" she asked.

"Guess what I just heard?"

"I'll never guess." Janey sorted through the pretzels in her bowl to find three chocolate chips in the bottom. She popped the pretzel and the three chips into her mouth together, the best treat on the planet.

"Tommy Ryan is back in town."

Janey let the chocolate melt against her tongue. "Tommy Ryan, my high school boyfriend?"

"Yes!" Annabelle shrieked. "And he's divorced, and you should totally go out with him."

Janey sighed, but Annabelle kept talking. "I know you don't date, but I really think you should break your vow of celibacy when it comes to him."

"I didn't take a vow of celibacy." Janey scoffed. "And I'm not interested in Tommy Ryan. Or have you forgotten why we broke up?"

"So he went out with another girl when he got to college."

"No, no," Janey said. "No. It wasn't a girl. It was his English professor, and it was more than one date, and we weren't even broken up yet."

"He was out of high school. It wasn't illegal."

"I'm not interested."

"Janey," Annabelle whined. "He even asked about you."

"You've seen him already?"

"He came into the shop." Her husband owned a sailboat shop. Rentals and purchases.

"Oh, is he in the sailboat market?"

"Maybe." But the tone of her voice said *Totally not.*

"I'm not interested."

"Come on, you—"

"I'm not interested, because I'm already seeing someone else."

A deathly silence came through the line, and a sliver of satisfaction squirreled through Janey that she'd rendered her mouthiest sister quiet.

"I'm sorry," Annabelle said in a freaky, calm voice. "I don't think I heard you right."

"I'm sure you did. In fact, he's why I called."

Another shriek came through the line, and Janey held the phone away from her ear while she collected another pretzel and it's accompanying chocolate chips.

"Who is it?"

"Oh, I can't say yet," Janey said, a teasing quality in her voice.

"So I know him."

"He's a native of Hawthorne Harbor, so yep." She could practically hear her sister's wheels turning, and Janey wondered if she'd already said too much. "Anyway." She cleared her throat. "This is okay, right? Me dating another man."

"Oh, honey." Annabelle's voice turned compassionate. "Of course it's okay. Matt's been gone for a long time."

Janey's attention wandered to the picture of her and Matt sitting on her bedside table. It showed the two of them up at the lake at the lodge, the day he'd asked her to marry him. It was just a quick selfie, but it was a day Janey didn't want to forget.

"I feel like I don't know him anymore," she said.

"You didn't get enough time to really know him," Annabelle said. "It's normal and healthy for you to move forward. Find someone new to spend your life with."

Janey snuggled deeper into her pillows, her reading device dormant beside the picture on the table. She'd stay up for another couple of hours after she finished with Annabelle, because reading in the middle of the night was the only time she truly felt free.

"So tell me about this mystery man. How many times have you gone out?"

"Just twice," Janey said.

"So no kissing, I assume?"

"Too early for that," Janey said, though she had thought about what it would be like to kiss Adam. It was kind of hard not to imagine it with the man's arm around her shoulders and the bells vibrating in the wind and the beautiful Washington countryside sweeping out in front of her.

"But you like him?"

Janey took a deep breath and said, "Yeah, I like him," as she pushed the air out of her lungs. It felt good to say it out loud to someone else.

"Well, I can't wait to hear who it is."

If Janey knew her older sister—and she did—she'd have already sent a text off to Lily Stoker, the owner of the bridal shop on Wedding Row. The dress shop was the hotbed of gossip in Hawthorne Harbor, as it had a constantly rotating door of women coming and going. Just because they were all engaged didn't mean they didn't know who was dating who.

Janey plugged in her phone and reached for her book, satisfied that she and Adam had kept their two dates as far from prying eyes as possible—and hoping they could continue to do so this weekend at the beach.

10

Adam ran down the beach on Friday morning, his feet matching the rhythm of his breathing as he kept his eye on Gypsy. She frolicked out in the surf, as usual, barking at an errant bird that hadn't flown south yet.

The summer had clung to Hawthorne Harbor for a few extra weeks this year, something his step-father was thrilled about because it meant better lavender growth for next year. Adam didn't mind it either, and he hoped the warmer weather would last through the weekend.

Ah, the weekend. He'd never spent a lot of time lying on the sand at the beach, but he'd looked through Gretchen's itinerary, and there seemed like there'd be plenty of time for relaxing in the sun.

He'd texted Janey early, before he'd started his run, and

said, Seems to be plenty of free time this weekend. Maybe we can sneak away for a stroll down the beach?

She hadn't answered by the time he'd put his headphones in and started his morning ritual. The house where they were staying this weekend was located at Double Bluff Beach, one of the sandier beaches on Whidbey Island. He wasn't sure what the running conditions would be like, as he didn't take many beach vacations. But there was an exercise room in the clubhouse nearby, and Adam thought he might use that.

Or he might not run at all. But running provided such a great way for his mind to work through things that he couldn't usually go too long without pounding the pavement.

Today, all he could think about was Janey, and while she'd haunted him for years, this was different. This was him holding her hand, and smelling her perfume, and having fantasies of more than that.

He'd never allowed himself to venture too far into those dangerous waters, because there was no point. Matt had claimed her on the very night Adam had wanted to make his move, and there was nothing he could do to change history. Sure, he'd dip a toe in when he took her presents, but he was always quick to remind himself that she wasn't really available.

But his last date with her had said maybe she was. And it was that slippery *maybe* that he clung to, hoped in, ran for.

When he got back to his car, his phone flashed with a blue light. His heart kicked up a notch as if he was still running. "Could be anything," he told himself as he reached for the sports drink in the console. Bypassing the phone beside the bottle, he pulled the drink out and guzzled it, silently hoping the blue light belonged to Janey.

Satiated and ready to shower, he sat behind the steering wheel and allowed himself to brighten the phone screen. Just to see who'd texted.

He had eight texts, one of which was from Janey.

We'll see.

What a perfectly diplomatic answer. He sighed as he ignored the texts from Sarah, his secretary, and Trent, the officer assigned to the early morning shift that day. He wasn't going in to work today, and their questions could wait until Monday. Or they could ask Milo, who should be walking in the door within the hour.

After showering, packing, and hunting around the shed for a football, Adam tossed his bag in the backseat and returned to the house to face the dogs. "All right, you two," he said. "Come on."

Gypsy almost trampled him in her enthusiasm to please him. "Sit down, sit down."

She complied, her smile infectious. He grinned at her and said, "Come on, Fable."

The husky approached more slowly, still licking his jaws as Adam had interrupted his breakfast. He stopped beside Gypsy, but Fable didn't sit. He would—if Adam had a treat to give him. But otherwise? He could stand, thanks.

"Brenda is coming over after work," he said. "You remember her, don't you?"

Gypsy cocked her head as if truly trying to figure out if she could remember Brenda. Fable just stared at him.

"She's taking you home with her while I'm gone. I don't want any trouble." He gave a stern glare to Fable. "All right?"

The husky yawned, extended his front paws out in front of him, and kept his hindquarters up in the air as he stretched.

"All right." Adam gave them both a scrub along the ears, grabbed his wallet and keys, and left the house. He drove out of town and down around Discovery Bay, marveling at how much lighter he felt just being outside the Hawthorne Harbor city limits.

It was miraculous, really, that he could drive for a couple of hours and end up somewhere that felt completely different from Hawthorne Harbor. While he loved his job, he didn't get outside the city limits much, and he rolled the windows down on the cruiser to let in the fresh air and the scent of freedom.

He took the ferry from Port Townsend, wondering how Janey was going to make it to Double Bluff Beach. The ferry from Port Townsend to Coupeville was about a forty-five minute ride, and to his knowledge, Janey hadn't been on a ferry since Matt's death. She rarely left town at all. He stood at the railing, the sound of the seawater splashing the sides of the ferry filling his ears, as well as the scream that he probably kept *too* close of an eye on her if he knew such things about her.

His mind drifted from Janey to Matt, and he wondered what had gone wrong that day. The findings of the investigation had been inconclusive as to why the fire had started, only that it had begun in the engine room and moved rapidly to consume the whole boat.

Shaking his head to clear the memories of that horrible day, he gazed out across the Puget Sound, the water, wind, and waves creating one of the most beautiful scenes in the world.

By the time he navigated to the beach house his brother had rented for the weekend, his stomach reminded him that he was going to grab breakfast on the way out of town and hadn't. Drew was always going on and on about the breakfast burritos at Duality. Adam was no stranger to the gas station-slash-eatery, and he stopped by the joint more often than he wanted to admit.

Drew opened the front door of the beach house as Adam straightened from the cruiser, a smile already on his face. "You made it."

"Pretty drive," Adam said. "Am I okay to park here?"

"Yeah, sure. Janey's coming with Gretchen and Dixie. Mom and Joel won't be here until later."

"Oh?" Adam strode toward his brother. "She didn't say they would be coming late." He climbed the stairs and embraced Drew. "How are you doing? Ready to get married?"

Drew chuckled and pounded Adam on the back. "Just about." They stepped back and Drew continued with, "Joel said he had to stay and take care of the animals this afternoon before they could leave. Then Dwayne Harper is going to come over on Saturday and Sunday."

Dwayne owned a small apple orchard several miles down the road from Adam's mother and step-father. They'd been helping each other for as long as Adam could remember. "So this is the place, huh?" He ducked through the doorway and looked around the bright, airy house. Light flowed from front to back and the entire wall before him faced the beach and was made of glass.

"Wow." Adam moved toward it, the idea to move to Double Bluff Beach invading his mind. Surely the small towns around here needed police officers, right? A deck extended beyond the house, with steps that led right down to the sandy beach. The wind whipped the waves against the shore, and Adam admired the bay beyond that.

He'd walked through a spacious living room, with a dining area on his right and the kitchen on the left.

"Two bedrooms on the main level," he said. "Four upstairs. You can have one to yourself." Drew gestured for Adam to follow him. "Main bath here." He pointed to the first door on his left. "I think this room for Mom and Joel."

Adam peeked into the room, and it was well-furnished

and seemed fresh and clean. "This is a nice place. Where did you find it?"

"Just on Your Home," Drew said. "There's a bedroom here with bunk beds. We'll probably put the kids here."

Drew took the tour upstairs, where he thought Adam and Janey, as well as he and Gretchen would each have their own room. One pair of bedrooms was hooked together by a Jack-and-Jill bathroom, and it had the largest counter.

"Women in there," Adam said.

"Probably." Drew stepped to the last door on the right side. "I was thinking this would be your room."

It was square, a box, with a queen bed opposite of the window. He moved toward the glass and said, "Beach view. Sold."

Drew laughed and said, "So you decided not to bring the dogs? You know this is a leash-free beach."

"Did you bring yours?"

"Of course. You didn't hear Blue whining when we passed my bedroom?" Drew stepped back out into the hall and opened the door next to Adam's. Blue, his over-eager German shepherd burst from the room like a jack-in-the-box, his whole body wagging as he flew toward Adam.

Adam loved Drew's dogs, and he crouched down to let Blue and then Chief lick his face, laughing as he scrubbed their necks and ears. "Did he trap you in that bedroom? Did he?"

"Should've brought Fable and Gypsy."

"Oh, can you imagine?" Adam straightened and chuckled. "Four huge dogs up here. It would've been chaos." He started for the steps. "I'm starving. Anything to eat here?"

Drew followed him back downstairs and into the kitchen. "Eggs and bread."

"Done." Adam set about cracking eggs to make a sandwich while Drew sat at the counter and cocked his head. He dropped two slices of bread into the toaster and set it. "What? You want one?"

"You seem...overly chipper."

Adam turned his back on his brother and opened a cupboard to find a pan, trying to find the right thing to say. "I'm on vacation. I never go on vacation."

"Yeah, that's true...but that's not it."

Adam set the frying pan on the stove and opened the fridge, muttering, "Butter, butter."

"In the door."

He found the fat and worked to put a bit in the pan to melt.

"Have you got a new case at work?"

"What? N—Yes. New case at work." If that would get Drew off this topic of conversation, Adam could stand to tell the little white lie. Besides, he thought about Janey a lot at work. Had solved a whole Rubix cube while his mind sorted through what to do about her, what to say to her, what move to make next.

He poured the eggs into the pan and they sizzled.

Drew let him cook in peace, and Adam said, "How's the lavender growing?" His brother had recently quit his job as a paramedic and renovated the house next door to their mom and step-dad.

"Growing great," he said.

"Do you miss the bus?"

"Every day."

Adam turned back to his brother, though he really shouldn't take his eyes off the eggs for too long. "Yeah? And that's okay?"

"It's okay, yeah." Drew shrugged and pointed to the pan. "Moving out there and taking over that farm was the right thing to do."

Adam grunted and pushed his eggs into a square the size of a piece of bread. The toast popped up and he slathered butter on it, then slid the egg patty onto the bread. He ignored the begging German shepherds and sat down next to his brother with a sigh. "I love eggs."

"That you do." Drew nudged him with his elbow while he ate.

"When is Gretchen getting here?" Adam asked, careful not to say Janey's name. He'd never told anyone—not even Drew—about his insane crush on Janey, but he didn't trust himself not to say much about her now that they'd been out a few times.

It was easier before, when Adam knew he didn't have a chance with her. But now that there was some hope, now that he'd held her hand, he couldn't imagine being able to say her name without using a softer voice than he normally did.

"Should be soon." Drew lifted his phone and looked at it. "They left two hours ago."

Adam ate his sandwich and had just gotten up to put the plate in the dishwasher when a horn honked outside. Drew whooped and headed for the front door, but Adam couldn't seem to make his feet move out of the kitchen.

He heard Gretchen squeal and giggle and a few moments later, she ushered her blonde daughter through the door, saying, "You two are sharing the room with the bunk beds. Go find it."

Dixie skipped toward him, saying, "Hiya, Chief," before turning and disappearing down the hall.

Jess came in wearing headphones and a backpack and a look that said he wasn't ultra-pleased to be here without Thayne. He met Adam's eye and pulled out one earbud. "Where are you sleeping?"

"Bedroom upstairs."

The boy came closer, and it took all of Adam's concentration to maintain eye contact with Jess instead of searching the doorway for his mom. "Don't you think I'm a little old to be sharing a room with a girl?"

"I—I don't—"

"We're not cousins or anything." Jess huffed and twisted back toward the front door, where Gretchen and Drew spoke to each other with stars in their eyes and whispers in their voices.

"You like Dixie."

"I do *not*," Jess said, spinning back to Adam, who definitely saw and heard something too vehement in the boy's statement. He cocked his head, trying to figure out what he'd said wrong to elicit such a reaction from Jess.

"Maybe I can sleep with you." Jess looked at him with hopeful eyes. "I'll sleep on the floor or whatever."

Adam had no idea what to say to him. And then Janey appeared in the doorway, and Adam forgot about Jess's dilemma. He only had eyes for her, and everything inside him urged him to cross the room and take her in his arms the way a boyfriend would.

He held perfectly still instead. Her eyes met his too, and an zip of electricity shot between them. Surely everyone in the room had felt it, but Jess didn't even turn toward his mom.

Gretchen, however, had noticed that both Janey and Adam had frozen and couldn't seem to look away from each other. She nudged Drew, which set Adam into action.

"Come on," he said to Jess. "Let's go check out the bunk beds and see what the real deal is." He put his arm around Jess's shoulders and steered him down the hall, the energy between him and Janey still crackling like lightning.

11

Janey refused to let herself clear her throat until she'd towed her suitcase upstairs and into the bedroom Drew had detailed. First door on the left. Once behind it, she pressed her back into the wood and exhaled.

It hadn't even been forty-eight hours since she'd seen Adam, and still the sight of him had rendered her weak. Breathless.

"Brainless," she muttered. "Pull yourself together." She didn't want to distract from Gretchen's planning weekend. The woman had sent a five-page itinerary, for crying out loud. And Adam's parents were here, and her son, and she couldn't go freezing and staring like that again.

She left her suitcase by the dresser and went into the bathroom. Staring at her reflection, she found a flush in her cheeks. A flush! Maybe she could pass it off as excitement to be at the beach, one of her favorite locations in the whole world.

"Mom!" Jess's voice came through the door, and Janey sighed as she went to see what he wanted. She already knew, but she needed to take care of this issue before he hurt Dixie's feelings. Or Gretchen's.

"Get in here," she hissed at him, and Jess ducked into her bedroom. She cast a furtive glance left and right like she couldn't be seen talking to her own child.

"Mom, I can't sleep in the same room as Dixie." He looked seriously upset about it, not just surly as he had been for the *entire* drive here. Even when she'd white-knuckled the railing on the ferry for forty-five straight minutes, he'd still sent her dirty looks about the sleeping situation.

She sighed and cocked her hip. "Why not, Jess? You guys get along great. She'll change in the bathroom."

He shuffled his feet, his face turning red. Janey hadn't seen Jess blush about anything since he'd won the spelling bee in fifth grade and the whole school had stood and cheered for him.

Two sharp knocks sounded on her bedroom door, and then Adam poked his head in. "He can sleep in my bedroom."

Janey nearly got whiplash as she looked back to Jess, and then back to Adam. Then Jess. "You talked to him about this?"

"I can't sleep in there," Jess said.

Adam cleared his throat. "Let him sleep with me, Janey. He has a good reason."

"Oh?" She folded her arms. "And what is it?" She glared at Jess. "Hmm?"

He looked at Adam, his puppy dog pleading eyes alerting Janey to a real crisis here. "Adam?"

"You might as well tell her," he said.

"Yeah," Janey said quickly. "Moms find out everything anyway."

"It's nothing," Jess said. "I just...." He lifted his chin and looked at Janey. "Please, Mom."

She warred with herself, and having Adam standing so close and smelling so good, she could barely think. "Fine," she said.

"Thanks, Mom!" Jess launched himself at her and wrapped his arms around her. The hug only lasted for a moment, which was more than she'd gotten from him since he'd started seventh grade, and then he stepped over to Adam. "Thanks, Chief." He fist-bumped Adam and walked out of the room. "I'm just gonna go grab my suitcase."

Janey waited until Jess's pounding footsteps faded, and then she trained her eyes on Adam. "So what's his reason."

"Oh, I can't say." He held up both hands in surrender and fell back a step into the hall. "He made me promise, and the Chief doesn't break his promises." He flashed her a smile that made her heart thump around like a lopsided bowling ball rolling down the lane, and followed Jess down the stairs.

"Well, at least they get along," she muttered to herself.

~

AN HOUR LATER, SHE SAT ON THE BACK DECK WITH A GLASS of peach lemonade in her hand, her sunglasses shading her eyes, and happiness spreading through her at the tranquil sight before her. Jess had changed into a pair of board shorts and followed Dixie down to the beach despite the wind coming off the bay.

Gretchen and Drew had disappeared into town to buy groceries, though Adam claimed the fridge was full of food, and Joel and Donna hadn't arrived yet.

Which was why she had one hand wrapped around the cold glass and the other laced in Adam's. "This place is really nice," she said for probably the third time.

Adam reclined in his lounger, his eyes closed. "Hm mm." He wasn't asleep, because his grip on her hand stayed firm, but she still stole a few seconds to simply stare at his handsome face.

A smile touched her lips, and she faced the waves again. "So do you like the beach?" she asked.

"I like running on the beach."

"So you won't go in the water?"

"It's September. That water is freezing."

"Dixie and Jess are in it."

He chuckled and squeezed her fingers. "It's on the itinerary, so I'm sure I'll do it."

One of Drew's dogs barked, and Janey's attention flew to the dog, anticipating a problem. But Blue was just chasing a bird, sand kicking up behind his paws as he galloped along the shore.

"Do you ever wish you could go back in time and change something?"

Adam opened his eyes and looked at her. He didn't seem like he found the question weird or comical. "Yes."

"What would it be?" She laid her head against the back of the chair and gazed at him, the moment between them soft now that they were alone.

"I don't...know."

"You're not a great liar, Chief." She giggled, as he'd tried to tell her he didn't know the answer to why he hadn't gotten married yet. Maybe he'd tell her now.

"I'd go back and tell my dad thank you before he died," she said.

"Oh yeah? You wouldn't keep Matt home on the day of the ferry fire?"

Janey normally would've flinched at the sound of his name, that single syllable the cause of so much turmoil in her life. But this time, she didn't. Her heart didn't clench, and her stomach stayed steady.

"No," she said. "Some things are just meant to be, you know?"

"I guess," he said.

"So I'd tell my dad thank you. He put up with a lot with us four girls, and I never really got to tell him how much I appreciated him." She smiled, but it did carry a hint of sadness. She cleared her throat and asked, "So what about you?"

"I'd, well, I'd—oh, wow. I don't know if I can say this out loud." He pulled his hand free and sat up straight, his eyes singular on the kids on the beach.

"You can," she said. "I won't judge you."

He rested his hands on his knees and took a great breath, like what he was about to say required strength and inner fortitude. "I'd go back to high school and ask you out."

She started to laugh, but he continued, his voice possessing a quiet strength. "Even though you had that other boyfriend. And if it didn't work out then, I'd make sure I called you *before* that stupid Fall Festival dance where Matt beat me to asking you to dance."

Janey's insides iced over, and she stared at the side of Adam's face, trying to make sense of everything he'd said. Everything he'd just admitted.

As if in slow motion, he turned toward her, his eyes locking onto hers. "I've liked you for a really long time, Janey. Longer than is even normal, or sane." Yet he didn't laugh. His dark eyes seemed electric and fiery, like the sky during a lightning storm. "So if I had one thing to go back and change, it would be to make sure you knew I was interested in you before twenty years went by."

His words sat between them like a hunk of cement, and try as she might, Janey had no idea how to respond.

He stood up, switching his attention back to the beach. "Excuse me."

She let him go though she wanted to call him back. Make him explain himself further. He'd been by her side through childhood. She'd cheered for him at the football games. He'd never given any indication that he wanted to go out with her.

Even on the night of the Fall Festival, when Matt had asked her to dance, Adam hadn't flinched. He'd said nothing. He'd stood beside Matt as his best man as she married him. Never once had she known he had feelings for her. Never until last week.

Her heart thundered in her chest, making breathing difficult. Now her stomach swooped, and she thought the crackers and lemonade she'd been snacking on would make a reappearance.

How had he endured all of that and not said anything? Had Matt known? The questions continued to pile up, but one broke free from the pack and screamed through her mind.

Had she kept herself from happiness with Adam because she was still hung up on a man who'd died twelve years ago?

12

Adam couldn't stay at the beach house, not after what he'd confessed. "You're so delusional," he muttered to himself as he drove down the highway. No way he could go back there and exist in the same space as Janey and keep the relationship a secret. Not after spilling one of his biggest secrets.

He caught sight of his mother as she and Joel passed him going the opposite way. He should go back. Go back and get everything out in the open so they could get on with the weekend. His and Janey's relationship didn't have to detract from planning Drew and Gretchen's wedding.

Did it?

He pulled over to the side of the road and said, "Call Janey Germaine."

The screen on his console blipped with blue light and said in a robotic female voice, "Calling Janey Germaine."

Adam looked out the window, every organ in his body rioting. He couldn't seem to settle on any one thought, especially as her phone rang twice, then three times.

"Hey," she said, overly chipper. "What's up?"

"You're with my parents, aren't you?"

"Yes, just a sec."

Scrapes and scuffles came through the line, and then she said, "Where are you?" in a much more hushed and urgent tone.

"I went for a drive."

"I don't suppose we're going to make it through the weekend without telling everyone about us, are we?"

"I don't know," Adam said, thinking of Jess's schoolboy crush on his best friend, Dixie. But Adam knew his crush was way beyond schoolboy stage. And he knew he'd blown things wide open for Janey by saying so much.

"I'm worried about Jess," she whispered. "He's going through a transition right now."

Adam half-chuckled. "Yeah, they're called hormones." He looked away from his reflection in the glass and said, "Look, I'll talk to him about it. See how he reacts. Then maybe we can go from there."

"I'm sorry," she said, her voice pitching up the slightest bit. "I had no idea."

"It's fine," he said. "It's not your fault at all. I shouldn't have said so much."

"Did you really like me in high school?"

"Do you really think the Chief of Police goes around lying to women?"

She giggled, which somehow broke the tension between them. "Come on back," she said. "Your mother already suspects something is going on."

"How so?"

"I told her you were my sister, but then had to go upstairs to talk to you. And she knows you should be here."

"Just tell her I went out driving. Wait." He exhaled, his immature behavior getting him stuck between a rock and a hard place. "Don't tell her that. She knows I only go out driving when I'm stressed. Then she'll want to know what's going on." He put the car in gear and eased back onto the road.

"Tell her I had to run and get some drinks."

"We have drinks here."

"What's Jess's favorite soda?"

"So you're going to sugar him up and then tell him we're dating?"

"If it kills two birds with one stone...."

She laughed, and he joined in. "What do you want?" he asked.

"Diet Coke," she said. "Jess too."

"Two Diet Cokes, coming right up." Adam pulled into a convenience store and stared at the cases of soda. He had no idea there were so many choices for Diet Coke. In the end, he picked what he hoped was regular Diet Coke

—no cherry, no vanilla, no zeroes in sight—and headed back to the beach house.

When he got there, he called, "Here's your soda," as if he'd planned to make a drink run all along.

"There you are." His mom came out of the kitchen, a wide smile on her face.

"Hey, Mom." He set the drinks on the counter and embraced her. "When did you guys get here?"

"Oh, just a few minutes ago. Joel's lying down."

Alarm pulled through Adam and he straightened. "He is? Is he okay?"

"He was up most of the night with one of the goats. He'll be fine once he gets in a little nap." She nodded toward the huge wall of windows. "Janey's on the deck. Kids are on the beach."

Adam picked up the sodas and moved that way. "Are you going to come out?"

"In a few minutes. Drew asked me to make those cheddar garlic knots to go with the pizza they're bringing back." She smiled, and nothing seemed too off. Adam nodded and went back outside, the sun warm but the wind chilly.

He sat beside Janey, in the same lounge chair he'd been in before, and set the bottles of soda on the table between them. "Drinks."

She looked at him, and he swore an hour could've passed and he wouldn't have known. Gazing into her eyes made everything else fade into nothing, as if she alone held the key to experiencing life.

Blink, he told himself. *Blink now!*

He did, and changed his gaze to the water. "Still goin' strong, huh?"

"You'll have to drag Jess off the beach," she said, as if he hadn't confessed his decades-old love for her only an hour ago, right in this very spot.

"Are we going to talk about what I said?" he asked.

She reached over and brushed her fingers along his forearm before picking up her bottle and twisting the lid. The hiss of carbonation escaping made a background as she said, "We already did."

"That's it?"

"Yeah, that's it."

Adam's chest tightened. "I was jealous of him for a long time," he said. He didn't need to say Matt's name. Janey would know. "Eventually, that faded. And then he died, and then I felt so guilty. And then...then my old feelings came back."

"I understand a little bit about feeling guilty."

"What do you have to feel guilty about?"

"Dating someone else." She took a long drag of her soda. "For a while there, I vowed I never would. But that's...unrealistic."

Adam didn't want to agree, so he said nothing. His mother poked her head out of the house and said, "I'm going to take a shower. Drew and Gretchen will be back in thirty minutes with dinner."

"Sounds good," Adam said, his voice just a touch too loud. His mom either didn't notice or didn't care, and she left.

He waited through a few agonizingly slow breaths. Then he reached over and took Janey's hand in his again. She sighed as if his touch healed unseen things and squeezed his fingers.

Letting his eyes drift closed once again, more joy than Adam had ever known spread through him.

∽

THAT NIGHT, AFTER DINNER, AFTER CARD GAMES, AFTER WAY too much bread, Adam went upstairs with a slightly sunburnt Jess. "You'll have to wear more sunblock tomorrow, bud," he said.

"It'll fade," Jess said. "It always does."

Adam had his doubts. If Jess could see the Rudolph quality of his nose, he wouldn't say that. Adam followed him into their bedroom and paused. "Okay, so Drew put your cot against the wall."

His brother had found a couple of hammocks and cots in the garage of the beach house and texted the owner to see if they could be used. When the answer was yes, Drew had brought one cot up to this room and hung the hammocks from the deck so people could nap there tomorrow.

"You can take the top blanket from the bed," Adam said, pulling it down. "There's another one underneath. I'll be plenty warm."

Once they were both lying in their beds, Adam gazed at the ceiling and asked, "Jess, can I talk to you about something?"

"Yeah, I guess."

"It sort of has to do with Dixie."

The boy sucked in a breath. "You didn't tell my mom, did you?"

"Of course not."

"Good. It's stupid anyway, and I don't want Dixie to know."

"It's not stupid," Adam said, trying to make his words line up. "It's okay to have a crush on someone."

"Right." Jess's tone indicated he didn't need a lecture on the birds and the bees.

"I sort of have a crush I wanted you to know about." His mouth was so dry. He hadn't even told his brother about his feelings for Janey. And telling her son—his best friend's son—was infinitely worse than talking to Drew about it.

The cot squeaked as Jess moved on it, but Adam kept his eyes on the ceiling, tracking the lines in the wood he could barely see with the moonlight coming in the window.

"It's your mom," Adam blurted. "I kinda like your mom the way you like Dixie."

Jess hissed. Or maybe he was simply exhaling. "Are you serious?" he asked.

"Kinda. Yeah." Adam cleared his throat. "See? Women make all men nervous, no matter how old we get." He chuckled, finding his center and seizing onto it. "How do you feel about that? I mean, what if I asked your mom out and we went to dinner or something?"

"I...guess, yeah. She never goes out. She'd probably like it."

"Why do you think she never goes out?"

"Because she still loves my dad."

Adam pulled in a breath, the words so bare and so full of truth they burned. He didn't know what to say to such a powerful statement, and he turned his head and looked out the moonlit window.

"It's not stupid how you feel about Dixie," he said, real quiet, almost like he didn't want Jess to hear him. Several seconds of silence passed, and Adam wondered if maybe the boy had fallen asleep.

"Yeah, probably not," he finally said. "And I can tell that you like my mom more than *kinda*."

"Yeah, probably." Adam chuckled, the sound rolling and gaining strength until they were both laughing out loud.

13

Janey stood on the back deck, the wind trying to take her hair right off her head. She kept her hands buried deep in the front pocket of her hoodie, not even willing to take them out so she could sip her coffee. It had likely gone cold in the few minutes she'd been waiting for the sun to rise.

The golden glow was almost over the mountains, and she wanted to experience the day at its birth. Wanted to see if there were any new possibilities for this Saturday. For her.

Finally, the edge of the star peeked over the mountain, and Janey tilted her head back and closed her eyes. A sigh passed through her whole body as the first rays of light touched the little bit of skin exposed to the elements.

"Watching the sun rise?"

She turned at the sound of Joel's voice, a fond smile lighting upon her lips. "Yes, come see."

He ambled over to her and faced the bay. "Did you hear Jess and Adam laughing last night?"

"The whole house heard them." Janey's curiosity had kept her awake for an extra half-hour, especially when neither one of them would answer her texts. She didn't expect Jess to be up for at least another hour, but Adam should be down at any time. She wanted to see him first thing.

"Donna's fixing to make pumpkin pancakes."

Janey smiled and threw a glance in Joel's direction. "How festive."

"She goes crazy this time of year with the pumpkin."

She wasn't sure if Joel appreciated that or not. He sipped his coffee and watched the waves. A rush of gratitude swept over her, and she half-turned toward him. "Have I told you thank you for always taking Jess when I need you to? For letting him ride the horses and go out to that wishing well, and...all of it."

Joel looked at her. "You say it every time I see you, Janey."

"Well, I am thankful."

"Drew does most of it." Joel put his mug next to hers on the railing. "Jess is a good worker. He takes care of the horses pretty much by himself these days."

"He's not out there every day," she said. "So that can't be true."

"When he is out there, he does it."

Janey nodded, glad her son wasn't being a burden to Adam's parents. With a realization that startled her physically, she realized that if she and Adam ever got married, Joel and Donna would become Jess's grandparents.

She wondered what Adam had said to Jess last night to make him laugh so hard. Had he confessed the same thing to him that he had to her? Her impatience made her feet shift and her stomach pinch.

"Have you seen Adam?"

"He took the dogs running." Drew stepped beside Janey. "Left about an hour ago, so he should be back soon."

Janey wasn't sure if she should be frustrated that Adam got up early and ran along the beach, or if she should admire him for exercising while on vacation. The man amazed her, and he was almost too perfect.

Don't forget he's Matt's best friend.

That was definitely a strike against him.

And that he's the Chief of Police. Not exactly a safe job. He could die at any time.

She recognized the absurdity of her thoughts at the same time she gave him another strike. One more, and would she throw him out?

She sighed, scanning the beach now as the sunlight started warming the sand. Sure enough, only a moment later, a man rounded the curve of the bay, running with two dogs beside him.

Drew's German shepherds flanked him, one on each side, their tongues hanging out of their mouths as they kept pace with the cop. He wore athletic shorts and a gray T-shirt that clung to his broad shoulders. Janey had never seen anything so magnificent, and all her muscles released from how tight she'd been holding them against the chill in the air.

"Ah, there he is now." Joel wore the smile in his voice Janey felt stretch her mouth.

Drew went down the steps to meet his dogs, one of which barked and ran circles around him. He laughed, and sand flew as he tried to catch the canine. Adam stretched, taking his time before he came up the steps.

Janey held very, very still, watching him advance.

"Morning," he said to Joel, his eyes looking past her instead of directly at her.

"Your mom is making breakfast," Joel said.

"Great." Adam moved to step around Janey. His pinky finger barely grazed hers, and she almost fell to her knees when her bones turned to marshmallows. "Hey, Janey."

"Hey," fell from her lips. Why she was going all melty, she had no idea. Because he was handsome? He'd been good-looking for years and years. Because he'd gone running with his brother's dogs? He probably did that every day back home, but with his own dogs. She inhaled some reason into her brain and turned.

He'd already moved all the way to the door. "Hey, what were you and Jess laughing about last night?"

He gave her a flirtatious grin and said, "I'll tell you later." He went inside without another word, leaving her to face two slobbery German shepherds who'd just launched themselves up the steps to the deck.

After breakfast, which she'd eaten between Gretchen and Jess, she sat with Gretchen at the dining room table, a binder spread before them. She peered at the columns labeled Flowers, Dress, Photographer, Reception Center, and at least half a dozen more.

"You're doing the flowers," Janey said, reading the notes. "How's that coming?"

"Pretty good. I'm making all the centerpieces. My bouquet, the boutonnieres, and flower crowns for the bridesmaids."

"Flower crowns?" Janey couldn't imagine herself wearing a flower crown. "What's that going to be like?"

Gretchen flipped to the *FLOWERS* divider and a sketch sat on the first page. "Something like this. It won't be too huge."

It looked huge to Janey, and she studied it for a few moments. "Is that a daisy?" Several smaller flowers ran along the forehead, with a much larger one over the right temple.

"Yes." Gretchen gazed at the sketch with fondness. "I've been engineering a hybrid daisy. It's an indigo daisy, and they'll be ready by the wedding."

"I've never heard you talk about an indigo daisy."

Janey's voice was laced with surprise and admiration at the same time.

"Oh, I've been cross-pollinating them for a few years." She giggled and turned the page. "Dreaming." She shrugged and said, "I guess sometimes dreams do come true."

Janey thought of Adam, and how long he'd been waiting to go out with her. Had one of his dreams come true when they'd eaten soup at the lodge?

The weight of fulfilling someone's dreams suddenly seemed crushing, and she leaned away from the binder. "So you knew Drew for a while before you guys started dating, right?"

"Yeah, well, sort of. He delivered Daisy, and we'd spent some time out at the lavender farm when I used to come as a teenager. Nothing serious."

"Nothing serious," Janey echoed, her thoughts moving away from the wedding preparations.

Gretchen didn't flip more pages, or move to a new section, or ask another question. By the time Janey felt the weight of her stare, it was too late to play off as nothing.

"Janey," she said in a cautious voice, almost a sing-song. "What's going on?"

"Nothing," she said quickly.

Gretchen tucked Janey's hair behind her ear. "You've never lied to me before. It's kind of cute how you think you can."

Janey smiled and laughed with Gretchen. "Fine. All

right." She straightened and tossed her head, as if preparing to do something wild and adventurous. "Okay." She cleared her throat.

"Are you dating someone?"

Janey pressed her lips together to keep them from smiling and nodded.

Gretchen bounced in her seat, her eyes alight. "Oh my gosh. This is huge!"

"I know." She glanced around. "Sh. No one knows yet. I haven't even talked to Jess about it." Of course, Adam was supposed to talk to Jess, but "later" hadn't come yet so she didn't know if he actually had. Or why they'd been laughing. He'd gone down to the beach with the kids and the rest of his family, leaving her and Gretchen to work on the wedding.

Gretchen quieted and leaned in farther, also glancing around. "Okay, I'll be quiet. But come on. You haven't dated in years. Or even seemed interested in it."

"That's not true. I've been thinking about it for a few months."

"Thinking is a lot different than doing." Gretchen cocked one eyebrow. "You won't even give me a hint as to who it is?"

Janey could give little clues, sure. But she liked the idea of just saying Adam's name. Maybe not as much as she liked keeping their budding relationship secret. So she oscillated between blurting out his name and bottling everything up.

"Just a hint," Gretchen said.

"He's an old friend."

"Oh, that doesn't narrow down the playing field at all." Gretchen flipped to the RECEPTION CENTER tab in her binder. "You grew up in Hawthorne Harbor, and so did just about everyone else who still lives there."

Janey didn't want to detract from her friend's weekend, so she focused on the binder. "Magleby Mansion will be beautiful at Christmas."

"Mabel is decorating it herself." Gretchen flipped a page. "I need to decide on the menu, though."

"Are you doing a full dinner or cake and refreshments?"

"Mabel said I could have whatever I wanted." She met Janey's eyes. "Aaron and I had a simple wedding, because we didn't have any money. Is it wrong of me to want to splurge?"

"Heavens, no." Janey looked at the paper. "So this is a full menu. Oh my goodness. This one comes with crab legs?" She scooted the binder closer so she could read the scrumptious descriptions of the food. "Mabel can do all of this?"

"She has three chefs that come in for weddings." Gretchen pointed to the second one down. "I was thinking of the salmon. It says Washington, and it's Drew's favorite fish...."

They worked through the menu, the cake flavor, as well as the design, and gushed over the photographer's online portfolio. By the time lunch rolled around, Gretchen was happy with their progress, and Janey couldn't wait another second to see Adam and find out the answers to her questions.

Gretchen got up and stirred the soup she put in a slow cooker after breakfast. "Can you get out the rolls and slice them?" She replaced the lid and moved to the back door. After going out on the deck, she called everyone in for lunch.

Janey finished slicing the rolls and set them in a basket next to the butter dish. She took pitchers of strawberry punch out of the fridge and braced herself for the fray as the dogs arrived first. Then Jess and Dixie. Adam entered, chattering with Drew, and he stepped right over to where she stood in the kitchen, sweeping one arm around her waist.

"Hey." He grinned down at her and twined his fingers in hers before realization made him freeze.

Everything had happened so fast, Janey hadn't had time to breathe, think, or react. Adam stepped back, but a hush had fallen over the kitchen.

"See?" Jess said to Dixie in a know-it-all voice. "He likes my mom."

14

Adam had lost his mind. Lost it completely. Maybe it had been addled by the sun. Or burned by the wind. Something.

He tore his eyes from Janey's stunned ones and looked at Jess. "Hey, that was a secret, remember?"

Jess's eyes rounded and his half-tanned, half-sunburned face paled when he added, "You want me to spill your secrets?"

The boy shook his head, and Adam nodded before looking at Drew, who gaped at him like he'd never seen Adam with a woman.

"Are you—?"

"We're dating," Janey blurted before Adam could say anything. She edged toward Jess as Adam's mom and Joel entered the house.

"Oh...okay," his mom said, taking in the scene. "What did we miss?"

"Janey and Adam are dating!" Gretchen squealed the words, her voice pitching toward intolerable levels by the last word.

A flurry of activity happened then, almost too much for him to catalog. Gretchen hugged Janey. Janey gripped Jess's shoulders and asked him something. He nodded. Smiled.

Drew clapped Adam on the back like he'd just gotten engaged instead of having gone out with a woman for dinner a couple of times. He kept one eye on Janey until the clamor died down. He wanted to lace his fingers through hers, but that was what had gotten him in this mess to begin with.

"So when did this happen?" his mother asked.

"Oh, I don't know," Janey said evasively.

"The night you two kept Jess while Janey went up to the lodge. We went to dinner." He'd enjoyed their secrecy, and he wanted it a little longer, at least with the people in town. "We were keeping things simple," he said. "Private, because of Jess, and because of my job."

"But Adam told me last night." Jess grinned at him, and a flash of love for the boy bolted through Adam. He'd spent the whole morning watching him and Dixie play in the water, build sandcastles, throw a football, and play with Drew's dogs. They were great kids, and Adam was glad he'd get to be Dixie's step-uncle. As for Jess...he wasn't sure what to hope for yet.

The thought of replacing Matt was laughable. Adam had never been as good as Matt, and he'd always known it. It was why he was on the offensive line in high school, while Matt was the quarterback. Why he'd faded into the background and let Matt date Janey. Why he'd swallowed his feelings until they went away. Why he'd thought for years that even if he'd gotten to Janey first, she still would've chosen Matt over him.

"I'd still like to keep it between us," Adam said, finally latching onto Janey's hand, glad when she squeezed back. "The people of Hawthorne Harbor like to...speculate about my relationships. Can we do that, as a family? Keep this to ourselves?"

Murmurs of assent and nods went through the group.

"Great." Adam looked at Janey. "Time for lunch?"

"Yes," she said, her dark eyes bright and filled with laughter. "Time for lunch."

∽

ADAM WOKE ON MONDAY MORNING, IN HIS OWN BED, THE ghost of Janey's hand still in his. Once he'd announced that they were dating, he'd got to walk down the beach with her and laugh easily with her. Jess hadn't said anything else about it, and they hadn't talked about Dixie either.

He'd run and laughed and played with her just fine, so he was obviously much better at hiding his feelings than Adam was—at least since that dinner at the lodge. He'd been quite adept at keeping everything hidden before the door had been opened and that soup had been consumed.

Who would've thought that soup would be the reason he'd finally get to be with Janey Germaine?

He rolled over and knew from the light streaming through the bedroom window that he'd overslept and didn't have time for a run before work. So he got the dogs fed and let them into the yard, packed himself a lunch, and went to the station.

"Morning, Sarah," he said as he passed.

"Messages on your desk."

He suppressed his groan and made it to his office before sighing. He'd known his job would come with a lot of desk time, but he didn't have to enjoy it. He worked through the messages, calling people back and setting up meetings with the appropriate people.

Public works, the traffic team in his own department, emergency services. All of them had to coordinate and work together to handle the influx of people for the Fall Festival. He pulled out his calendar and realized he only had a month to get everything in place.

He'd been able to stay on task at work while dating before, but there was something different about Janey. She seemed to consume his every thought, take almost all of his mental energy, and he couldn't devote so much attention to her. At least not while at work.

The alarm on his phone went off at the same time his phone beeped. "Trent's ready for you," Sarah said over the intercom.

He swiped his phone off his desk and left his office. "Where is he?" he asked.

"Conference room two." Sarah swiveled toward him. "You need this." She handed him a folder and he perused it as he maneuvered through the desks and down the hall to the conference rooms.

Trent and two other officers were already inside, fiddling with the projector. "Maybe if I push this button." Trent did and twisted to look at the screen. "Ah, got it." He met Adam's eye. "Hey, boss. How was the beach?"

"Relaxing," he said with a smile.

"At least the rain held off until today," Lex said, one of the leaders of the traffic crew at the department.

Adam glanced out the window, where a steady drizzle had made most of the landscape gray and foggy. "Yeah. Lucky, I guess." He exhaled as he sat at the end of the table, facing the screen. "So where are we with our parade route?" He tapped the folder. "Lisa is getting pretty anxious to get the website updated."

"Right," Trent said. "We've got that info for her. As well as a schedule of when the roads will be blocked, and which officer will be where that Saturday."

The Fall Festival went for a full week, with a culminating parade on Saturday, which was the most work for Adam's department.

"All right," he said. "Lay it on me." He managed to listen and contribute while Trent went over their plan, and then while Lex detailed how many cops they'd brought in from Bell Hill and Port Williams to help with crowd control and general peace-keeping.

By lunch, he couldn't wait to escape to his office and eat his simple peanut butter sandwich. Because then he could think about Janey. Maybe even text her.

Before he could do any of that, a text came in from a number he didn't have saved in his phone.

Hey, Adam, this is Jess. I was wondering if I could come over and we could work on that motorcycle sometime?

Adam smiled, the thought of tinkering in the shed with Jess more appealing than Adam even knew.

Sure. Tonight?

Let me ask my mom.

I can swing by and pick you up on my way home from work. Make it easy for her.

Several minutes went by, and Adam waited to text Janey until he heard from Jess. He'd reached out, and Adam wanted to give the boy a chance to make his plans.

She says she can bring over dinner and then we can do the motorcycle. Is that okay?

Is she cooking?

Haha, Jess responded. *She said she'll get pizza.*

I like pizza. What time?

Six-thirty?

See you then.

Six-thirty came quickly, as Adam always had too much work to do and not enough time to do it in. He'd just finished straightening up the living room when Jess knocked and then entered the house without waiting for an invitation.

"Hey," he said, carrying a skateboard under his arm and dripping rain from his waterproof poncho. Gypsy barked from the kitchen and came running toward the front door.

"Hey." Adam grinned at the boy and fist-bumped him as the dog arrived. "Where's your mom?"

"She let me skateboard over while she went to get the pizza. She's always running late." He put his board down, pulled off his poncho, and scrubbed Gypsy's head. "At least she let me have my board back."

"Oh? Did you lose it?"

He dipped his chin. "Yeah, for a week. I shouldn't have skipped school, and I promised I wouldn't again."

"Smart move," Adam said. "And not only to get the board back." He walked down the hall and into the kitchen. "You want something to drink? I have Diet Coke."

Jess followed him, his wet shoes squeaking against the floor. "Yeah, sure." He crouched down to pat Gypsy, and even Fable came over for a quick scrub. "Hey, I wanted to ask you something too, real quick before my mom gets here."

"Shoot." Adam pulled out some paper plates and plastic cups, wondering if he should use real dishes for pizza or not. He normally wouldn't, so he stuck to the decision.

"Will you teach me how to cook?" He straightened and looked at Adam. "Your mom's been doing some stuff, and I really like it."

Adam glanced at him, wanting to stare but not wanting to make him uncomfortable. "Yeah, sure."

"I know you're doing soups for the Fall Festival. I could just watch until that's over."

"You can help." Adam leaned his weight into his palms and looked squarely at Jess. "I mean, everyone has to pick up a knife sometime, right?"

Jess chuckled. "Yeah, just don't tell my mom."

"Don't tell me what?" Janey appeared, a stack of pizza boxes in her hand. "Door was open. Hope you don't mind that I came right in."

"Not at all." Adam's smile felt giddy and foolish, but he couldn't straighten it or tame it. He took the boxes from her and set them on the counter.

"So." She stepped over to Jess and drew him into her side. "What are we not telling me now?"

Adam spread the boxes out and started opening them to see what kind of pizza Janey had ordered.

"Oh, it's nothing," Jess said.

"I've heard that before." Janey cut Adam a look.

"He's just going to teach me how to cook. That's all."

Jess met her eye, and Adam realized that they were very nearly the same height now.

Something pinched crossed Janey's face, but she wiped it away quickly. "Sounds great. Now, I'm starving. Should we eat?"

The conversation stalled for a few minutes while they selected slices and poured drinks. When they were all seated around his tiny table, Adam said, "Are you sure you're okay with Jess learning to cook?"

"Your mother does it."

"She hasn't let him pick up a knife," Adam said, watching her, keenly aware Jess was too. "And I will."

Janey nibbled on her pizza. "It's really okay. It'll be good for Jess, and if I'm not here, I don't have to see it when his fingers get cut off."

A beat of silence passed, and then she laughed.

Adam wasn't sure if he should join in or not, but Jess did, and when the tension broke, he said, "I'm certified in first aid, in case you didn't know."

Janey rolled her eyes. "Of course you are."

"Oh, wow," Jess said. "Watching you two flirt is almost painful."

Adam's eyes flew to Jess, and Janey's chair scraped the floor she jerked so hard. "We're not...." she started. "Flirting."

Jess rolled his eyes and said, "Can we go out to the shed now?" He got up without waiting for Adam to answer and left through the back door, taking the dogs with him.

Though Adam wasn't finished eating yet, he stacked two more slices on his plate and picked it up. "We'll talk later, okay?"

She nodded, and he left her sitting at his kitchen table.

15

Janey remained at the table, her piece of pizza only half consumed. Keeping the relationship with Adam under wraps was almost easier than being able to flirt with him in front of her son.

Jess hadn't seemed *bothered* by the flirting, just...disgusted by it? Maybe.

When she'd suggested dinner, his enthusiasm for the evening had dropped a bit. Maybe he wanted to spend time with Adam alone. Janey could certainly understand that. She'd like to be out in the shed with Adam too. Watching him get his hands dirty, fitting little parts together to make a much more powerful machine run.

She left her dinner behind and moved to the front porch while dialing her sister. It was time to figure things out and make sure she wasn't doing damage to her son by dating Adam.

"Hey, there. Are you all tan and glowy now?" Annabelle laughed and then said, "Don, can you take him?" in a much quieter voice.

The unhappy squeal of Annabelle's one-year-old came through the line. "All right. You have all of my attention. You're calling about your mystery boyfriend, right?"

Janey sighed. "Yeah." She didn't want to deny it. "We told Jess about us, and he seems okay with it, but I'm not sure."

"You know, it would really help if I knew who he was okay with."

Janey looked at her Jeep parked beside Adam's cruiser. The rain dripped steadily against the windshield. Any of his neighbors could see it. Would know that it wasn't the first time she'd been here in the past week. Any number of conclusions could be formed.

"It's Adam Herrin," she said, preparing herself for an unearthly scream from Annabelle by holding the phone away from her ear.

It came, and Janey smiled.

"I can't believe it," Annabelle said breathlessly. "I mean, Adam Herrin. He's so handsome, and tall, and wow. Matt's best friend."

The enthusiasm hushed, and for some reason tears pricked Janey's eyes. "It's okay for me to date him, right? I mean, Jess seems to like him. They're in Adam's shed right now, building a motorcycle together. I could never give Jess an experience like that."

"Oh, honey, you've always been too concerned with what kind of experiences you can give Jess."

Janey nodded. "I know. I know that. I just—" She just wanted him to have what other kids did. A loving family. Fun vacations. Awesome birthday presents. "He asked Adam to teach him how to cook."

"Well, that's not bad," Annabelle said. "Why do you sound so upset?"

She shook her head. "I don't know."

"Well, let me go all big sister on you for a minute." She drew in a deep breath, all pretense of giddiness gone. "Adam Herrin is the Chief of Police. There is no better man in this whole town. You shouldn't feel guilty for going out with him. Heck, you should be enjoying every last moment of it."

"I know, I—"

"No, you don't know, or you wouldn't be sitting wherever you're sitting, talking to me about this."

Janey pressed her lips together, knowing Annabelle would continue whether she spoke or not.

"Jess will likely struggle with parts of you dating him, but in the end, there is no better man to take Matt's place."

"No." Janey shook her head. "No one's taking Matt's place."

"And Adam won't want to," Annabelle said. "But he's perfect for you, and he'd make a great step-dad for Jess. So Janey, listen very carefully to me. Don't get too far into your head on this. Just enjoy it. Act first. Think later." She scoffed and gave a short, barking laugh. "That's the opposite of everything I tell my kids right now. But you tend to overthink things, right?"

"Maybe a little," Janey said.

"More than a little," Annabelle teased. "It's a miracle Matt was able to sweep you off your feet so easily."

They continued talking for a few minutes longer, and then Annabelle said, "Eli won't stop crying. I have to go." She sighed like being a mother was the worst thing in that moment, and Janey smiled as she said goodbye.

She'd certainly had her fair share of moments like the one Annabelle was going through right now. But she'd been all alone, with no one to pass the fussy infant to so she could chat with her sister. No one to take a turn changing the diaper. No one to get up with the crying baby in the middle of the night.

Adam had been there that first night, and she had her anonymous angel that had kept her going when things got really rough. She got up and collected her umbrella from where she'd left it against the front door when she'd come in.

It flipped open and she moved down the steps and along Adam's front sidewalk. Janey loved the rain, everything about it. The scent as it hit the dirty pavement. The sound of it against the roof, the windows, the umbrella. The way it cleansed everything for a new start.

She walked slowly down the street, looking at the

cheery yellow lights in the homes neighboring Adam's. He probably knew every single one of them, took them soup on rainy days like tonight, and begged his forgiveness when his dogs went rogue in the neighborhood. Well, at least Fable. Gypsy probably knew the exact blade of grass that didn't belong to her anymore.

Janey smiled thinking about his dogs. Thinking about him.

Don't think. Annabelle's voice rang in her head. *Just act.*

She'd overthought her rapid relationship with Matt, but she'd been so enamored with him that she hadn't had much time to get too far inside her head.

"But you've been living inside it for twelve years," she muttered to herself. The magic of the rain kept her melancholy thoughts at bay, and she wandered the neighborhood until her phone sounded.

Where did you go? Your car's still in the driveway.

She smiled at Adam's name on the screen, the concern in those simple words.

Went for a walk, she typed out clumsily with one hand. *Be back soon.*

After all, it was time Janey came back. Back from Matt's death. Back to living a full life. Back to herself and finding her own happiness.

She returned to the shed and leaned in the doorway with the rain dripping off her umbrella. "Hey, you two."

Jess looked up from where he sat on the ground, a

variety of tools surrounding him. His hands held the grease she'd imagined, and his face beamed the brightest smile at her. "Hey, Mom."

Adam's gaze flew to her, and he jumped to his feet, already wiping his hands on a blue mechanic's rag. "There you are. I was worried when I went inside and you were gone." His eyes carried that worry in their ocean-blue depths, and Janey felt herself slipping outside of her mind. Maybe even slipping down the slope toward love.

"Sorry about that," she said. "I worked a lot at my desk today, so I thought I'd take a walk." She put the umbrella down and stepped further into the shed, surveying the scene before her and noting the metallic smell of machinery and the sharp scent of oil. "Wow, this looks like it's in more pieces than before."

"Oh, it is." Adam turned back to it. "But we're making progress."

"How is more pieces considered progress?" She slipped her hand into his, and he pulled his attention back to her, his eyes full of questions. Janey didn't know any of the answers, and for right now, that was okay.

"Sometimes things have to be taken apart before they can be put back together," he said, his voice on the edge of husky and hoarse and sending a rumble through Janey's whole body.

She nodded. "All right, then. I'll leave you guys to it." She looked at Jess. "Can Adam give you a ride home when you're finished here?"

"Yeah, whatever." Jess barely looked at her.

She pressed her free hand against Adam's chest and said, "Not too late, okay?"

He nodded, and Janey ducked back out into the rain, not bothering with her umbrella this time.

∽

Oh, I forgot to tell you not to mention that Adam and I are dating. Janey sent the message to her sister the following morning as she made her way out of town and up to the National Park. She loved the drive along the shore and through the trees, even if it did add thirty minutes to her day. The rain had stopped sometime in the night, and everything felt shiny and new.

Oops....

Janey almost rammed her foot on the brake. She hit call and hoped she'd have service long enough to find out who Annabelle had told. "Annabelle," she said when her sister picked up. Complete chaos came through the line, from children crying to talking to something sizzling that probably shouldn't have been.

"Who did you tell?" she practically yelled into the phone.

"Just Esther and Opi."

Janey groaned. "Not Opi. She'll tell everyone at the salon, and it'll spread like wildfire down Wedding Row by the end of the day." She kicked herself for telling her sister and not remembering to warn her to keep the info to herself.

"They're old friends," she said. "They knew Matt and Adam in high school too. They thought it was sweet."

"Adam doesn't want the whole town buzzing about it," Janey said. Truth be told, she didn't either. She'd always lived just outside of the spotlight, and she liked it that way. But Adam Herrin was as in the spotlight as someone could get.

"Everyone talks about everything he does—oh."

"Exactly."

"I'll tell them as soon as I get my kids off to school." Annabelle said something to one of her kids that made it sound like breakfast wasn't going so well.

"All right." Janey hung up, not sure what else to do. If Opi Gunnison didn't say anything about this juicy piece of gossip, it would be a town miracle. She pulled over to the side of the road and sent a quick text to Adam, confessing what she'd told her sister and who Annabelle had then told.

I'm sorry, she ended with. I'm headed through the forest right now and won't have service for about twenty minutes.

She sent the message and got herself back on the road, a sense of dread hanging over her she couldn't describe.

When she got to her office, Maya was already there. "Oh, good morning," Janey said. "Am I late?"

"No, I don't know." Maya grinned at her. "I just wanted to hear how pizza and motorcycling went with your secret boyfriend." She stood from Janey's chair and moved around to the other side of the desk.

"You owe me forty dollars for pizza." Janey stowed her purse in her bottom desk drawer.

Maya laughed and pulled two twenties from her pocket. "Worth it, though, right?" She'd been the one answering Jess's texts yesterday while Janey was in a meeting. When she'd finally gotten away from the camp managers, Maya had her whole evening planned for her, the pizza already ordered online.

"It was fun," Janey said. "Jess spent more time with him than I did."

Maya sighed a happy little sound and fell back into the chair. "Sounds wonderful."

"So what did you do last night, Maya?" Janey pressed the button to turn on her desktop computer, almost desperate to stop talking about Adam. It was too much to think about him all the time, get lectured by her sister, and then completely disrupt her evening reading routine because she couldn't focus on the words in her book.

"The same old thing," Maya said. "Yoga downtown and then I stopped by the Anchor, hoping the firemen would be on their dinner break."

"And were they?"

"No such luck. They must eat in shifts now or something." A little frown appeared between her eyes. "Do you know how hard it is to meet a man in this town?"

Janey did, and she hmm'ed and yeah'ed in all the right

spots until Maya got up and said, "I guess I better go get ready for the Tuesday Trailhike."

"Yep," Janey said. "I'll meet you out there."

Adam still hadn't responded to her text, and she wondered if he was angry or just busy. Hopefully not busy dealing with a storm of gossip about his new girlfriend.

She set her thoughts aside and reached into her cabinet to pull out her hiking boots. Once they were properly laced, she set out for the back patio of the lodge, where the Tuesday Trailhike met every week at ten o'clock.

They usually had school groups midweek, but today there were several families also in attendance. Maya ran the Trailhike. All Janey had to do was hand her the rock samples and tree branches when she spoke about them.

She also kept records of how many people attended the Trailhike, and how many went up the half-mile walk to the waterfalls. She loved the hike through nature, and she answered questions along the way.

When they arrived, the sound of rushing, tumbling, falling water soothed her. She'd always found it strange that she could love the water and be terrified of it at the same time. But she'd made it across the sound to the beach house, and as the memories of the first time she and Matt had made this hike to the waterfalls came to mind, she didn't push against them.

She didn't have to hide her tears. She smiled at the

sweetness of them, at the way he'd held her hand and snapped a selfie with the falls in the background. Though their life together had been short, it had been sweet.

Not bitter.

After she'd returned to the lodge and done her daily trail checks, she met Maya in the break room. "Great job today," she said. "You get better and better at that every week."

"You think so?"

"Everyone was laughing today." Janey stuck her leftover pizza in the microwave and turned back to her friend. "So yeah. I think so."

Maya beamed under the compliment. Janey pulled her pizza out and sat across from her friend. "So I'm dating Adam Herrin, and I think I might be ready to move past Matt."

Maya's eyes rounded and her spoon paused halfway to her mouth, loaded with raspberry yogurt. "Adam Herrin?"

"Yeah, you know. Chief of Police."

"Yeah, I know." She stuck the yogurt in his mouth. "Wow, Janey. You go big or go home."

Janey laughed, sobering quickly. "Is it bad that I can think of Matt now without wanting to cry?"

Maya put one hand over Janey's their tan skin blending together in an array of fingers. "Of course not. He's been gone a long time."

Janey nodded, and as her mind started sucking her

down a path about the dangers of Adam's job, she pulled herself right back out.

Think less. Act first.

16

Adam left the station about mid-afternoon and went home to make another batch of soup. He'd heard a rumor that the judges strongly favored an autumn themed recipe, and as he looked back through the previous dishes he'd won with—pork with roasted apples and heirloom beets when the theme was apples, and a pumpkin chocolate chip soufflé when the theme was pumpkin, and sausage with sweet potatoes and pecans when the them had been sweet potatoes.

So he couldn't serve beef stew at the Fall Festival. He'd stopped by the grocery store and picked up several autumn squashes—acorn, butternut to be precise. They, along with three heads of garlic, were currently roasting in the oven with olive oil, salt, and pepper while Adam studied a recipe card that had been used so many times, the edges were curled.

He picked up the phone and called his mother, saying, "Hey, Ma," when she answered. "I'm looking at Grandma's recipe, and I can't read one of the spices." He lifted the card and peered at it on a slant. "It says spicy curry powder, and cumin, and then smoked...something. What is that?"

"Paprika," she said immediately. "And cinnamon. And cayenne pepper. Are you making that for the Fall Festival?"

"I'm trying it."

"It's different. Granny Stevie will like it if you win with her recipe. She switched out some of the butternut for acorn squash you know. And she used to add a single carrot for color too."

Adam frowned at the card. "She did? That's not written here."

"Well, write it in. I was with her the last time she made it, and she added a single, peeled carrot with the other squashes when she roasted them. It gave the soup a richer orange color." She laughed and Adam heard something bang in the background. "My mouth is watering just thinking about that soup."

"I'll bring you some before City Council meeting."

"If you have time," she said. "I know these Council Tuesdays are busy for you."

With all the new ingredients—from coconut milk to goat cheese to smoked paprika—he wasn't sure he'd have time to get out to the lavender farm before his meeting.

He loved cooking while the afternoon sun slanted through the windows along the back of his house, and before he knew it, the soup had come together nicely.

It did look a bit pale, halfway between yellow and orange, and he scratched out a note to add a carrot for color next time he made it. He swirled the coconut ginger cream on the top, and added the goat cheese, the roasted pistachios, a bit of chopped cilantro, and a few arils of pomegranate to the top of the soup. The white, the brown, the pink, the green, and the yellow made a beautiful food picture, and Adam smiled at the soup.

He knew the judges awarded points for presentation, and he wondered if he needed more of a crunchy element. Maybe croutons? He could easily herb up squares of bread and toast them while the soup cooked and add a few to the medley of garnishes.

He snapped a picture and sent it to Janey, along with *What do you think of this for the Fall Festival?*

I want to eat that right now, she sent back immediately.

Where are you? He checked the time and realized he only had an hour until his meeting. *I'm headed out to my mother's to drop off some of this. I can swing by your place too, if you want.*

Not home yet, she messaged. *Don't worry about it.*

A sense of loss Adam didn't quite understand enveloped him. He pushed it away and messaged, *All right. City Council tonight. Talk later,* before shoving his phone in his back pocket and packing up the soup.

He arrived at his parent's farm and went in the back door to find Joel washing his hands at the kitchen sink. "Hey, brought some soup." He put the containers on the table and faced his step-dad. "How's the farm?"

Joel smiled as he dried his hands. "Just fine. Did Drew tell you he's thinking about getting another dog?"

Adam's eyebrows shot up. "No, he didn't say that."

"He wants a smaller one," Joel said, opening the fridge. "How are you and Janey?"

It had been two days since the beach trip had ended. What did Joel think could happen in two days? "Just fine," he said, echoing Joel's comment. "Look, I have City Council tonight. I just stopped by to drop this off. Tell my mom hello, okay?"

He wondered where she was, but he didn't want to ask.

"She's just getting up," Joel said. "She should be out any second."

"Getting up?"

"She took a little nap this afternoon."

Adam cocked his head to the side and looked at his step-dad. For the first time, Adam realized how old he looked. His hair had gone white at some point, and while he was still tall and wiry, he looked like he'd lost some of his strength.

"Is she okay?" Adam asked. He wasn't alarmed. No sense in worrying over a nap if it was nothing. He took naps sometimes, too.

"She caught something at the beach," Joel said. "A cold or something. She'll appreciate this soup."

A moment later, footsteps sounded, and Adam glanced toward the doorway that led into the living room. His mother appeared, and she looked older than the picture in his head. And pale.

Her smile was the same, as was the warmth she exuded whenever she looked at him. The only time he'd seen her anything but welcoming and wonderful had been which his father had passed away.

"Adam." She swept over to him and gave him a hug. "Good to see you."

He chuckled, though he loved a good hug from his mom. "We just spent the weekend together."

"Oh, no." She stepped back and glanced at the soup containers. "You spent the weekend with Janey. We barely saw you."

Adam scoffed. "That's not true. She spent hours and hours planning the wedding. I was a glorified babysitter for her and Gretchen."

His mom laughed and picked up a soup container. "So are we. We like it."

Adam grinned at the two of them, glad he could come here and bask in the memories of his childhood, feel his mother's love, and see what great people she and Joel were. He hooked his thumb over his shoulder. "All right. I'm going to be late." He nodded at the containers. "You put most of that on top. It's pretty good."

"I'll let you know." Joel stepped between Adam and his mom and plucked a container from the table and put it in the microwave.

Adam ducked out the door and got back in his cruiser. He had five minutes to spare when he arrived at the city offices, and the number of cars in the parking lot didn't soothe him. Sometimes these meetings could go for hours, and he was foolish to think tonight's would be different. It was the last City Council meeting before the Fall Festival, and there was a group of people who wanted to take the city funding for the festival and put it toward road improvements.

As soon as he walked in, he spied all of those people, and he couldn't help the sigh that blew through his lips. It was definitely going to be a long meeting.

∽

By the time he got home, his exhaustion reached all the way into his bones. He pulled into his driveway, his headlights cutting a swath across a green Jeep. His heart pumped out an extra beat, and he hoped Janey had gone inside as autumn had chosen the last two days to arrive with a vengeance.

She sat on his front steps, both dogs crowded around her and her hands buried in her coat pockets.

"Hey," he said as he climbed the steps slowly. "Why didn't you go in?"

"It's locked."

"How long have you been here?"

"Oh, only about a half an hour."

"Don't you know that everyone has a spare key hidden under their mat?" He chuckled and extended his hand toward her to help her stand. "Now, since I do know that, I keep my spare key in a *much* more secure place." He reached up to the top of the doorjamb and swiped his hand along the narrow ridge there as she came to his side. His fingers brushed metal and he pulled the key down, presenting it to her with a flourish.

"I honestly can't believe I locked the door when I left. I had so much stuff in my hands." He smiled down at her, her beauty striking him right in the chest. She held his gaze, her eyes bright under the porch light and her cheeks tinged with pink because of the chill in the air.

She didn't fit the key into the lock and go inside but held his gaze. The desire to kiss her made his whole body tingle, and he let his natural instincts take over.

He lifted his hand and cradled her face, bent down slowly, ever so slowly so she could stop him if she wanted to. He closed his eyes and heard her whisper something, but it wasn't loud enough for him to decipher.

And then his mouth grazed hers and lightning struck his heart. She'd given her permission by not pulling back or pushing him away, and Adam kissed her properly the second time his lips touched hers, his other hand curling around her waist and keeping her close.

He barely had time to think about what he was doing when the kiss ended. His eyes flew open and met hers, and the powerful electricity flowing between them made Adam feel more alive than he ever had.

He had no idea what to say and she didn't seem to either as the silence stretched. At least it wasn't an awkward silence. She broke their connection and laid her cheek against his chest, a sigh passing from her and into him.

"Okay?" he finally got up the courage to ask.

She giggled and wrapped both arms around him. "Okay."

"So we can go in?" he asked. "I'm starting to freeze out here."

She extracted herself from his arms and fumbled the key in the lock, finally fitting it in and opening the door. The dogs streaked past her and he waited for her to enter first.

"It's late," he said. "Aren't you tired?"

"I have tomorrow off," she said.

"I thought you had to work Wednesdays for the next few weeks because of the beach weekend."

"I begged off tomorrow." She drew in a deep breath and exhaled. "I'm just going to lie around in sweats and drink hot cocoa." She glanced at him and laughed. "I should probably hide those flaws, shouldn't I?"

Adam set his wallet and keys on the kitchen counter and said, "You don't have many flaws, Janey. If wearing sweats on your day off is one of them, I think you're doin' just fine." He flashed her a smile, his earlier exhaustion returning. He yawned and unhooked his police belt, ready to be in sweats himself.

"I stay up late and read in bed," she said with a small laugh. "But I can see you're tired. I just wanted to...I don't know. See you, I guess."

Adam leaned his hip into the countertop. "You wanted to see me?"

She gave him a coy smile that made his pulse beat irregularly. "I wanted to see you, so I came to see you."

"Well, you've seen me, and it's late, and with your car in my driveway all the time, I don't think this relationship is going to stay private much longer."

"No, probably not." She inched closer. "Do we have time for soup now, or do you not eat at eleven o'clock at night?"

"You know eating this late is bad for your digestive system, right?"

"I eat pretzels and chocolate chips until two a.m. pretty regularly."

Surprise and delight bolted through Adam and he tipped his head back and laughed. "So soup is nothing. I'll heat it up." He went about making her a hot, pretty bowl of soup while she told him about her Tuesday hike to some waterfalls.

"And I want you to come sometime," she said.

"I don't know if I can get away on Tuesday."

"We can go anytime," she said. "Jess likes the hike and we can take a lunch or something."

"What about this weekend?" He sprinkled the nuts and other toppings on the soup and slid it over to her.

"We can go on my lunch hour," she said, picking up her spoon.

"And Jess can ride over here in the morning, and we'll cook." He wasn't really asking, though they hadn't made plans. "What does he normally do on the weekends?"

"Oh, he sleeps late, and then he's usually home alone on Saturdays. On Sunday, Gretchen usually takes him out the lavender farm or over to her place."

"He can come here anytime," Adam offered. "I think he likes it here."

Janey rolled her eyes. "You think? He talks about your dogs and your motorcycle non-stop. You're like a god to him."

Adam blinked, unsure if he should laugh or scoff or what. She dished up a bite of soup and put it in her mouth, a moan emanating from her throat a moment later.

"Oh, yeah." She nodded. "That's the winner right there."

17

Janey wanted to curl into Adam's side on his couch and watch whatever he put on, but he seemed a couple of minutes away from passing out. So she finished her soup and put on her coat. He walked her to the door, and she wanted to kiss him again.

So, just like she'd done to get herself to his house tonight, she didn't think. She acted. Tipping up on her toes, she kissed him, taking a few extra seconds to really experience him before pulling away.

"See you tomorrow?" she asked.

"I thought you were going to drink hot cocoa in your sweats all day."

"I think I can spare an hour for lunch. Do you want to go out here in town? Really make everything known?"

A flash of alarm passed through his eyes. There, then gone. "Sure," he said. "Do you like Mexican food?"

"I never say no to chips and salsa."

"Great, I'll call you." He opened the door and leaned into the doorjamb with one arm. "My schedule is a little unpredictable."

"All right, let me know." She trailed her fingers along his chest before stepping out into the cold night. By the time she got home and slid under her covers with her e-reader, a slight sense of panic had descended upon her.

She'd snuck out of the house after her teenager was asleep, to go meet her boyfriend, and kiss him on his front porch. A smile tugged at the corners of her mouth, pulled against her panic. And what a kiss it had been. Beautiful, and slow, and filled with emotion.

"So nothing to worry about," she told herself. Jess had been fine here alone. And she'd gotten to see Adam.

She started reading, and when Jess woke her in the morning, her device had been wedged under her arm somehow. "I can drive you," she said, flinging the covers off.

"It's fine. I'm skating over with Thayne and Greg."

"Greg?" Janey padded after him and entered the kitchen, where Jess grabbed a couple of slices of toast from the counter. "Who's Greg?"

"Greg Grigsby," he said. "His mom works at the school, remember?"

"She's a counselor, right?"

"Right." Jess stepped past her and headed for the front door.

"Are you okay to go to Adam's this weekend to cook? He asked if you wanted to come on Saturday."

"Yeah, fine." Jess opened the door and left without looking back. Janey sighed, wishing she'd set her alarm and gotten up so she could spend longer than thirty seconds having a conversation mostly with herself.

The door opened, and Jess ran back in.

"Did you forget something?"

He hugged her and said, "Bye, Mom. Love you," before ducking his head and retracing his steps.

Janey smiled after him, wondering what she'd done to get such a good son. "He's just like Matt," she muttered. Good-natured. Kind. He could use some lessons in hard work, but he seemed to do okay in school, and he worked around the farm when he went out there with Joel and Drew and Donna.

She did stay in her pajamas for a while, and she sipped hot chocolate while she watched the sun melt the fog. Then she showered and got dressed and went over to her mom's house. She hadn't visited with her in a while, and she tried to get over to see her, assess any household needs she had, and let them visit with Jess as often as she could stand it. With her dad gone now, sometimes her mom didn't take care of things the way she should.

"Mom?" she called as she pushed through the front door. They lived in an old brick house, the same one where Janey had grown up, on the northeast side of town. She lived in almost a straight diagonal line from them, closer to the Lavender Highway and thus the National Park.

"Janey?" Her mom perked up from her spot in the recliner. She set aside her sewing and stood. "What are you doing here?"

"Just came to say hello." She glanced around. Everything seemed to be okay. There were no foul smells in the air, and nothing seemed to be about to explode.

"Where's Jess?"

"Oh, he's at school. It's Wednesday, Mom. My day off." She followed her mom into the kitchen.

"Coffee?" Her mom bustled around, already filling the coffee pot.

Though her mom didn't make great coffee, Janey said, "Sure," and opened the fridge to see what was inside.

Not much. No cream. No milk.

"Mom, do you need to go to the grocery store?"

"Oh, I'm not going there anymore."

Janey let the fridge swing shut. "What do you mean?"

"I mean, they were rude to me last time I was there, and I'm not going back." She set the empty pot on the burner, her eyes flashing.

"Rude to you? At the grocery store? What happened?" And where did she think she was going to get groceries? There was only one store in town that had everything she needed. Sure, she could try Duality and probably get the staples. But they didn't sell fresh fruit or vegetables.

As her mom ranted about the boy who'd offered to

help her take her groceries to her car, Janey realized she was confused. "Mom, he *was* helping you."

"He didn't bring them out."

"You told him not to."

"I did not. I said...." She turned from the cabinet. "I can't remember what I said."

"Mom, you have to get groceries. You don't have anything to eat."

"Oh, I'm fine. I've got loads of stuff in the storage room downstairs." She waved away Janey's concerns, the same way she always did.

Exasperation filled her. "Mom, you can't go up and down the stairs." Her oldest sister's husband was supposed to come move everything upstairs for their mother a few months ago—and lock the door that led to the basement. "Do you want to have another hip replacement?"

"Oh, I'm fine." She set the sugar bowl on the counter with a little too much force, causing the lid to rattle against the bowl.

Janey gritted her teeth. Nothing irritated her more than her mother telling her she was fine. The evidence said she wasn't fine. "Didn't Bruce come and put all the food storage in the utility room?"

"Oh, that's right," she said. "See? I don't go up and down the stairs."

But Janey was a mother of a teenager, and she could spot a lie from a mile away. She accepted the mug of coffee and put in as much sugar as she could stand since there was no milk or cream. After sipping and making small talk for a few minutes, she said, "I need to use the bathroom."

She moved down the hall and went in the bathroom. Then, quietly, she opened the door again and darted over to the door that led to the basement. It had very clearly been sealed off at some point. But her mother had obviously taken the nails out and was definitely going downstairs for some reason.

Janey slipped through the door as quietly as she could and tiptoed into the basement. Her father had finished it himself, to make room for all the kids. Once it was done, Janey had gotten her own room down here, and she'd loved it.

Her old room held a few things from her childhood she'd never claimed. Nothing important. Junk that should be thrown away. Still, she enjoyed the memories of playing the clarinet in the band and the dance costumes she'd thought were too extravagant to throw away.

Annabelle's room had been down here too, and it sat spotless and empty. The bathroom had a note on the door that said, *The water's been turned off in here. Do not use!*

It looked like Bruce's handwriting, and Janey made a mental note to call him and let him know that his handiwork had been undone. The furnace room contained a couple of filters, and nothing else. The living room was empty.

So what was her mother doing coming down here?

Janey glanced up the steps as she passed them, darting into the storage room and closing the door. She used to sneak her friends down here every summer to get popsicles out of the deep chest freezer in this room.

She opened it, and the scent of warm rubber met her nose. She wrinkled it and closed the lid on the empty, unplugged freezer. The shelves her father had built to hold her mother's canning, big bags of flour and sugar, and buckets of oats were all empty. Bruce had come over and moved everything upstairs, just as Janey had thought he had.

The only thing in the storage room was a bookcase, with an old rocking chair next to it. Her mother had told all four girls that she'd sat in that chair and rocked them to sleep at night when they were babies.

Janey touched the top of it, setting it into motion. It was clear this was where her mother had been coming. Baby books and photo albums lined the shelves, none of them out of place. She sat down in the rocking chair, this memory corner of the house so quiet and peaceful.

She thought of Matt, bracing herself for the powerful, debilitating emotions that came whenever she conjured up a picture of him in her mind.

Today, though, she rocked and smiled, no tears in sight.

"I've moved on," she whispered to the cement storage

room. The idea was as wonderful as it was sad, and she let herself experience both emotions.

"Janey?" Her mother's voice broke Janey's solitude, and she leapt from the rocker.

"I'm coming," she called as she went up the steps. She pulled the door closed behind her and went back into the kitchen. "Mom, you really can't go up and down the steps." She picked up her coffee mug and took a sip, keeping her eyes on her mom. "I'll bring that rocker and bookcase up this weekend, okay?"

Her mother pressed her lips together and nodded, hiding behind her own coffee cup.

"Well, I can't. I have to work. But I'll send over my boyfriend."

Her mom wasn't so far gone that she didn't understand what it meant for Janey to have a boyfriend. She whipped her attention to her and said, "What?"

"I'm dating the Chief of Police," Janey said with a smile. "Big, strapping man named Adam Herrin. He and Jess will come over on Saturday and bring up the photo albums and the rocking chair. Okay?"

Her mother patted her flat curls as if she'd be meeting a king this weekend. "Oh, my. The Chief of Police."

Janey laughed, feeling happier than she had in a long time.

∼

"What kind of apples?" she asked her mom, a plastic bag at the ready and dozens of apple varieties spread out before her at the grocery store.

"Fuji and gala," her mom said.

Janey bagged them up for her and walked ahead of the cart to get a couple of cucumbers. "Then you can have that salad you like," she told her mom.

They went up and down the aisles, slowly filling a cart almost all the way to the top. Janey had finally gotten out of her mom that she hadn't been to the store in five weeks. She'd vowed to check in on her more often. It wasn't like it was hard. A few miles separated them, and Janey had two days off every week. She could probably do her mother's shopping for her from now on.

"Bread?" she asked, finally in the last aisle. "Wheat or white?"

Her mom acted like she hadn't spoken. "Mom," Janey said louder. "Wheat or white?"

"Oh, wheat."

Janey picked out a loaf that looked good and put it in the cart. "Anything else?"

"Did I get ice cream?"

"Yes, mom. Two different kinds." And that had taken several minutes of Janey yelling the flavors out for her mom to pick from.

A pair of women went by, both of them looking at Janey with wide smiles on their faces. She searched her memory to see if she knew them, but came up blank.

Shrugging it off, she swung the cart around. "Oh, what about cat food?" Her mom had a little black cat named Peanut. He only liked her mother, and he usually hid when anyone else came over.

"Rat food? Why would I feed a rat?"

"*Cat* food, Mom. *Cat*." Janey's throat was starting to feel raw from all the yelling. "For Peanut."

"Oh, right. Peanut. He likes scrambled eggs."

She hadn't had any eggs, so Janey had no idea what her mom had been feeding the cat. She pushed the heavy cart back a few aisles to the pet food. Another woman stared right at her, not even trying to hide it.

Janey wondered if she'd forgotten to do up one of her buttons on her blouse, but when she checked, all was well. So what was everyone staring at?

She got the cat food and some new kitty litter, and started for the check stand. It seemed like every eye in the place found her and held on. Surely she was just imagining things. She was no one special.

The girl started ringing them up, and all at once, her face brightened. "Are you Janey Germaine?"

Again, Janey tried to figure out how she knew this Carol ringing up her mother's groceries. Maybe she'd come out to the lodge at some point. But no, she didn't know her.

"Yes," she said slowly. Maybe she was one of Jess's friend's mothers. Or maybe—

"You're dating Chief Herrin, aren't you?" The woman

looked absolutely giddy as she slid a can of black beans over the scanner.

"Oh, well—"

"I heard he runs along the beach every morning." She sighed as if that was the most wonderful thing on the planet. "Makes a girl want to start running, don't you think?"

Janey had no idea what to think, but all the staring suddenly made sense. Two check stands away, another woman had turned around to stare at her, and Janey ducked her head and willed Carol to scan faster.

The town had obviously gotten the memo on her and Adam's relationship, and Janey wasn't sure how to feel about being recognized in the grocery store.

18

Adam waited outside Janey's house on Saturday morning, the rain pounding against his car. He'd called Jess and told him not to skateboard over. Adam was afraid the boy would get washed right off the streets, what with the way the weather had turned during the night.

Janey had texted and said she'd made it up to the lodge okay, and Adam hadn't gotten in his run on the beach. With the Fall Festival only three weeks away, he was already starting to check the long-range weather forecasts to see if they'd need to move everything indoors.

They had contingency plans for that, of course, but he hoped they wouldn't have to use them. His officers had a hard time working long hours in the rain, and less people would show up for the festivities if Mother Nature didn't get her act together before the festival.

He was just about to call Jess again when the front

door opened and the boy dashed down the steps. He ran across the grass and practically dove into the front seat of the cruiser. "Whew! It is so loud in the house." He brushed water from his shoulders and hair.

"And still no jacket, I see," Adam commented, remembering when he was thirteen and it was *so uncool* to wear anything that provided any protection whatsoever. It seemed like that hadn't changed.

"I figured I'd be in the car or the house most of the time." Jess grinned at him. "Surely we're not still hiking to the waterfalls today."

"Nope." Adam flipped a U-turn and headed down the street to get back to his place. "But we are meeting your mom at the lodge for lunch."

Jess groaned, and Adam asked, "What?"

"I don't like the food at the lodge."

"You can eat the soup we're about to make." He turned right and then left to get out of Janey's neighborhood, went down the road a ways, and pulled into the grocery store parking lot.

"We have to go grocery shopping first?" Jess peered out the windshield like Adam had brought him to the dump.

"The food doesn't magically show up in your fridge by fairies," he said. "I take it you've never been grocery shopping."

"I mean, I've come with my mom."

"It can be fun." Adam unbuckled his seatbelt. "I always get to buy whatever I want."

Jess laughed and together, they ran through the torrential rain to the safety of the store. "Will you let me buy whatever I want?"

He handed Jess the list he'd made for the corn and crab bisque they were making. "You get all of this. And one other thing. One thing. Your choice."

Jess's dark eyes glittered like this would be a great adventure, and Adam was reminded of Matt so much, his breath petered out of his body. He trailed along behind Jess, who pushed the cart and selected onions, vegetables, butter, and cream. Adam had never had a problem spending time with Jess; he wanted to do it. First, to help Janey if he could. Second, he genuinely liked the boy.

Of course he saw Matt every time he looked into Jess's face. He'd just never been hit by such a wave of longing to have his best friend back before.

They moved into the canned area, and Jess got chicken broth. The crowd at the grocery store seemed thinner today, and Adam remembered it was dumping buckets outside. He was suddenly glad for the terrible weather, as it probably saved him and Jess from more curious stares.

As it was, everyone who passed looked at Adam and smiled. When they saw who he was with, they either blinked like they couldn't believe it or grinned wider. Thankfully, Jess didn't seem to notice.

"I don't know how to choose crab." Jess turned back to Adam, the anxiety on his face. He looked back to the seafood counter, his feet shifting.

"You just ask," Adam said, leaning his arm on the meat case. When Taylor Locke, the butcher came over, Adam grinned at him. "Hey, Taylor. We're making crab bisque. We want the best crab you've got. Anything good today?"

"Sure thing. How much do you think?" He glanced at Jess and back to Adam. He was used to people staring at him, making judgments about who he was with and what he bought, and he could practically see Taylor's wheels turning.

So the rumors are true. He is dating Janey Germaine. Here he is, with her son.

"How much, Jess?" Adam looked at the paper, where he'd written down what to get.

"One pound," Jess said when he found the info.

"Comin' up," Taylor said.

Jess beamed at him and crossed off the last item on the list while Taylor wrapped the crab. He put it in the cart, and said, "Okay, I just need my one thing." He pushed the cart toward the front of the store.

"What are you going to get?" Adam asked when Jess didn't detour toward the cookie aisle, or turn back toward the bakery—both of which Adam would've done at his age.

Almost to a check stand, Jess paused where a bunch of boxed baked goods were displayed on the end of the aisle. "These." He picked up a box of oatmeal pies, and brandished them toward Adam.

"You want boxed cakes?" Adam looked at them with disgust.

"My mom never lets me get them, and Thayne always has them at lunch." Jess took the box back and put it in the cart. "You said I could get one thing. Anything I wanted."

Adam's eyes flickered to the price tag. Two bucks. "That's fine. I'm just surprised you don't want an apple fritter bear claw. I mean, they make those fresh every day."

"These are good." He pushed the cart toward the check stand. "Are you going to get something?"

"Yeah, you start loading those groceries on the belt, and I'll be right back." He headed over to the bakery and procured his bear claw. He'd just turned around to rejoin Jess when he nearly plowed into Mabel Magleby.

"Oh, good morning, Mabel." He tried to step to the side, but the old woman blocked him again.

"Are you dating that sweet Janey Germaine?" she asked, her voice creaky and crotchety at the same time. At least she'd come right out and asked him, no staring, no speculating.

"Yes, ma'am," he said, almost saluting her. He wasn't sure why Mabel was frowning so deeply. "What's wrong with that?"

Mabel stepped in closer and pointed one knobbled finger at him. "You better not break her heart."

"Oh, Mabel, come on now." He chuckled and noticed a few other shoppers watching the exchange. He leaned in closer and lowered his voice when he said, "If anything, she'll break mine."

He nodded and whistled as he stepped around her and hurried back to where Jess had already unloaded the whole cart's worth of groceries onto the belt. He nodded back toward the bakery, which could just be seen from where they stood. "What's with Mabel Magleby?"

"Do you know her?"

"Yeah, of course. Everyone knows Mabel."

"More than that, I mean." Adam glanced back to the bakery too, and then focused on Jess.

"Yeah, she always brings leftovers when there's a big event at the Mansion. She's been doing it for years."

"Huh." Adam stepped forward to pay for the groceries. "Your mom never told me that."

"We have someone else who leaves stuff for us too," Jess said. "We don't know who it is. Mom calls them our anonymous angel."

Adam's movement stuttered as he swiped his debit card through the reader. "What kind of stuff?"

"Food, cookies, sometimes presents. They left me a scooter once on my birthday, and Mom says they left diapers and clothes when I was a baby."

Adam lifted the bags back into the cart and said, "You stay here. I'll run out and pull the car up."

Jess agreed, and Adam walked away from the boy before he spilled his guts and confessed that he was their anonymous angel. *Why does it matter?* he thought as he jogged through the rain and took shelter in the cruiser.

"And you're going to have to tell them sometime." He pulled up to the store and he and Jess loaded the groceries into the trunk with at least some shelter from the rain. Once Jess was back in the car, Adam looked at him and asked, "Can you keep a secret?"

"Yeah, sure."

"This has to actually stay secret," Adam said. "Not like when I told you I liked your mom and you blabbed to Dixie the first chance you got."

"I didn't—" Jess ducked his head. "All right. So I did. But I swear I won't say anything to her—to *anyone*—about this."

Adam drove through the rain, his words taking their sweet time to align. He'd made it all the way back to his house and put the car in park before he turned to Jess. "So your dad was my best friend. Did you know that?"

Jess nodded, his eyes serious. "Yeah, Mom's mentioned that."

Adam exhaled. "So a few days before he and your mom got married, we went to dinner, and he asked me to take care of her. And any kids they might have. You know, if anything ever happened to him."

Jess's eyes widened and he blinked.

"He didn't know something would happen," Adam said. "He just wanted to know I'd be there if he couldn't be. And I have been, Jess. I stayed with you and your mom the night he died. And I'm your anonymous angel."

"*You've* been leaving stuff all this time?"

Adam nodded. "And I don't want your mom to know quite yet."

"Why not?" Jess asked.

"I don't know. I just...it's always just been something I do. I don't need thanks, and I knew she'd never ask for help." He looked at the front door, wondering if he and Jess could get all the groceries inside in one trip. "All right? This is just between you and me, right?"

"Right."

"All right. This bisque isn't going to make itself. Let's go."

～

"Hey, you made it." Janey rose from the couch in the lobby of the lodge as soon as Adam walked in. She embraced him, and he held her tight, taking a deep breath of her floral scent before stepping back.

"He has all his fingers, as you can see." He beamed at Jess, who launched into telling her how he'd diced carrots and chopped onions for the corn and crab bisque.

"And I sautéed, Mom. And made a roux—that's this thickening thing with flour and butter. And the soup was *sooo* good."

Janey laughed at him and looked back to Adam. "So a successful morning."

"And now he wants to go play a video game on your computer. I guess he said you let him do that sometimes?"

She smoothed his hair off his forehead. "You don't want to eat lunch with me and Adam?"

"I already ate." Jess looked at her with those dark, puppy dog eyes. "I never get to come up here and play on your computer anymore. And I don't even like the food at the lodge."

"That's true." She looked at Adam, who shrugged. It was her call. He wouldn't mind dining alone with her again. "All right," she said. She reached into her pocket and pulled out her keys. "Lock the door behind you."

He whooped, gave her a quick hug, and high-fived Adam on his way out of the lobby. Adam chuckled and watched him go, his fondness for the boy expanding.

"You should've seen him in the kitchen," Adam said as they walked over to the restaurant and got a table. "He was a little nervous at first, but he did great."

"He really chopped and diced and sautéed, huh?"

"Oh, yeah." Adam pulled her chair out for her and bent down to kiss her. "He's such a great kid, Janey. You've done so well with him."

Something crossed her face, but he couldn't catalog what before she turned away. "You think so?"

He sat down across from her and tilted his head. "You don't think so?"

"How much of it do you think is me, and how much of it do you think is just him being him?"

"I think it's a combination of both." Adam opened the menu, needing something more than soup this time. "But your influence shouldn't be discounted. A boy can easily go the wrong way without the love of a good mother."

19

Janey let Adam's words tumble around in her head. *A good mother.*

She'd never given much thought to how good of a mother she was. She was doing the best she could, that was all.

"I'm going for the bacon wrapped filet mignon." He snapped the menu closed "What about you?"

"Oh, I don't know." She looked at the entrees, even though she had the menu memorized and had eaten there hundreds of times over the years she'd worked at the National Park. She wanted to make new memories with Adam here. Things she could think about while she was here, where he starred in the scenes in her head instead of Matt.

"Are you ready for the Fall Festival?" she asked.

"Getting there." He flashed her a smile, and Janey

loved the formation of it, loved the way it transformed his handsome face into something akin to a heavenly vision.

The waiter arrived and she ordered soda and the appetizer platter and then indicated Adam should order his steak. Once the waiter left, he lifted his right eyebrow into a cute quirk and asked, "The appetizer platter?"

She sighed and tugged her shirtsleeves father down before placing her hands on the table. "Sometimes a person just needs a large quantity of fried foods." She grinned at him and took his hands in hers. "Thanks for coming up here."

"Yeah, of course."

Her courage felt a little wobbly, but she wanted to be honest with him. "I have so many memories of Matt here," she said, looking down to fiddle with her silverware. "And I like that you're coming here, making new memories in this space with me."

Everything about Adam softened, and he squeezed her hands. "I want to make all kinds of memories with you." His smile was kind and beautiful, and Janey thought for the first time since Matt's death that she could fall in love with someone new.

∼

THE WEEKS PASSED, WITH RAIN FALLING MORE DAYS THAN IT stayed dry. Janey didn't mind, though she knew that as the days marched closer to the Fall Festival, every drop of rain caused Adam grief.

Because it was almost the end of October, and crowds in the National Park normally thinned about this time of year, she managed to get another Saturday off so she could go to the Fall Festival with Adam and Jess.

They'd been spending the weekends together, and she'd been making new memories with Adam on Wednesdays and Mondays, determined to eat lunch at a new spot until they'd gone everywhere in Hawthorne Harbor.

Janey was used to the staring now, and sometimes she smiled back at the prying eyes. She'd talked with Adam about it, and he said he'd gotten used to living in the public eye. He'd asked her if it bothered her, and he seemed really anxious about that.

She didn't answer right away, because she'd never thought about if it bothered her. In the end, she'd said, "Not really," and that had seemed to appease him.

He'd decided on the butternut squash soup for his entry in the Fall Festival, and Jess was going to make the corn and crab bisque. When she asked Adam if he was worried her son would beat him, he'd remained straight-faced and said, "Absolutely. He's good in the kitchen, and it's a great recipe."

On Saturday morning, Jess woke her by jumping on her bed. "Mom, I'm going over to Adam's to start on the soup."

She groaned and rolled toward him. "What time is it?"

"Seven."

"Is it raining?"

"Nope. Gonna be a great day." Jess bounced to the edge of the bed and laughed. "See you at the festival, okay?"

"Okay," she called, listening for the smack of his board against the hard floor and then the slam of the front door. She styed in a bed for a couple more minutes, warm and cozy and completely satisfied with her life.

She wasn't sure she'd ever felt this way before and she wanted to hold onto it for as long as she could. Eventually, she got up and showered. She'd made plans to meet Adam and Jess at the festival after they'd turned in their entries, which were due by ten-thirty.

A buffet-style lunch was then served from all the entries, and the public had an opportunity to vote for their favorites. The top three from the general vote then went to a panel of judges, who decided on the final winner.

The festival had been running all week, and she'd hardly seen Adam at all. The parade was that morning, but he'd made sure other officers could cover it, and Jess didn't seem to care to run out and get the salt water taffy that was thrown by businesses and high school groups.

Janey had attended the Fall Festival parade every year, and she didn't want to miss it this year. So she called

Gretchen and asked, "Where are you sitting? Is there enough room for me?"

"Of course," Gretchen said, the wind scratching across the line too. "We're right in front of the Anchor."

"I'll be there soon."

Janey drove the half-mile to downtown and parked on a side street to avoid the traffic. It felt good to walk when it wasn't her job, and she arrived at the Anchor after only a few minutes. Dixie sat on the curb, a blanket beneath her, with Drew and Gretchen sitting in camp chairs behind her.

"Hey." Janey sidled up next to Gretchen, who jumped up.

"Hey." She laughed as she hugged Janey. "How are you?"

"Great." She waved at Drew, who smiled back at her. "Have you got someone in the shop this morning?"

"Oh, I just closed it for the day. We won't die."

Janey's eyebrows rose as surprise flitted through her. "Really?"

Gretchen's face said otherwise, and she'd confessed to Janey more than once that money was tight for her. That she had to keep the shop open as much as possible.

"I just don't want to be consumed by it anymore," she said.

Drew took her hand and squeezed it, and Janey admired his silent show of support.

"Everyone's here anyway," Janey said. "No one's going to be buying flowers today. It's not the Lavender Festival."

"Yep, you're right." Gretchen turned as the police sirens started. "Is Adam leading the parade?"

"He's at home, making soup," Janey said.

"He's not here?" Drew asked.

Janey looked at him and found the incredulity on his face. "No...why? Is that a problem?"

"He's the Police Chief," Drew said. "He's led the parade for six years."

Janey didn't know what to say. He hadn't acted like it was a big deal that he have Milo drive the cruiser in the parade, and she'd never asked how he'd entered the competition in the past. Maybe he got special privileges because he was the Chief of Police.

She didn't know, and she didn't want to spend the whole parade thinking about it. So she shrugged and edged forward a few feet. "Can I sit by you, Dix?"

"Sure." She scooted over. "Where's Jess?"

"He's making a soup for the festival." She smiled at the girl and leaned closer. "If I tell you what kind, you could vote for his."

Her face lit up and she whispered, "Which kind?"

"Corn and crab bisque."

Dixie's cute face scrunched up. "Ew. I don't like crab."

"Have you ever had it?"

"Yeah, sure."

The police sirens neared, screaming so loudly that

talking was impossible. Several cars passed, and the colors followed. The crowd stood as if doing the wave, and Janey joined everyone in placing her hand over her heart.

She loved the horses clippity-clopping down the street. Loved the trucks that had been decorated by hand-drawn banners. Loved the children's bike troupe, which Jess had ridden in for a couple of years.

By the time the parade ended, her tailbone ached. She stood and stretched, stole one more piece of bubble gum from Dixie's stash, and said, "I'm headed over to find Adam and Jess. You guys want to come?"

"I'll take the chairs to the truck." Drew shouldered them both, as well as the blanket Dixie had been sitting on, and Gretchen linked her arm through Janey's.

"So things with Adam are fairly serious?"

"Well, I suppose you could say that," Janey said, a coyness to her voice she liked. "I like him a lot, and I think he likes me."

Gretchen giggled so loud, several people turned and looked at her. "Janey, that man is head over heels in love with you."

Janey ducked her head and giggled too, the thought of being loved by someone like Adam almost too overwhelming to think about. So she once again, employed Annabelle's suggestion, and didn't think about it.

She paused at the statue in the middle of the park. "They're supposed to meet me here." Turning in a circle, she scanned the crowd for them and didn't find them. She pulled her windbreaker tighter, glad the sun was out but wishing the wind wasn't quite so whippy today.

"Mom!"

She turned in the direction of Jess's voice to see him working his way through the crowd. The taller, boxier form of Adam followed him, and they reached the statue in a few seconds.

"Hey," she said with a chuckle. "How did the soup-making go this morning?"

"Great." Jess glanced at Dixie and cleared his throat. "I mean, it was okay."

"Did you get yours turned in on time?"

Adam's arm snaked around her back and she leaned into him. "We did." He pressed a kiss to her forehead. "Jess said he wanted to eat and then go over to the—"

"It's nothing," Jess said over him, and Adam swung his head toward the boy. Something silent passed between them, and Janey didn't like it.

"What's going on?" she asked.

"Did you want to look at the booths with me?" Dixie asked. "My mom said I could have ten dollars for whatever I want."

Jess looked at her, and his face brightened. "Yeah, sure. Are you gonna eat first?"

Janey sucked in a breath as all the pieces clicked into place. She twisted to face Adam, her excitement almost through the roof. "He...."

Adam shook his head and she spun back to her son. "So let's go eat," she said in a falsely bright voice.

Jess looked at Dixie again and they set off together. Dixie leaned over and said, "Your mom told me which soup you made, so I'm gonna vote for you."

The very tips of his ears turned bright red, and giddiness danced through her. "He has a crush on her," she whispered to Adam.

He nodded, his mouth remaining steadfastly closed.

"How long have you known?"

"He told me at the beach. It's why he didn't want to sleep in the same room as her."

Janey shook her head, still in a bit of disbelief. "I had no idea."

"He'll grow out of it."

"I think it's cute."

"What's cute?" Gretchen asked.

"Jess—"

Adam's grip on her waist tightened, and Janey said, "Jess...cooking with Adam."

"What did you make, Chief?" Gretchen asked.

"Oh, can't tell you that. It's anonymous."

Gretchen snorted and laughed. "You'll be the only one who hasn't told everyone they know to vote for them."

"I'm sure that's not true," Adam said. "Where's Drew?"

"He took the chairs to the truck." Gretchen looked over her shoulder. "He'll be here in a minute."

Janey picked up a bowl and a slip of paper with all the choices on it. "There's a lot of entries this year."

"Soup is very Fall Festival," Adam said. "The public vote is kind of dumb with this many choices. How can anyone possibly sample every kind?"

As they moved down the line, there were small, white plastic tasting spoons at every pot of soup. She tried a half a dozen before coming to Jess's. She tasted it too, surprised at how rich the flavor was, how smooth the texture.

"This one's good," she said loudly, and Adam rolled his eyes. She checked it on her paper with a chuckle and kept moving.

She very nearly tasted all the soups, even though Adam had said such a thing wasn't possible, and she turned in her paper with her top three choices. Adam's butternut squash, and Jess's bisque, and a potato chowder with bacon and chives.

"The voting will be closing in fifteen minutes," a voice over the loudspeaker said. "Please put your votes in the blue box at the front of the meal tent."

She linked her hand in Adam's and said, "You promised me a funnel cake."

"You want to cash that in right now? We just ate."

"Little sips of soup," she said. "Hardly anyone takes a bowl and gets one kind, the way you did."

"That wild leek with sausage and mushrooms is going to win." He glanced around the fair as if his police training had taught him how to read minds. "I wish I knew who made it."

"Well, if it wins, then you'll know." She danced in front of him, hoping to lighten his mood. "Come on, Chief. It's sunny and they're not going to announce the winners until later anyway. Get me a funnel cake, and let the kids shop the booths, and I think there's a pumpkin carving contest later too."

A smile cracked his stoic expression and he relented. "All right. But I don't think Jess brought any money."

She turned to find the kids several paces ahead. She called them back and gave him a twenty dollar bill from her purse. "Share with Dix if she doesn't have enough for something, okay? You've got your phone?"

"Yeah, Mom. Right here."

"Adam and I are going to get a funnel cake. Gretchen and Drew are around somewhere. We'll meet you over in the booths in a few minutes."

Dixie grabbed Jess's arm. "Come on, Jess! They'll sell out of the llamas if we don't hurry."

He grinned as Adam said, "Be good. Take care of her," and then ran off.

"They're so cute," Janey said, her heart warming at the sight of them. She'd always loved their friendship, and she hoped Jess's heart wouldn't be too wounded with this childhood crush.

"Come on." Adam took her hand again. "Let's go get you sugared up."

20

Adam's senses were heightened as he walked through the food booths and the sales booths with Janey and the kids. He kept his head moving from left to right, noticing all the little details just in case.

He couldn't relax at the Fall Festival; he'd never been able to. He worked it. He'd told Janey that, but she seemed to have forgotten. He wasn't wearing his uniform; he was just one of six plain-clothes cops in the crowd.

The idea was that having cops in uniform reduced problems simply by them being present. The plain-clothes cops provided another layer of security, and he'd lectured them to keep their eyes open while they played carnival games with their families. He had to do the same.

He managed to enjoy himself. Heck, he would've enjoyed himself anywhere, doing anything, if his hand was secured in Janey's. Her touch kept his nerves over the soup contest at bay, something he'd used his uniform to do in the past.

He watched Janey carve out a blocky pumpkin face while Jess and Dixie worked on one together. They were terrible, but Adam acted like they should've won the carving contest. He waited with Dixie while she got her face painted, and he bought the kids apple cider.

"We better get back over to the meal tent," Janey said, and Adam checked his watch.

"Oh, right." He glanced around for the kids. "Jess, come on. They're going to make the announcement in a few minutes."

They wandered back over to the main square of the park, where a small crowd had gathered to hear the announcement. Probably just the people who'd entered, as this contest wasn't nearly up to the level of the Lavender Festival competition. No crowns awarded, no public panel tasting the food, no speeches to be made at podiums.

"What was your number again?" Janey asked.

"I was thirty-seven," Adam said.

"I was sixteen," Jess said.

"I hope you win," Dixie said, clenching her arms around herself. "Do you win anything?"

Jess turned to Adam. "I don't know. What do you win?"

"A bit of money," Adam said. "Not much, mind you. A couple hundred dollars. Just the recognition."

"A couple hundred dollars?" Jess's voice lifted into the air. "Wow!"

"We're ready to make the announcement of this year's Fall Festival cookoff, with the theme of soups. In third place, number forty-two, Ira Mansville, with the wild leek, sausage, and mushroom soup."

Adam applauded along with everyone else as Ira, a gentleman about a decade older than Adam, whooped and danced toward a couple of people near the voting box. Adam's hopes crashed and burned. There was no way his butternut squash soup had beaten that wild leek concoction.

"In second place, number thirty-seven, Chief Adam Herrin, with his butternut squash soup with ginger coconut cream."

Janey squealed and Jess spun on him. "You got second!" he yelled as if Adam hadn't heard the man over the loudspeaker.

"Go on," Dixie said, her face one bright ray of happiness.

Adam went through the crowd and shook hands with Beth Yardley, the director of the Fall Festival.

"Good job, Chief Herrin," she said, handing him an envelope and nodding for her assistant to continue with the winner. Adam stayed by her and Ira, smiling for the people.

"And our winner this year...number sixteen, Jess Germaine, with his corn and crab bisque."

Several cheers went up, and Adam watched as Jess ran down the aisle to Beth. She shook his hand and presented him with an envelope and Jess pranced over to Adam, his grin so wide it had to hurt his face.

"I can't believe it," Jess said. "The soup wasn't that good, was it?"

"It's because you got Dixie to vote for you," Adam said out of the corner of his mouth.

Jess started laughing, and the sound was so joy-filled that Adam couldn't help joining in. Later, when he pulled up to Janey's house to drop Jess off, the boy paused before getting out of the cruiser.

"Adam?"

"Yep?"

"I—I had a great day with you. Thanks for letting me come over and cook."

Adam looked evenly at the boy, his heart completely open to him. "Anytime, Jess." He smiled and said again, "Anytime."

Jess nodded and got out of the car. He took a couple of steps away and then came back. "My mom wants to talk to you," he said through the window.

Adam got out of the car to see Janey haloed by the porch light and as Jess went up the stairs, she came down. They paused and said a few words, and in that brief moment, Adam knew he loved them both.

The emotion hit him so strongly, he gasped. The love

moved through him, making his muscles warm and everything around him soft along the edges.

He moved around the car and met Janey at the front hood. Taking her into his arms was as easy as breathing, and she said, "Thank you for a great day."

"I can't believe Jess beat me," he whispered into her neck. She giggled and he laughed lightly with her. "Greatest day ever."

She pulled back and gazed up at him, and when she kissed him, he thought maybe she could love him too.

~

HALLOWEEN CAME AND WENT, AND ADAM TURNED ALL HIS focus to the Festival of Trees. Honestly, he sometimes wished he would've grown up in a town with slightly fewer festivals on their schedule. He supposed four a year wasn't too bad, but he felt all he did was maintain relationships with his officers and prepare for big events.

One Thursday in mid-November, he was able to sneak away from the office and get behind the wheel to just drive. He loved nothing better than to drive around, looking at the neighborhoods in town, speed down the beach highway, and loop back around to town on the Lavender Highway.

He'd been in the car for about an hour before he stopped at Duality for something to eat and something caffeinated to help him through the rest of the afternoon.

Back in the car, he ate his sidewinder fries and kept his eyes open as he eased onto Main Street. As he drove along his beloved beach, the rain started to fall. By the time he made it back to town, it was freezing rain and he needed to return to the station.

"Weather alert," bubbled over the radio. "Sending out the warning to all radios, televisions, and Internet stations."

Adam recognized Sammy Puth's voice, the weather expert out of the bigger town of Port Williams.

Only moments later, Trent came on Adam's shoulder. "Where you at, boss?"

"Heading back." He turned the corner, the heavy cruiser sitting right down on the road and sticking. He hit a slick patch, but the car righted pretty quickly.

A horn sounded, and Adam scanned, searched, scrambled to find where it was coming from. The volume of it increased, and he still couldn't see anything. He tapped the brake, but the car slid—and that was when he saw the ice cream truck emerge from the alley between the grocery store and the bakery.

He couldn't avoid it, so he braced for impact. Time slowed as he looked right into the headlights of the massive truck, only a few feet from his eyes.

He inched by—maybe he'd make it past.

Time jumped forward again, and he gripped the steering wheel as the front of the huge vehicle clipped the rear door on the driver's side.

He spun, his headlights facing the truck's now. A yell tore from his throat as the truck hit his car again and pushed it across his own lane. More bright light flashed in his peripheral vision and he had just enough time to look out his side window to see another pair of headlights as they bore down on him.

The car that had been behind him smashed right into his door. The sound of breaking glass and crunching metal filled Adam's ears. Panic pounded through him, and pain shot up his left leg and sliced his face.

The air bag deployed. Something hot lanced his forearm. He pulled his hands from the wheel and sucked in a breath as everything came to a halt.

Panting, he took a few moments to figure out where he was and that he was still okay. He touched his cheek, and his fingers came away sticky with blood. He depressed the button on his shoulder radio.

"I've been in an accident. Sixth and Main. Send an ambulance." His head fell back against the seat and his first instinct was to jump from the ruined cruiser and see if everyone else was okay.

But the freezing rain—now diving into the car because the windshield had separated from the car, and his side window had been completely smashed. He tried to pull his left leg from the bent metal on that side, and it didn't budge.

"Chief? A car accident?"

"With another civilian vehicle and an ice cream truck.

I can't get out." His head swam and he wasn't even sure why. He could breathe okay. He knew nothing was too hurt, though things were starting to throb now.

"Call my brother and my parents," he said. "Call Janey." His voice weakened, and he knew he was going to pass out. "Send an ambulance."

The last words he heard were, "Help is on the way, Chief."

21

"Janey Germaine, please report to the security desk. Janey Germain to the security desk."

Janey's heart leapt to the back of her throat at the sound of her name over the loudspeaker at the lodge. When the rain had started, they'd pulled everyone in off the trails, despite their complaints. Tourists didn't understand how dangerous freezing rain could be, and she'd just stopped in front of the fireplace to warm her hands.

Her hair was plastered to her skull and she tried to fluff the water from it on her way over to the visitor's center, where the security desk was.

It's fine, she told herself. Jess was at school. Maybe they'd cancelled the rest of the day. If so, he could stay home alone for a few hours. Before Adam had come into their lives, he used to stay home alone all day on Saturdays.

Everything's fine.

One step through the door, and she knew everything was not fine. Bekka, who worked the security desk, wore a somber yet anxious look on her face and waved for Janey to hurry.

"What's going on?" she asked from several paces away, her wet boots making squeaky noises on the tiled floor.

"Adam's been in an accident. The police just called. They're sending someone up to get you."

Janey's ears stopped working after the first sentence.

Adam's been in an accident.

She'd heard those words before, but with a different name. Every fear she'd been ignoring, tamping back every time one of them tried to come forward and make her think too hard, surged to the front of her mind.

Bekka said something else, but Janey could only hear the sound of her own blood rushing through her ears.

See? His job is too dangerous.

See? You can't guarantee that he'll be around for very long.

See? You're better off just trying to get Jess raised and on his own.

"Janey?"

She came back to herself when Bekka touched her hand. "Are you okay? Did you hear what I said?"

She pressed her lips together and shook her head. Surprisingly, no tears came. The numbness that had spread through her at the news of Matt's death didn't come.

Looking right at Bekka, she said, "Tell me again."

"They're sending someone up to get you, because the rain is really bad right now. You can call them back and talk to Sarah there. She'll let you know more of what's going on."

Janey didn't even know how to call the police station if it wasn't an emergency. And she knew that went to dispatch, not someone at a desk. "Did Sarah leave a number?"

"Right here." Bekka shook the paper she'd been holding out. Janey hadn't even seen it.

She took it and said, "I'll go call right now." She spun on her heel and marched back to her office, her head high. She would not dissolve into tears, not until she knew what there was to cry about.

After locking the door and seating herself at her desk, she drew in a deep breath and blew it out. "All right." She dialed Sarah and while the line rang, she turned up the setting on her space heater so she could finally get warm.

"Sarah Farnsworth," she answered.

"Sarah, it's Janey Germaine."

"Oh, my goodness, Janey." Her voice turned personal instead of professional, and she said, "He wanted us to call you. Milo's on his way up to get you, but it's slow, as I'm sure you understand. The Chief gave him your cell number, so he can call when he gets there."

"So Adam's awake? He's okay?" He was obviously giving out directions, so he must not be too badly injured.

The whispers in her mind wouldn't cease though, and she pushed against them again.

"He called in the accident okay," she said. "We've got an ambulance there now, and I'm waiting to hear how he is."

So Sarah didn't really know any more than Janey did. She sighed, wishing for more news and faster relief than *Sit and wait and we'll let you know.*

"Can I give you my cell too?" Janey asked. "You can just text me whatever you find out, as soon as you know."

"Yes, go ahead and give it to me," Sarah said.

Janey recited the number, and said, "Well, I guess that's it. Thanks for calling up here to let me know."

"Drew's on his way in from the farm," Sarah said. "We'll know more soon." Something beeped really loudly on her end, and she said, "Oh! That's Trent."

"Sarah, come back."

"Here, Trent."

Janey bit her lip, waiting, hoping.

"He's passed out, that's why he won't answer. The bus is here, and they're working to get his leg free. Looks like he's been cut on his face and neck a bit, probably from the broken glass. Russ says he's breathing fine, and Pete's in the car with him, trying to get him awake."

"I've got Janey on the line," Sarah said.

Janey felt like she was hovering outside of her body, but she said, "Thank you, Trent."

"He's okay, Janey," Trent said. "He's going to be just fine. Nothing life-threatening."

The relief she wanted flowed through her, and the tears came. "Thank you," she said again, her voice choked and full of emotion.

"Trent, out."

Janey wiped her face and her phone buzzed and chirped, indicating she'd received a text. "Thank you, Sarah," she said.

"Of course, dear." The other woman sounded like she was crying too, and Janey realized Adam had a whole police department family who loved him as much as she did.

She hung up and stared at her phone, unseeing.

Because she was in love with Adam Herrin, and she'd just now realized it.

∽

SHE SQUEEZED JESS'S HAND AS THEY ENTERED THE emergency room waiting area. Milo came puffing in behind them, and he turned to the right as if he'd been here numerous times before. He probably had.

He stepped up to the desk and said, "Chief Herrin?"

It had been at least almost ninety minutes since the accident. The National Park was a good half an hour from town on a sunny day, and she'd asked Milo to stop by the junior high so she could get Jess. He deserved to know what was going on, be there for Adam too.

"He just got out of x-ray." The receptionist looked up. "I can let him know you're here, and talk to the doctor and see if it's okay for you to go back."

Milo shook his head. "It's okay for us to go back." He stepped around to the door and pushed it open. The receptionist did not think it was okay for them to go back, and she met them in the hall through the door.

"You're not family. He might not be fit for guests." She wore a stern look, and Janey's heart pounded. She needed to see Adam right now. Right *now*.

"We're family, Roberta," Milo said in a low voice. "Just point me toward where he is, and we'll only stay a minute. We just want to see him."

"You and every other cop on the force," she said, folding her arms. "We can't have the whole department in the emergency room."

"Just them, then." Milo stepped back.

Roberta surveyed Janey and Jess, and she softened a little. "Fine. But if I get in trouble for this, I'm telling them I told you no."

"That's okay," Janey said. "I'll tell whoever I need to that Jess held you back or something."

"Yeah, totally." Jess shifted next to her. "I just want to see him. He taught me how to cook, you know? It was his recipe that I won with in the Fall Festival."

Janey looked at him when she heard the tightness in his voice.

"It's not fair," Jess said, swiping at his eyes. He straightened and put on a stoic mask. "Just five minutes."

"He's in curtain seven," Roberta said, stepping out of the way.

Janey didn't waste a second. She hurried down the hall, glad Milo was with her to say, "It's to your left, Janey. Left."

She turned and saw curtain four ahead. Around a bend in the hall, and curtain seven came into view on the right. She slowed, suddenly unsure. "Maybe I should go first," she told Jess as she stepped in front of him. "Trent said he'd been cut on his face and neck."

Jess looked up at her with those dark-as-night eyes. "I'll be fine, Mom."

They faced the curtain together, and she pulled it back a bit and said, "Hello?"

Adam lay in bed, partially propped up. It took a long moment for him to turn his head toward the sound of her voice, and she saw in his dull eyes that he'd been given some heavy painkillers.

"Hey," she said again, softer and sweeter now.

"Janey," he said. "Jess." He motioned for them to come closer with his right hand. Almost everything on his right side seemed untouched. His arm, his leg, his side, his face, all fine.

It was his left side that had been battered, bruised, and

buffeted. He had nicks and cuts from his fingers to his elbow, and gauze over his neck and ear, and one large spot on his forearm.

Janey went to his right side and reached up and ran her fingers through his hair before placing a kiss on his forehead. "You're okay." She took a deep breath of him, but he smelled more like antiseptic and plastic bandages than the Adam she knew.

"My left leg is broken," he said. "Just got back from x-ray. They're talkin' about it with Drew and my mom now." His voice slurred and his eyes closed.

Jess took his hand and said, "It's just your left leg, Chief. You barely need that one."

Adam chuckled but he didn't open his eyes.

"We should go, Jess."

"No." Adam opened his eyes. "Don't go."

The area in curtain seven wasn't that big, especially when a doctor, two nurses, Drew, Joel, and Donna came back.

"Oh, you made it." Donna hugged her and then Jess, and Janey tried to stuff herself into a corner so the doctors could examine Adam's leg.

"He'll be going into surgery in just a few minutes," she said. "The waiting room is on the third floor, just to the right of the elevators. When he's done, I'll come talk to you about how it went." She nodded in a no-nonsense way but wore a kind smile as she did.

And with that, they lowered Adam's bed until it was

flat, and they pushed him and all of his equipment out of the curtain area.

"Okay, then." Drew sighed and ran his hands through his hair. "Let's go wait on the third floor."

⁓

Janey bought Jess a can of soda from the machine and met Donna's eye. She mimed that she was going to go make a quick phone call, and Donna nodded, tucking Jess against her side in a silent *I've got him.*

Janey walked away, her legs feeling rubbery and like they might not hold her up for much longer. She ducked around the corner and dialed AnnaBelle.

"I've been waiting for you to call," her sister said in a rush. "Is Adam all right?"

"How did you know?"

"He got in an accident on Main Street over two hours ago. Everyone knows."

Janey sighed and leaned her head against the sterile wall behind her. She slid down and sat on the floor, her knees tucked to her chest. "They just took him into surgery. He has a broken leg. Other than that, he's got a few bruises and cuts. I think the term the doctor used was 'lacerations' on his hands, arms, neck, and face. And a burn from the airbag."

AnnaBelle sucked in a breath. "I'm so sorry, Janey."

This time, Janey's tears poured down her face. "Why

does this stuff always happen to me? I mean, you've been married to Don for nine years now. He's never gotten in an accident. Never broken a bone." She calmed and quieted as someone in a white lab coat went by. "Maybe I'm bad luck."

"Don't be silly." But AnnaBelle didn't sound like Janey was being silly at all.

She tilted her head back and looked at the ceiling tiles. "What should I do?"

"What do you mean?"

"Jess and I get along just fine. Maybe I should...I don't know. Cut Adam loose."

"Janey...." But she didn't finish. Didn't reassure Janey that if she married Adam, they could grow old together. Janey supposed there were no assurances of that for anyone.

Her eyes filled with tears, and they trickled down her face. "I'll call you when I know more, okay? Will you tell everyone else?"

"Of course."

"Bye." Janey hung up without waiting for AnnaBelle to say anything else. She stayed against the wall until her tears dried and her backside went numb. Then she got up and went into the bathroom to clean herself up. After all, she didn't need Jess to see that she'd fallen apart over a broken leg.

It's more than that.

And she knew it was, but she didn't know what to do

about her feelings for Adam, which had grown and swelled in only a few short months. And she couldn't ask him to quit his job for her. He was a cop, through and through, obviously not exempt from the dangers of freezing rain.

She returned to the waiting area to find Jess fast asleep, his head in Donna's lap, and Janey knew that if she broke things off with Adam, she'd be dealing with two broken hearts.

22

Loud beeping kept pinging against Adam's blissful slumber. He really wanted it to stop. He needed to figure out where he was, and how he'd gotten there. Bright flashes of light kept sweeping in front of him, like headlights or the swift passing of a lighthouse beam.

People spoke, but whether the questions were directed at him or not, he couldn't tell. It felt like a long time went by in this state, while only a few minutes passed at the same time.

Eventually, he was able to open his eyes, but it was still mostly dark, with that incessant beeping in the background.

He groaned, his mouth dry and tasting like someone had filled it with wallpaper paste. His leg ached and itched and he tried to pull it toward him to scratch it.

Pain tore through his hip, and that was when he

remembered everything. A yelp left his mouth, and the scratching of a chair sounded in the room.

"Adam?"

"Janey?" His parched throat could barely push the word out.

"Let me get the nurse." Her silhouette crossed to the door, which had a yellow-lit window, and she left. A few moments later, she returned with a nurse who flipped on the overhead lights.

He squinted and held back another groan.

"Hello, Chief. Good to see you awake." Nancy Runsom smiled at him, but he couldn't quite return the gesture the way he normally did.

"I wish I was still asleep."

"Oh, nope." She grabbed his chart and looked at it. Wrote some things down from the source of that annoying beep and said, "We'll have you up and moving by morning."

He gaped at her. "I obviously have a broken leg."

"And some great big biceps to propel yourself around." She grinned at him like they were conversing at a party. "What's your pain at? Scale of one to ten, ten being so bad you're about to cry."

"Four." He reached up and scratched his face, only to have his fingers meet gauze and tape. "I itch everywhere."

"That's a side-effect of the anesthetic they use during surgery. It'll wear off soon."

Not soon enough, in Adam's opinion. Nancy flitted

around and took his blood pressure, put some more painkillers in his IV, and finally left him alone with Janey.

"Hey," he said. "Come here."

She moved to the right side of the bed, her arms wrapped tightly around her.

"You okay?" he asked.

She shook her head, a single tear splashing her face. He lifted his right arm, and she carefully curled into his side, her breath and tears hot against his chest.

"I'm okay," he finally whispered. "People break their legs every day."

She nodded but still didn't say anything. Adam didn't know how to reassure her, because the simple fact was, he couldn't. So he simply held her close to his heart until she quieted, until her breathing evened out and she fell back asleep, until he could whisper, "I love you," into the darkness and be the only one who heard it.

∼

NINE DAYS AFTER THE ACCIDENT, HE FINALLY HOBBLED BACK into the police station. Sarah jumped from her seat with, "Chief! You're back!" She hovered around him, her hands flapping like bird's wings. "Let me get the door to your office."

He'd had a steady stream of people helping him at home too. His brother came every morning to make sure Adam could get in and out of the shower. Up and down the stairs. Janey came on Monday and Wednesday to bring him lunch. Jess came after school to take the dogs out for a run. Joel and his mother had come every night with dinner.

Adam just wanted to be alone. Needed to be able to take care of himself. His leg hardly hurt anymore, and the physical therapist he saw twice a week said he was making great progress. His cuts had healed nicely, though he wore a bandage over the biggest ones. He had two—one over a particularly deep cut on his neck and one over the burn on his arm from the explosive that detonated to inflate the airbag.

He could file paperwork, though. And answer emails. And sit in meetings. So he did all of that, growing more and more weary with every passing hour. Around two-thirty, Sarah said, "You should go home. You look gray."

He felt gray, so he asked Trent to take him home. He didn't have a new cruiser yet, as the insurance was being slow to come through on the appraisal of the one that had been totaled. It had been hit three times, in three different spots, so he wasn't sure what the hold up was.

Doesn't matter, he told himself as Trent turned into his driveway. *You can't drive anyway.*

He waited for Trent to come give him something steady to hold onto as he heaved his considerable weight onto his good leg. Trent stayed by his side along the walkway and up the steps. Adam collapsed into a chair on his front porch, his breath laboring in and out of his lungs.

"Thanks."

"You sure you're okay?"

"I'm just going to sit right here for a while," Adam said. "Jess will be by after school. I'll make him cook me dinner." He put a smile on his face so his officer would leave. Trent did, and Adam's smile disappeared with the departure. He needed Gypsy's happy face, so he got himself to his feet and opened the front door. "Come on," he called, and both dogs came running.

Fable had been less standoffish since Adam had returned home, and both dogs sat at his feet. He absently rubbed them, taking their friendship and strength as his own.

A while later, the tell-tale sound of a skateboard on asphalt filled the air, and Adam watched as Jess came down the road. He kicked his board up and caught it under his arm before coming up the driveway. When he saw Adam sitting on the porch, his face burst into a grin.

"Hey, man."

Gypsy left Adam's side and went to greet Jess, who knelt down and let her lick his face while he laughed. Adam's heart swelled with love for the teen. He didn't have to come here after school. He probably had friends he'd rather hang out with.

"I'm starving," he said. "Can I...?"

"Bring me some crackers or whatever my mom put in the cupboards."

Jess went inside, taking Gypsy with him, the glutton. She knew where to get treats, and it wasn't from Adam. He returned with two boxes of crackers and a cheese ball. Adam opted for the wheat ones, no cheese ball necessary, and Jess sat in the chair on the other side of the table, Gypsy begging at his feet.

"How's school?" Adam asked.

"Great. Almost the end of the term."

"What are you guys doing for Thanksgiving?"

"Going out to your parents. Or Drew's, I guess. They're doing dinner out there."

Adam nodded. He'd been invited to Drew's too. And while Janey hadn't stopped coming over, and they texted and talked a lot, Adam felt something different between them.

"How's your mom?"

"Okay."

And that about summed it up. Before, things had been going great. Now they were just okay. Adam wasn't quite sure what was on Janey's mind, because she hadn't told him. Their lunches had been quiet affairs, and she rarely came in the evenings, because his parents did.

"She's been saying some weird stuff." Jess paused in his rapid consumption of the crackers and dip.

"Like what?" Adam looked at the boy. "I mean, you don't have to tell me. Probably none of my business."

Jess shook his head. "I don't know. It's probably nothing."

Adam let a beat of silence go by, and then he said, "Hey, remember when you were making the bisque, and I said to listen to your gut? You gotta do that all the time. You say things are nothing a lot, but they rarely are. They're something."

Jess looked at him with Matt's eyes—his best friend's eyes—and Adam smiled. "Okay?"

He nodded, emotions storming through those eyes. "Okay. So then...I mean, how interested are you in being my dad?"

Adam blinked at the question, not quite prepared for it and not expecting it to come up right now. "I'm totally interested in that," Adam said, his voice thick and hoarse at the same time. "I love you, Jess. You're a great kid." He cleared his throat, glad Jess's chin had started wobbling a little bit too.

"I'll tell my mom."

"Why? She thinks I don't want to be your dad?"

"She thinks you won't be around long enough." Jess went back to his crackers. "Or something. She stays up real late, you know? Thinks I don't know she's lying in bed reading. Except this week, she's been crying." He glanced at Adam. "She talks to herself when she's stressed. Did you know that?"

Adam nodded. "It's hard work being as awesome as she is. Makes sense she'd want to talk some things out with herself." And a bowl of chocolate chips and pretzels.

"Anyway, she keeps saying she's not being fair to you, but I don't know what that means. Last night, she said you probably wouldn't be around long enough to...do something. I couldn't quite hear."

Adam sighed and surveyed the front lawn, the quiet street in front of him. "You probably shouldn't be eavesdropping on your mom."

"Yeah, probably not."

Adam ate a few crackers, trying to think of something to say. He finally came up with, "I can't control everything, Jess, just because I'm the Chief of Police. You know that, right?"

"Yeah, sure."

"We don't have a lot of violence or problems here in Hawthorne Harbor, but my guess is your mom thinks my job is too dangerous for me to be...." He cleared the emotion from his voice. "Her husband and your dad."

Adam wanted to be both. The possibility of it had been drawing closer and closer, but now it felt distant. A dot on the horizon he couldn't reach. Would never reach.

"How interested are you in me being your dad?" he asked.

The box of crackers made a crumpling noise as Jess dug into the plastic bag again. "I'm real interested in that."

"You don't think it'll cramp your style?"

"What does that mean?"

"You know, me being the Chief of Police and all that. You think your friends would still want to hang out with you?"

"Maybe not all of them."

"Maybe not the ones who want you to tag buildings."

Jess looked away. "Yeah, not those ones."

"Maybe they're not real friends, then."

"Maybe not." Jess scooped up more dip and made a sandwich out of two crackers. "But I wouldn't mind."

Adam leaned back in his chair and closed his eyes. "I wouldn't mind either, Jess."

23

Janey pulled into the driveway at home at the same time Jess opened the garage door, his skateboard tucked under his arm.

She rolled down her window before pulling into the garage. "Hey, bud. How's Adam today?"

"Went back to work," he said before walking away.

Janey's motherly instincts fired, and she eased into the garage and parked. Once inside, she found Jess standing in front of the fridge, looking for something to eat. "Everything okay?"

Jess closed the fridge but wouldn't look at her. "We have nothing to eat."

"We could go see Grandma Germaine. She's been asking about you." Janey tried to get Jess over to see Matt's parents as often as possible. They took him on weekends sometimes too, but they hadn't for a while, not since LouAnn had started having some health problems.

"I already texted her. They're in Seattle for a couple of days."

Janey simultaneously loved that Jess had a phone and didn't. At least he was texting people like the Chief of Police and his grandmother. "Then let's go get pizza or something."

"I don't want pizza."

Janey knew then that something serious had happened. Was it school? Or Adam? "Hey," she said, reaching out and touching his shirtsleeve. "What's going on?"

Jess turned toward her, his face a perfect storm of anger and confusion. "I hear you crying at night, Mom."

Janey fell back a step. "I'm...fine, Jess."

"You're not fine."

She'd been getting up and going to work every day. Nothing in their routine had changed, except for she'd taken sandwiches and salads to Adam's house for lunch last week. Jess skated over there after school. That was all.

"Yes, I am."

"Was this how you were when Dad died?"

She sucked in a breath and held it. "No, because Adam's not my husband *or* your dad, and he didn't pass away."

"So you were worse. Great." He opened a cupboard,

didn't find what he wanted, and slammed it shut. "Are you going to break up with him?"

She stared at him, her heart thundering in her chest. He'd just asked the same question she'd been battling for nine days.

"It's not fair to him or me to keep stringing him along."

"Stringing him along? Did he tell you that's what I was doing?" Because if he had.... Janey's anger kicked into gear, and it took a lot to get her mad.

"He told me not to ignore my gut, and my gut says you're not sure about him, but you haven't told him anything."

How her thirteen-year-old knew so much, Janey couldn't comprehend. He had no idea what she'd said or not said to Adam. He had no idea what it was like trying to balance a dozen different very breakable plates, hoping you didn't drop one that was too valuable, or too important, or that would come back to haunt you later.

"I don't know what to do," Janey admitted.

"You can do hard things," Jess said in a mildly sarcastic tone. "Isn't that what you're always telling me?" He gave her a disgruntled look and added, "I'm ordering pizza," before lifting his phone to his ear.

Helplessness filled her, choked her, made her feel like she was drowning. She sat down at the kitchen table while Jess ordered more pizza than would be possible for the two of them to eat. He asked for cash from her wallet to pay for it, and she gave it to him. She barely noticed when the house filled with the scent of marinara and garlic, or that Jess's friend Thayne had come over.

She rarely allowed friends over on weeknights, but she didn't have the energy to bring it up, argue about it, or any of it. She got up and got herself some pizza and then retreated to her bedroom.

The door closed around nine, and she knew Thayne had gone. Jess usually poked his head in her room and said good-night, but tonight his footsteps took him right into his bedroom, where that door closed too.

She cleaned up the kitchen, packed herself a lunch for the following day, and hunted around for her phone. She finally found it in her purse, dead, so she plugged it in and retreated back to her bed.

But she didn't pull out the e-reader, or open the top drawer of her nightstand to get out her secret stash of treats. She simply stared, trying to sort through all the various thoughts in her head and find a solution to her issues with her relationship with Adam.

Don't think so hard.

But every time she thought about him, with those crutches and needing help for the most basic of things, all she could see was that he was hurt.

Hurt on the job.

A job he wasn't going to give up.

She leaned back against the pillows, wondering if she could maybe just see how things went. That had been her plan in the beginning, and it had turned out pretty well.

She wasn't planning to see Adam again until Monday for lunch, but she decided she didn't want to wait almost four more days.

The covers got flung to the side relatively easy, and she stuffed her feet into her slippers. She paused at Jess's door and only heard silence. Rapping lightly with her knuckles, she pushed open the door. He was sitting up in bed, a real book in his hands and his earphones in.

After getting his attention by flipping the lights, she said, "I'm going to go talk to Adam. I'll be back later."

Jess just stared, and Janey nodded once before leaving the house. At Adam's, she sat in the Jeep and stared at the rectangles of light in his house, trying to get up the courage to go in and talk to him. She'd done it before, been here late at night, unannounced.

But it felt different this time, and she wasn't even sure why.

His front door opened and he filled the doorway with his broad shoulders and those crutches. She had to get out now, so she sighed and unbuckled her seat belt to get out of the Jeep. She tucked her hands in her coat pockets and approached slowly.

"I thought that was you," he said when she reached the bottom of the steps. "I don't usually have people sitting outside my house."

She climbed the stairs and stopped, still trying to figure out what to say or why her heart suddenly wanted to leap from her body and flee.

"You want to talk?" he asked, shifting his weight to make room for her to squeeze by. She started toward him, thinking he'd go in first and she'd follow him. But he didn't. He stayed right where he was, leaving a small space for her to pass.

As she did, he wrapped his strong fingers around her wrist. "Please don't make this harder than it needs to be."

She looked up at him. "What do you mean?"

"I can tell there's something different between us," he said. "I'm not stupid, and you're not my first girlfriend. If you're going to break up with me, just say it."

"I don't want to break up...." She hung onto the last two words, trying to decide what she did want.

"Then what do you want?"

Her mind spun, and she hated how it wouldn't stop. "I want things to go back to how they were at the beach house," she blurted. "Fun, and new, and not too heavy. Light. I can't do anything heavy right now, and this...." She gestured to his stormy face and cast leg. "This, this feels heavy."

"This is real life," he said. "Sometimes it's beach houses and sometimes it's broken legs. There's only one person I want to do all of the above with, and that's you."

A flicker of a smile touched her lips, but it was quickly followed by a half-sob. "I'm scared. I think maybe...maybe I just need more time to make sure this is right. For me. For Jess."

"Don't bring Jess into it. We talk every day, you know. He tells me stuff, and I tell him stuff."

Janey narrowed her eyes at him. "What kind of stuff?"

"Guy stuff."

"Like who he has a crush on?"

"Among other things." He dropped his hand from hers. "I don't want you to use him for an excuse. You're better than that." He hobbled backward on his crutch. "My door is always open. Come on back when you know how you feel and if you think we could be right for each other."

He nudged the door with the rubber tip of his crutch and it started to swing closed. Janey wanted to throw her hand out and stop it, but she didn't. "Are you breaking up with me?" The door snicked closed right as she finished her sentence.

She heard him say, "You know where the key is."

Janey stared at the closed door just a few inches from her nose, every cell in her body unsure of what to say, what to do, how to react. She turned on wooden legs and took slow steps away from his front door.

At the bottom of the porch, she turned and looked back half-expecting him to have returned, his sexy smile back in place and his leg miraculously healed. The door was still stubbornly shut.

She sat down on the bottom step, unwilling to go home and face her son. Adam was right; she *had* used her son as an excuse, and she *was* better than that. She also didn't want to get into a serious relationship with Adam just because Jess liked him.

A while later, she got up and drove home When she checked in on Jess, she found him asleep, his book nowhere to be seen. His earbuds still trailed from his ears, and she crossed the room and switched off his lamp and pulled the headphones out of Jess's ears. "Love you, bud," she whispered.

She went to what comforted her and allowed her to get outside of her own head. Her digital books. Her chocolate chips. And her pretzels.

24

Adam pulled his new cruiser into his parents' farm, Janey's forest green Jeep like a siren's call to him. He couldn't look away from it though it made his heartbeat snake through his veins in a strange way.

He missed seeing it parked in front of his house at ten o'clock at night. Hated that they weren't still going to lunch at every restaurant in Hawthorne Harbor until they'd tried them all. Wanted to curl up and cry every time he felt like texting her and then remembering that he couldn't.

He'd put the ball squarely in her court, and she hadn't bounced it back yet. Or even picked it up, from what he could tell—and he had spies on the inside.

Jess skated over to the police station after school now, since Adam was working full days again. His leg was getting better and better every day, but he was letting Jess come over on Saturdays and make him lunch and dinner. The kid was a whiz with a knife and a recipe, and Adam was so glad that he hadn't lost Jess just because Janey needed time to figure things out.

His phone buzzed, and he checked it, half-hoping for a major fire or ten-car pile up that he'd need to leave for immediately. Unfortunately, it was his mother. *We can all see your car out there. Are you coming in? Do you need help?*

He thought about telling her he was on a call with dispatch, but the fib felt bigger than he was comfortable telling. Instead of answering, he reached for the door handle.

He technically shouldn't be driving by himself, but since his injured leg was his non-driving leg, he'd been using the new cruiser for a couple of days now.

Send Jess out to get the pies. He sent the text as he swung his legs out of the car and put all his weight on his good leg and the top of the car. He'd just gotten himself stabilized when the screen door slapped closed and Jess came running down the front sidewalk.

"Hey, man," he said, coming all the way around the front of the car with a big smile on his face. "Dixie wants to know if you'll take us out to the wishing well after dinner."

"You drivin' the ATV?" Adam knew Janey worried when Jess even rode on the ATV, and he wasn't sure if the boy even knew how to drive one.

"Yeah." He spoke without hesitation, and Adam grinned at him.

"Then, sure." He nodded toward the passenger side. "Pies over there. There are three. Make two trips, okay?"

But Jess balanced the pumpkin pie on his forearm and gripped the pecan and the key lime in his fingers before setting off for the side door.

"Mom!" he yelled, and someone opened the door for him, and Adam caught sight of Janey's beautiful face and heard her admonish Jess for carrying too much at once before he disappeared inside.

His heart twisted in his chest, and he faced away from the farmhouse and drew in a huge breath. Drew's back door opened, and he came out with Gretchen. They held hands and talked, their faces the picture of happiness and love.

Adam couldn't go inside. Not with them there. Not with Janey present. He wanted to hold her hand and kiss her and tell her he loved her. Having her so close and so out of reach was like torture. Torture he'd already endured once and couldn't do again.

"Hey," Drew wove through the fence posts that created a gate between the two properties. "You made it."

"I can't do it." Adam shook his head, his jaw clenched.

Drew's face fell as he frowned. "Do what?"

"He and Janey broke up," Gretchen said. "Remember I told you that?"

Drew whipped his head to her and back to Adam. "No, I don't remember that. What happened?"

"I got hurt."

"That's not why," Gretchen said.

Adam looked at her, a growl starting somewhere in the bottom of his gut. "Oh, no?"

"She's just scared," Gretchen said.

"Of what?" Drew asked.

What a great question. Adam wanted to know the answer too. Surely she understood that people got in car accidents. Survived broken legs—and much worse.

"I don't think she even knows what she's afraid of," Gretchen said, her blue eyes wide and worried. "She's here?"

Adam nodded, short little bursts of movement. She walked away, her feet crunching on the gravel before she reached the house.

"You're really not going to come in?"

"How can I?" Adam looked at his brother, his emotions rolling through him like an angry wave. "She broke up with me because I got in a *car accident.*" He leaned his weight against the cruiser to alleviate the pressure of the crutches under his arms.

Drew joined him, and together, they faced the water in the distance. "You've loved her for ages," he said. "You've loved her from across a table for twelve years, man. What's one more meal?"

He stayed for a few more moments and then said, "I'll buy you some time."

Adam wasn't sure how Drew would do that, but he let him go without asking.

What's one more meal?

Adam took a moment to enjoy the Thanksgiving sunshine, and then he turned and made his way inside. The kitchen was a flurry of activity, with Jess, Dixie, and his mom manning different pots and pans on the stovetop.

"There you are," his mother said. "Take these napkins into the dining room." She tucked them between his arm and the crutch, leaving him little choice but to do as she asked. Joel was the only one in the dining room, setting out plates, and he smiled and retrieved the napkins from Adam.

"How's the leg?" he asked, placing a burnt orange napkin beside each cream-colored plate. If there was something his mother knew how to do, it was make a meal festive.

"Getting better every day," Adam said. "The doctor says I'll be off the crutches by the wedding."

"Great news. What about getting back to running?"

"She wants me to wait until the new year, and then I have to go into the physical therapy unit to use the treadmill so they can test the strain." Adam missed his morning beach runs more than he thought he would. For the first few days, he'd enjoyed lying in bed later than he normally did.

He did *not* enjoy the attitudes and high-energy shenanigans the dogs got into when he didn't run them for an hour in the morning. With the rain this fall, his yard hadn't been a great option, especially because Gypsy gravitated toward mud like it was beef liver.

Joel nodded and said, "You lay out the silverware, and I'll be right back with the cups."

Adam did as his mom had taught him, and put the knife and spoon on the napkin, on the right side of the plate, with the fork opposite them. He'd only made it halfway around the table before Joel returned.

Working together, with the busy kitchen as background noise, they had the table ready in only a few minutes. Janey entered the room from the door that led to the living room, in the middle of a conversation with Gretchen, and they both froze when Adam glanced up from where he'd been adjusting the salt and pepper shakers at the end of the table.

Silence fell on the room; even the happenings in the kitchen seemed to mute. Joel had disappeared somehow, and Adam hadn't even seen him leave.

He could barely take in a breath, but he did. His lungs still worked. All the necessary functions, so it was nice to know he wouldn't die from a broken heart.

"Hey," he said. "Place cards?"

She nodded, her big brown eyes wide and beautiful.

Now that Adam had held her hand, kissed her, smelled the scent of her hair, he didn't have to fantasize about how wonderful those things would be.

The loss of them hurt, and badly.

"I want to sit by Jess," he said. "If that's not too much trouble."

"He made the same request," Gretchen said, plucking a couple of cards from Janey's fingers and starting around the table away from him. Janey followed like a lost lamb, and Adam thunked his way after them until he could escape through the door they'd come through. He went past the bathroom and down the hall toward the living room, and right on out the front door.

The air out here wasn't as filled with Janey's sweet scent, and he simultaneously enjoyed that and loathed it. He took a few breaths to cleanse his mind before turning to go see what else his mother needed him to do.

He caught sight of her back as she went in the dining room, leaving the kitchen empty. The stove was off, and it looked like a bomb had detonated.

"Where's Adam?" she asked.

"Coming," he called, hurrying as fast as the crutches would allow him to. He entered the dining room last, which made for an awkward dance between chair legs and people as he tried to get to his spot in the far corner.

Janey and Gretchen had placed him beside Jess and Drew, thankfully. Next to Drew was Gretchen, and then Janey, Dixie, and his parents. She was in his direct line of sight, and practically across from him. Where was he supposed to look for the whole meal?

He focused on his plate as Joel said nice words about being grateful and gathering together as family and friends. A bitterness entered Adam's throat, and it wasn't until Joel finished his speech and everyone reached for their sparkling cider glasses that he could swallow it away.

"Okay, so there's turkey, mashed potatoes, sweet potatoes, and gravy," his mother said. "Creamed corn, rolls, butter on both ends of the table...." She scanned like she'd forgotten something. "Leave room for Adam's pies. He outdoes himself every year." She beamed at him and sat down. "Let's eat."

Adam reached for the stuffing that had been placed directly in front of him and scooped some onto his place. He offered it to Jess, who said, "I only like the crispy parts on the edge."

"Then that's what you get." Adam gave him some, and dishes got passed around, and conversations started. Laughter rang out, and Adam was able to endure one more meal with Janey where she wasn't his.

It *was* different though, and the feeling writhed deep down in his stomach. Because this time, she knew how he felt about her. Every glance her way said something to her he didn't want to say. Every time he heard her say something, he tensed.

But he made it through and even managed to ask her for the pepper once without acting like a fool.

Adam gripped the overhead bar on the ATV tightly, hoping Jess didn't smash into the wishing well. He brought the vehicle to a stop—herky jerky style—and Dixie hopped out of the backseat while Adam was still making sure he had all the right pieces in all the right places.

"Hey!" Jess yelled after her. "You said I could go first." He twisted and pulled the key out before racing after her.

Adam chuckled, glad the actual meal of Thanksgiving had ended. The real grown-ups—the people with significant others and too much to do during the day—had been pouring coffee when he'd left with the kids. They'd probably converse and laugh and reminisce before pie made an appearance.

He'd much rather be out here than stuffed in the too-small farmhouse, wishing Janey would say something to him. Heck, at this point, he'd take a glance from her.

Sighing, he got out of the ATV and followed the kids over to the wishing well. Both of them stood on their tiptoes, peering over the edge at something inside.

"You guys don't tell each other what you wish for, do you?"

Dixie rounded on him, her cherubic face set on serious. "No way. Drew said the wish won't come true if you tell."

Adam leaned his right hip against the stones to give

his injured leg a break and looked down at the brackish water too. "Sometimes that's true, and sometimes it's not."

Jess copied his stance but looked at him. "What do you mean?"

"My dad built this well," Adam said. "Because I wanted to make the football team. Everyone knew that was why I ran out here every morning before school and every day after school too. After a while, he bought me weights to carry. But the wish stayed the same."

Dixie started nodding before Adam finished speaking. "My teacher was just talking about this."

"About Adam running out to the wishing well?" Jess asked.

She glanced at him and then Adam, her bright purple coat making her pale skin seem even more translucent. "No, about not just sitting back and wishing for things to happen. She said you have to work for them."

"A-ha," Adam said. "What was I really doing when I came out to the wishing well?" He watched the line between Jess's eyes deepen as he frowned, thought, worked through the problem.

"You ran out here," he said. "You were conditioning."

"Exactly. I didn't have an ATV, and it's what? A mile out here? Maybe more." Adam smiled at the kids. "So sometimes, even if someone knows your wish, it can still come true. If you work at it."

Dixie fished a coin out of her pocket. "I've made lots of wishes here." She flipped the coin up in the air and caught it again. "I've learned that it's best to only wish for something you can actually control."

Adam looked at the twelve-year-old who was wise beyond her years. "That's also true," he said. "Like it would make no sense for me to wish that, oh I don't know, that one of my officers would start bringing me lunch every day."

"Or for me to wish my mom and Drew would get married," she said.

"But your mom and Drew *are* getting married," Jess said.

"Now they are," she said, giving him a small glare. "But I spent a lot of wasted wishes on it, and it wasn't even something I could control." She flipped the coin again, but Adam snatched it out of the air.

"So, what are you going to wish for today?"

Her cheeks grew rosy. "I don't want to tell."

Jess peered down into the well. "I wish I could get my coin back. I think I've been wishing for the wrong thing." He spoke in a hushed, emotional voice, and Adam's heart twisted in his chest.

He wanted to make everything right for Jess. Give him whatever he'd been wishing for. Drive him to school and spend time with him on the weekends.

Not up to you, he reminded himself. But he could wish Janey could figure things out faster. Couldn't he?

Probably not. He couldn't control her.

He handed the dime back to Dixie. "Go on, then. The

wind's starting to pick up and if we don't get back soon, all the pecan pie will be gone. My mother loves that stuff."

Dixie grinned at him, pressed the silver coin to her lips, and tossed it in the well. She turned away, a proud smile on her face.

"What did you wish for?" Jess asked, falling into step beside her. Adam liked that neither one of them seemed concerned about his crutches and this uneven, rocky ground.

"I can't tell you, Jess." Dixie's voice suggested her statement had come with an eyeroll, and Adam made his way back to the ATV with a genuine smile on his face—his first since Janey had left his house and cut off all communication with him.

25

One Friday night a couple of weeks later, the doorbell rang. Janey was curled up on the couch, the television blaring something she wasn't watching. Jess was with Matt's parents, so she got up and went to see who it was.

Mabel Magleby stood on the porch with a huge tray in her hands. Janey lunged forward to take it from her at the same time she said, "Mabel, how good to see you. Come in." She backed up with the heavy tray, wondering how in the world the older woman had carried it.

"It's quick bread," she said as she followed Janey inside and closed the door behind her. "We had a reception at the Mansion for this tech business something or other." She spoke with disapproval, like technology shouldn't be developed.

Janey put the tray on the counter in the kitchen and

swept the aluminum foil off the top. The scent of lemons and sugar met her nose, and her mouth started to water. "Wow, this looks amazing."

"There's chocolate chip." Mabel pointed to one wedge of the tray. "This is orange marmalade. Coconut lime. And lemon zucchini."

Janey selected the lemon zucchini and took a bite of the top part of the bread, where the sugary lemon glaze was. A party exploded in her mouth with sweet and sour, and of course, the lovely, dense bread.

"This is so good." She smiled at Mabel and gave the old woman a hug. "Do you have time to sit and talk?" It had been so long since she'd shared an evening with someone. Jess got home about the same time she did each evening, and promptly went into his bedroom. He always said he wasn't hungry, and claimed to have homework that required his utmost attention.

Never mind that he usually ate a couple sandwiches for dinner, or several bowls of cereal, or half a pizza if she'd ordered in. Never mind that he normally sat on the couch with her to do his homework, asking her questions about the math he already knew the answers to.

Jess was simply upset with her that she'd broken up with Adam, despite the fact that she'd told him that Adam had ended things with her.

Not that you gave him much choice, she thought.

"I always have time to sit and talk." Mabel gave Janey a smile, and she returned it, more relieved to have company than she expected to be. As Mabel moved back toward the living room, she asked, "How's Jess doing?"

"Oh, he's okay." Janey switched off the TV and tucked her legs under her as she took her spot on the couch again. She wrapped her arms around herself and tried to give Mabel a smile that would smooth over the worry that had come through in her voice.

"And you?" Mabel perched on the wingback chair in front of the window, the coldest spot in the house. Janey needed to put in more energy-efficient glass, but she didn't have the time to research it, nor the money to actually get the job done.

Janey glanced away. "I'm doing okay too."

Mabel scoffed, drawing Janey's attention back to her. "I took one look at you and knew you weren't okay," she said. "Why do you think I brought you a platter of bread?" She cocked her head, her eyes as sharp as a falcon.

The front door opened and Jess came inside with both of Matt's parents. Janey jumped to her feet. "Hey, everyone." She smiled at them, Matt's eyes looking back at her from Jess's face and from Mav's.

He stepped up to Janey and hugged her. "Hey, Janey-girl." He'd always called her that, and she held onto him for an extra moment as a rush of love flowed through her.

"Hi, Mav. How's the tile business?"

"Thrilling." He let his wife step in and embrace Janey too.

"Something smells good," she said as Jess walked away.

"Hey," Jess said from the kitchen. "Can I have some of this?" He stood down at the end of the hall, a slab of bread in his palm.

"Of course," Janey called. "But Mabel's still here. Come say hello."

He obliged, returning to the living room with a stack of chocolate chip bread. "Hey, Mabel." He gave her a quick hug, gave each of his grandparents a slice of bread, and collapsed onto the bean bag. "This is great. What's it from?"

She told him, and Janey marveled that he spoke more to her in the next few minutes than he had to her in days.

"Well, I should go," Mabel finally said, exchanging a glance with Mav and LouAnn. "It's already dark, and Jaime's waiting for me to get back so he can go on home." She scooted to the edge of the chair and pushed herself up.

Jess leapt to his feet and steadied her with his elbow, his dark eyes smiling down on her.

"You're such a good boy." Mabel looked up at him. "Don't change that, all right?" She seemed to say more than that with just those words, but Janey didn't understand the message.

Jess obviously did, because he nodded.

"She'll come around," Mabel said, walking past Janey with a steady glare. She paused, Jess just on the other side of her, and both of Matt's parents standing there watching. Janey felt like they'd all ganged up on her and she wasn't even sure how it had happened.

"You broke up with the Chief." Mabel wasn't asking.

Janey blinked, uncomfortable talking about Adam with Mabel, and in front of Jess and Matt's parents. She wasn't exactly sure what her hesitation with Adam was, which only complicated explanations. "I...needed some time to think."

"Oh, boo." Mabel waved her hand like thinking was the stupidest thing to do. "You think too much. He's a good man." She took a few more steps and called back over her shoulder. "I told him not to break your heart, and he told me it would be the other way around. I didn't believe him."

"I didn't break his heart." She got to her feet and followed Mabel and Jess around the corner to the front door.

"Yes, you did, Mom," Jess said in a real quiet voice.

Mabel, however, wasn't nearly as nice. "Of course you did, Janey. He's in love with you, and you're trying to figure out an answer to an unanswerable question. He's confused. Lonely."

Janey held up her hand. "All right, Mabel."

Her blue eyes sparked with lightning. "Don't let him go because you're scared," she said. "You'll regret it forever."

Jess opened the door and Mabel shuffled through it.

He went with her to make sure she got down the steps and into her car okay, leaving Janey numb and frozen to the spot.

"We're okay with it," LouAnn said. "In case you were wondering."

"You've done so great with Jess," Mav said. "He's so much like Matt." He pressed his lips together for a quick minute. "Grief sneaks up on me sometimes." He looked away, and Janey felt the pinch of emotion in her heart too.

"I don't want to be disloyal to Matt," she whispered.

"Oh, honey, you're not." LouAnn put both hands on Janey's shoulders and looked right into her eyes. "You deserve to be happy. Don't be afraid of that." LouAnn gave her a smile and a nod, and then she waved that she and Mav should leave too.

They did, and Janey gripped the door as she watched them cross the porch to the steps. Mav kept his hand on LouAnn's elbow to steady her as she took the steps one at a time until she made it to the sidewalk. Their love was palpable, and she'd enjoyed being their daughter-in-law.

She'd always have them, just like Jess would always be Matt's son. As she stood there, the only part of her body that seemed to be working was her brain, and that thing never shut off.

Don't think. Just act.
Don't let him go.
Don't be afraid.

Everyone had such great advice. But no one told her

how to *do* the things she needed to do. No one told her how to be brave enough to push past her fears. No one told her how to explain things to Adam, or how to get him to understand where she was coming from.

Probably because you don't even know where you are or where you're coming from.

Janey sighed as Jess bounded up the stairs and back into the house. "Jess."

He didn't look at her or speak to her, but simply walked past, collected another stack of sweet bread, and went into his room.

The sound of his bedroom door clicking closed felt so final to Janey, and her chest tightened until she could barely breathe. Since she didn't know how to ease the tension or make things right, she got her own stack of sugary bread and went back to the TV.

~

"I SWEAR I USED TO BE A SIZE SIX," JANEY GRUMBLED, thinking of all that coconut lime bread she'd eaten this past week. But the size-six bridesmaid dress would decidedly not zip up. The shade of pale pink played nicely with her dark hair, but she definitely needed a bigger size.

She opened the dressing room door to find Moira standing right there. "Need a different size?"

"Eight, at least," Janey said, wondering how the other women were faring. She hadn't stepped foot in any of the shops on Wedding Row in years. Thankfully, the same anxieties she'd been entertaining since Adam's departure from her life hadn't reared their ugly heads yet today. She'd survived brunch with Gretchen and four more of her friends. Then they'd walked down the street, ogling the window displays in every shop though none of the rest of them were engaged.

Flowers, photographers, videographers, shoe stores, jewelers, photo booth rentals, party supply stores, two salons, a men's wear store and now the dress shop. Gretchen had scheduled an appointment, and each woman had her own attendant.

Moira returned carrying two pink dresses as well as something that looked like an oversized gauze wrap. "Let me help you with the shaper," she said.

Janey didn't even know what a shaper was. But she let Moira follow her into the dressing room and help her out of the pale pink dress that reminded Janey of cotton candy.

"You step in here," she said, holding the gauze open. "And it just shimmies on." She tugged and sure enough, the shaper slid right over Janey's hips, stomach, and chest. "It keeps you all straight."

Moira grinned as she turned to the dresses. "I think the eight will be just fine now. We could try the six again."

"Eight," Janey said. No amount of stretchy gauze was going to get that size six dress to zip up. Moira helped her get into the dress, which zipped right up. She even had a little room in it and she smiled at her reflection.

Thoughts of her own wedding flashed through her mind, and the grin on her face flipped upside down.

Her own wedding?

Who was she kidding?

She wasn't even dating anyone anymore. Her heart tumbled in her chest and tears sprang to her eyes.

"You are beautiful," Moira said. "It's okay to get a little teary."

Janey sniffled and shook her head. "It's not that."

"Oh." Moira busied herself with hanging the size six dress on another hanger.

"Are you married?" Janey asked.

Surprised crossed Moira's perfectly made up face, and a small, placating smile appeared. "Yes, I am."

"For how long?"

"Seven years now." The smile grew, then faltered. "I heard about you and Chief Herrin."

Janey's defenses immediately flew into place, though Moira had obviously put two and two together and arrived at the cause of Janey's tears.

"I'm just so confused by it all," Janey said, smoothing her hands down her waist and hips.

"What are you confused by?" Moira asked.

Knocking interrupted them. "Let me see, Janey," Gretchen called.

Janey met Moira's eyes and quickly made to wipe hers.

She nodded when she was satisfied she didn't look like she'd been a bit teary. Moira opened the door and Janey walked a couple of steps forward before cocking her hip and putting her hand on it.

"How do I look?"

Gretchen gasped and covered her mouth. "So beautiful."

"How are the other women doing?" Janey asked.

"We're mostly done. Betty is getting a different size."

Moira slipped out of the dressing room with the two dresses that weren't the right size. "Just leave those in the room, Janey," she said. "I'll get them."

"Isn't this place great?" Gretchen asked as she entered the dressing room to help Janey get the dress off.

"So great," Janey said.

Gretchen's fingers stuttered along the zipper. "You're having fun, right?"

She met her friend's eyes in the mirror and lifted one shoulder in a shrug. "I can't stop thinking about Adam. That maybe, one day, this would be me, shopping with my bridesmaids."

Even as she spoke, she realized it wasn't true. She wouldn't do what Gretchen was doing for her second wedding. She'd want a simple affair, with just her family there, and his family, and him in his best uniform and her in a pearly dress that wasn't quite white and wasn't quite pink, but somewhere in between.

There would be roses everywhere, and Jess would be

wearing a tux and she'd dance with him first before dancing with Adam. She sighed, and Gretchen slid the dress off her shoulders and hung it on the hanger.

"You know what that sigh just told me?"

"What?"

"That you're in love with him."

Janey slithered out of the body shaper and reached for her jeans, silent.

"I know you are. *You* know you are. What are you so afraid of?"

Janey pulled her sweater over her head and faced Gretchen. "I had perfect once, and it shattered. I can't go through that again. So...I think maybe I'm better off if things just stay the way they were. Jess and I are fine." A laugh came out with the last word. She'd barely spoken to her son since Adam had broken up with her.

"Things aren't perfect, but we've always been happy."

Why didn't she feel happy then? Why didn't she and Jess talk over dinner the way they used to? Why couldn't she sleep, even when she'd read for hours and eaten herself into a chocolate-chip-pretzel stupor?

Gretchen smoothed her hair off her face. "Oh, honey. A blind man could see you're not happy." She flashed a sympathetic smile and stepped out of the dressing room with the pink dress.

"I miss him," Janey whispered to herself. "I miss him so much."

And she didn't mean Matt.

∽

The Monday before Gretchen and Drew's wedding, Janey kept Jess home from school. It had been almost six weeks since her last encounter with Adam where they were still dating, and Jess was starting to thaw slightly. Very slightly.

This whole time, she'd been worrying about what he would think of her dating again, and he'd gone and fallen for the man before she had.

"I need your full attention during the fitting," she said as she drove across town to the men's wear shop on Wedding Row.

"Didn't I already do the fitting?"

"Right, yes. The suit should be ready. You just try it on one last time to make sure all the alterations are correct." She glanced at him, but his focus was on his phone. "And then we'll go get lunch."

"Can we take some to Adam?" Jess glanced up and out of the corner of his eye.

Janey sighed. He'd been doing that a lot more lately. Sneaking in a question about Adam, or trying to get her and Adam in the same room together.

"Jess," she said, unsure of how to continue.

"Why can't you just get back together with him? He's *miserable* without you, Mom."

Janey looked out her window, her heart ricocheting

around inside her chest. Jess had not said one single word about Adam. Not one. In all these weeks.

"His birthday is coming up," Jess said. "I'll do extra chores to earn more money. I want to get him something."

Janey looked at her son, at the determined lift of his chin. "That's fine."

"And I want to spend the day with him. He shouldn't be alone on his birthday."

"Jess—"

"You could come too. I know! Let's make him his favorite dinner and a birthday cake."

"Oh, bud, I don't even know what his favorite dinner is."

"I do. Ribeye and macaroni and cheese. Not the boxed kind. The homemade kind. I made it a couple of weeks ago." He sat up straighter. "I can make it again. Please, Mom?"

She pulled into the parking lot and swung the ancient Jeep into a stall. She met her son's eye, and she couldn't deny him.

"I know you're in love with him," Jess said, his voice quiet yet powerful. "And it's okay. I asked him if he wanted to be my dad, and he said yes."

Janey's breath froze in her lungs.

Jess swiped at his eyes. "Even though Dixie told me not to, I've been wishing for you and him to get back together. Every time I go out to the lavender farm." He turned away from her and sniffed, wiping at his face again. "I'm so stupid."

"You are not." Hesitantly, she reached out and touched his shoulder. "You asked him if he wanted to be your dad?"

"A long time ago, before you guys even broke up." Another sniff. He didn't twitch a muscle toward her.

Janey stared out the front windshield, so deep inside her mind she couldn't see a way out. She loved Adam. Gretchen was right. She wasn't happy, and she just wanted to be happy. She wanted her son to be happy, and he spent more time with Adam than with her.

"Can you keep a secret?" she asked, an idea occurring to her.

Jess shifted halfway toward her. "Sometimes." He shrugged. "I'm actually not that great at it."

She swallowed, and pushed away all her thoughts, all her fears. "I love him," she said, tears springing to her eyes.

Jess searched her face, a light of hope shining in his eyes she hadn't seen in a while. "Yeah? And?"

"So I have an idea...but you *have* to keep it a secret."

26

Adam showed up at the Magleby Mansion several hours before the wedding was set to happen. Drew had asked him to come help him get ready and then keep him company during the formal photography session.

He got out of his cruiser with only a hint of pain from the break in his lower leg, and the beach just down the lawn called to him, begged him to come run along the shore. Just for a few minutes. The cast had come off last week, and Adam had celebrated with ice cream and homemade brownies. Well, Jess had made the brownies.

Gretchen would be happy about today's sunshine, even if it was weak and barely lent any warmth to the air. He turned away from the glorious water and faced the Mansion. This wouldn't be a terribly big wedding, but Janey would be here. Adam was hoping to avoid her, but as the best man and with her as the matron of honor,

Drew had told him he'd have to be in at least one picture with her.

Maybe one with just the two of them.

His stomach warred with his other internal organs. He'd rather be anywhere but here, but his brother needed him, so in he went.

The Mansion had been transformed from a beautiful, old building into a Christmas spectacular. Wreaths hung from every arch and a Christmas tree no shorter than fifteen feet loomed before him. The steps curving up and to the left bore pine boughs and poinsettias, and Adam stopped and took it all in.

No wonder Gretchen wanted to get married here. It was magical. Even the functional items, like tables and chairs, held an elegance that demanded people stop and breathe it all in before they continued.

"Chief Herrin."

He turned toward the weathered voice to find Mabel standing a few arches down. She wore a frown of disapproval, but Adam had dealt with her differing opinions before.

"Mabel." He moved toward her and shook her hand. "This place looks great."

"Of course it does," she said. "We're having a wedding today."

"Right. Do you know where Drew is?"

"The groom's room is upstairs," she said. "He got here about five minutes ago."

"Thanks." Adam turned to go, but Mabel's veined hand shot out and grabbed his arm. She was surprisingly strong for an elderly woman, and he looked down at her. "Something I can help you with?"

"She'll come around."

He frowned at her. "Who?"

"Oh, you know who, you brute." She released his hand and turned to go back through the arch, which led into the kitchen. "She loves you, and when she figures it out, she'll come back to you." She stepped through the door, leaving him with those words.

He wanted to believe Janey loved him, but all the evidence pointed to the contrary. *Doesn't matter*, he told himself. If she ever came back to him, ready to throw the ball back to his court, he'd take it. He wasn't sure if that made him romantic or pathetic.

He found the groom's room on the second floor easily, and he knocked as he pushed open the door. His garment bag was starting to get heavy, and relief spread through his shoulder and bicep when he was able to hang it on a clothing rack just inside the door.

"Hey." Drew stood at the window, gazing out the glass. Adam joined him to take in the spectacular view spread before him. Though the gardens weren't as green and full as they would be in the spring and summer, the winter version was still beautiful. And the beach beyond was stunning, calming Adam's heart and reminding him that he was as steady and predictable as the waves that washed ashore day and night.

"You ready for this?" he asked as a sleek silver sedan turned from the highway to come up the drive to the Mansion.

"Yeah." Drew didn't carry an ounce of hesitation or resistance in his voice. He'd come a long way in establishing who he was and what he wanted out of life since leaving Hawthorne Harbor years ago, being disappointed in Seattle, and returning to town.

Adam was the one who'd always known what he wanted to be. He'd gone to school, gotten trainings, everything he could to enhance his career. Drew had too, getting several certifications as a paramedic, and then becoming a firefighter too. Neither was particularly easy, but neither had been a perfect fit for him.

Funny that lavender farming was the perfect fit for him. And now with Gretchen and Daisy, a measure of jealousy tickled the back of Adam's throat as he realized Drew was about to get everything Adam had always wanted.

Different woman. Different kid. But still. Adam could become the director of the FBI and it wouldn't be enough if he didn't have Janey and Jess. In fact, nothing really compared to having them in his life. He didn't need anything but them.

The urge to leave the Mansion and find Janey, talk to her, make her understand, filtered through him until he thought he'd go mad. But Dixie had said it was best to wish for things he could control, and he absolutely couldn't control Janey.

So he got himself dressed, and helped Drew with his bowtie and cufflinks, and looked into his brother's eyes.

"I wish Dad were here," Drew said, his voice almost a whisper.

Adam smiled, but it felt pinched on his face. Sometimes he didn't think about his father for weeks at a time. And other times, it was like he was constantly present in everything Adam did. "I know."

Someone knocked and called, "Mister Herrin? It's Alicia Bagley, the photographer."

Adam held Drews' gaze for one more moment before turning to get the door. The photographer swept into the room and scanned everything.

"Right over here, please," she said, indicating a spot in front of the window. "We'll get some shots of you as if you're getting ready, and then we'll go outside. Gretchen is almost ready, but you need to be in place first for the first look."

"First look?" Adam asked as her assistant lifted a flash above her head.

"I haven't seen Gretchen's dress," Drew explained.

"Okay, so yeah," Alicia said, clearly perturbed by the explanation and interruption. "Put your hands on your bow tie, like you're adjusting it...good...look down to your right...good...." The camera went *click, click, click*. Alicia made him pretend to tie his shoes, do up his belt, all of it.

Adam had a hard time believing they'd paid money for someone to do this, but he stood silently to the side, as instructed.

"Done," Alicia finally announced. "Let's go outside. Tara, you take them both. I'll go check on Gretchen."

Tara led the way outside, and Adam was thankful for his jacket once they hit the gardens. He followed instructions, kept his brother company, smiled when Drew finally got to turn and see his bride in her wedding gown.

Each event, each minute was captured on camera—and brought Adam closer to when he'd have to see Janey.

She came out with a handful of other women, all of them wearing pale pink bridesmaid dresses. She wore pearls around her neck and diamonds in her ears, and her hair swept up on top of her head like a princess.

He couldn't breathe. And he absolutely couldn't look away. She caught him staring, and he didn't even care. The pull that had been between them since he'd confessed his feelings to her seemed to tug until he couldn't resist taking a step toward her.

He felt the weight of all the female eyes in the near vicinity, but he was used to them. Janey didn't look away from him either, and it was like he'd parted the Red Sea as the other bridesmaids flowed around him until he was face-to-face with her.

The woman he loved.

He didn't say anything. His emotions stormed through

his chest, but everything else around him had gone quiet, still.

Someone called his name, but he ignored it easily, like swatting away a fly.

"They want you," Janey said quietly, a flush staining her tanned cheeks.

Did she want him too?

Why couldn't he say anything?

"You better go. Everyone's staring."

"Adam?" Drew arrived at his side and put his hand on Adam's shoulder. "Come on, Chief. Alicia only has about twenty minutes to get these pictures done." He glanced at Janey. "Hi, Janey."

"You look so handsome, Drew." Her face bloomed with a smile, and she ducked her head, tucking a hair that wasn't there out of old habit. "You too, Chief."

"Come on," Drew said. "You can talk to her later, when I'm not paying for it." He turned, and Adam looked at Janey for one more moment. His beautiful, wonderful Janey.

She linked her arm through his and gently turned him around. "I think he's going to hurt you if you don't fall into line," she said. "He's stressed. So let's make it easy for him, okay?"

He could listen to the magical, musical sound of her voice all day. Her words bounced around inside his mind and he managed to listen to the photographer enough to stand where she wanted him, look at the camera, put his hand in his pocket with the thumb out.

Let's make it easy for him.

Was that what she was doing? Being nice to him because it was easier than trying to avoid him?

For some reason that made him angrier, not more hopeful that they could get back together. Sure, his arm felt like she'd shocked it with her bare hands, even through his suit coat sleeve.

"Done," Alicia announced. "Thanks, everyone."

"We have a light lunch for all of you in the conference room upstairs," Gretchen called. The women started mincing their way back to the Mansion, their heels sinking into the gravel as they went. Adam hung back with Drew and Gretchen, not wanting to be trapped in a small space with Janey.

"I'm supposed to go get Jess," he said. "So I'll skip lunch if that's okay."

"Be sure to just grab something," Gretchen said. "I got the roast beef with avocado just for you." She looked at him with anxious eyes, and Adam hated that he'd caused problems for her.

"Thank you, Gretchen," he said, his voice catching on the last syllable of her name for a reason he couldn't fathom. His emotions vibrated just underneath his skin, and it didn't feel like an adequate barrier for keeping them contained.

"She'll come around," Drew said.

"She already has," Gretchen said.

"I couldn't say anything to her," Adam said. "I don't know what to say. I feel like I've said it all already."

"Just don't zone out so much," Drew said, waiting for Adam to open the huge doors for him and his bride-to-be.

"Definitely cut back on the zombie staring," Gretchen said, a teasing quality in her voice.

"Was it that bad?" Adam watched his brother's face and saw that yes, it was.

Gretchen laughed. "We all shouted your name simultaneously and you didn't even flinch."

"Great," Adam mumbled. He headed up the steps to collect his sandwich because he really didn't want Gretchen to be upset with him on her wedding day. Then he got out of the Mansion as fast as possible so he wouldn't have another apocalyptic encounter with Janey.

27

Janey finished vacuuming and decided to leave the bathrooms for another day. Her back ached from the five-mile climb she'd done in the park the day before. That, combined with scrubbing the shower, and the couch and a fistful of ibuprofen were calling her name.

Rain started to fall steadily against the kitchen window as she downed the painkillers and tore a banana off the bunch. Armed with the fruit and a mug of her favorite dark roast coffee, she headed into the living room to put on a movie she'd seen a dozen times before. With any luck, she could doze for an hour or two.

She wouldn't see Jess until evening, when Adam pulled up in his new cruiser and dropped him off. But she wanted to get a few more recipes into the book she'd been putting together on her days off, when Jess wasn't around.

It was a gift for him, and she hoped to be able to present it to him at Adam's birthday dinner. The plans for that had been going great, as Jess had suggested they do it at his house. "I cook for him all the time anyway," he'd said. "I'll just tell him I'm making steak and mac and cheese, and he can sit back and relax."

"You cook for him all the time?"

"Yeah, every weekend," he said. "He cooks during the week, or he buys me a hamburger. It's...nice."

Janey supposed it was nice, and while the fact that Adam cooking for and feeding her son triggered some guilt in her, she didn't want to take it from Jess.

"Besides," she told herself as she shut the blinds so the living room was dark. "If you can pull off this birthday dinner and get him to take you back, he can cook for you too." With that thought in her head, and the soft strains of a romantic movie on the screen, she ate her banana and sipped her coffee.

The wind blew like it had a personal vendetta against the Washington Peninsula, and Janey was glad to be home, tucked under a warm blanket. She wouldn't want to be outside in this gale, which only made the pounding on her front door more upsetting.

She flung the blanket off her legs and darted around the corner, her heart flinging itself against her breastbone.

The knocking came again, not quite as loud but just as urgent.

She strode forward and pulled the door open only to come face-to-face with a dripping wet man.

"Adam." She pressed one hand to her chest as two wet, muddy, and slobbery dogs misseled past her and into the house she'd just cleaned.

"I can't do it," he panted. He wore a pair of black gym shorts that felt to his knee and showed the bright red scar from his recent surgery. His gray T-shirt was plastered to his body by the rain, and water dripped from the ends of his hair.

"Can't do what?" She ignored the slipping and sliding of dog claws on her hard floor. She didn't dare turn to see what they'd done to her house.

"I can't give you up." He blinked at her and wiped his hand down his face. "I just can't do it. Tell me what to do to get you back, and I'll do it."

Of course he would. Janey didn't know what to say—he didn't need to *do* anything—so she backed up and said, "Come in." She waved him forward when he hesitated. "Come on inside. It's freezing out there." The wind whipped the rain horizontally, and though her porch was covered, Adam was still getting sprayed.

He stepped through the door and closed it behind him. Now she had three huge animals dripping all over her floor.

"Janey—"

"Don't," she said. A sigh ripped through her body, and she paced away from him. She hadn't imagined making up with him while he stood in her foyer, dripping wet. She'd fantasized about showing up at his house on his birthday, the cake Jess had made in her hands as she walked through the door wearing a green party dress that complemented her hair and eyes.

But she was wearing a pair of sweats and a ratty navy sweatshirt that fell off her left shoulder clumsily.

She looked at him and wanted to be with him. Wanted him to know. So though her nerves batted around her chest, she said, "I love you. Jess and I were planning this big birthday surprise for you, and he's going to be so upset you ruined it."

Adam blinked, a frown pulling at his eyebrows. "I'm sorry. Did you say you loved me?"

She exhaled a laugh. "Desperately. Madly. Terribly."

He moved with the power and grace of a panther, sweeping her into his arms and pressing his lips to hers. The water from his clothes seeped into hers, but she didn't mind so much, not when he kissed her with so much love and emotion in his touch.

"I love you, too," he said.

She pressed her forehead against his, enjoying the weight of his hands on her hips. She laughed, this time with a little more mirth in the sound. "Come on. I want to show you something."

She took his hand and turned around, stopping in her tracks after only one step. "Oh my goodness. Your dogs—" Janey didn't know how to finish. Mud and water had been splattered on the walls and now ran down. Dozens of footprints marred the floor and she couldn't even imagine what her carpet looked like. Gypsy peeked her sopping, dirty head out of the living room, and a groan issued from Janey's mouth.

"I'll call a maid service." Adam stepped around her and said, "Come on, Gypsy. Get outta there. Fable?"

The husky appeared down the hall, in the kitchen—which at least didn't have fibers on the floor.

"They can go on the back porch," she said. "It's covered."

He towed the golden retriever through the kitchen and out the back door, commanding Fable to follow. The husky did, but reluctantly, and he turned around and pressed his nose right against the glass again, begging to be let back in.

Janey moved to the living room doorway and peeked in. At least Gypsy had stayed on the floor. Adam joined her at her side, wrapping one strong arm around her waist and pulling her against him. The touch made her jump, and a nervous giggle escaped her mouth.

"Sorry." Adam edged away, but Janey cozied right up to him again.

"I've just—I'm not used to you touching me, that's all," she said, smiling up at him. "I like it."

"So are you going to tell me what the problem was?" He shivered, and she stepped away from him.

"Are you working today?"

"I was going to, yeah." He ran his hands through his hair, sending water everywhere. "I can probably call in though."

"I'll drive you home, and you can shower. Then you go on in to work and I'll bring you lunch."

"Lunch in my office? So soon?" He shook his head. "Nah. I'll bring over some of that Thai you like, and then I can check in with the maid."

"You haven't even called anyone."

He unzipped a pocket on the side of his shorts and removed a phone encased in a plastic bag. "I'll do it right now." He stepped away from her to make the call, and Janey rubbed her hands up her arms.

His low voice rumbled through the hallway, and he said, "Great, thanks, Monica," before returning to her. "They're on their way."

"I got scared," she blurted. "I got scared when you got hurt, because I thought maybe I was a curse on the men in my life. Or something." She paused, now that she'd started talking, her heart and mind calming a little.

"I was worried that you had a much more dangerous job than a ferry engineer, and Matt had died. I was sure it was only a matter of time before you had something bad happen to you, something much worse than a broken leg." She clenched her arms around her waist. "I sometimes get really deep inside my head, and I can't see reason."

He nodded as if he understood. But how could he? *She*

didn't even understand her neurosis. "I get it. My job is dangerous sometimes."

The atmosphere between them turned charged, and Janey said, "I'm willing to take the risk to be with you," her voice trembling the slightest bit. She stepped past him to collect her purse and keys from the kitchen counter.

"You really are going to have to explain to Jess why his perfectly planned birthday dinner and birthday cake are now ruined."

"Oh, I don't know." Adam pressed a kiss to her temple. "Maybe we can keep this on the down-low for the next ten days."

~

Curling up with the couch that evening was one of the hardest things Janey had ever done. Not as hard as losing her husband, but tough. Because the man she loved was with her son, and she had to pretend to still be lonely and miserable at home. By herself.

And she still kind of was.

She resisted the urge to text Adam, and instead called her sister. "I have some news for you," Janey singsonged once AnnaBelle had answered.

A shriek came through the line, and Janey yanked the phone away from her ear. "Okay, not a good time for a phone call," she yelled to her sister.

"Bring Harvey's," AnnaBelle called. "We can chat once they've eaten."

Janey chuckled, got herself to her feet, and drove over to the fast food joint that would save her sister from an evening of wanting to tear her hair out. When she arrived at the modest home on the east side of town, Janey could hardly contain her excitement.

She pushed open the door and held it with her hip as a wave of noise rolled over her. "Hey!" she called. "I have chicken fingers and French fries!"

Shouts and footsteps raced toward her, and Janey grinned at her niece and nephew. "This one's for you," she said, handing a colorful bag to Macey. "And this one has extra ranch for you, Henry."

"Aunt Janey!" He practically knocked her to the ground with the exuberance of his hug. "Mom! Aunt Janey brought *fooood!*" He skipped away from her as AnnaBelle came around the corner, her baby on her hip. Both of them looked liked they'd been crying.

"Let me take him." She took the one-year-old from her sister, trading Eli for a bag of food. "Where's Don?" She cooed at the baby and bounced him up and down.

"He has business in Seattle until Friday." AnnaBelle pulled a box of fries out of the bag and plucked two from it. "Mmm." Her eyes rolled back in her head. "You're a lifesaver."

Janey grinned at her sister, almost bursting with her news. She held it in long enough to take Eli into the kitchen and strap him into his highchair. She tore up a few fries and put them on the tray before taking out a piece of chicken and cutting it into chunks.

The other kids had disappeared down the few steps into the living room, where a cartoon blared while they ate. At least they were being quiet. AnnaBelle was too, and Janey's enthusiasm for her renewed relationship with Adam bubbled just beneath her skin.

"So you said you had news?" AnnaBelle asked.

"Oh, it's nothing." Janey waved her hand and bit into a bacon cheeseburger.

That caught AnnaBelle's attention and her darkhaired head cocked to the side. "You're lying." Her eyes glinted in a way that said she'd get the information she wanted, one way or another.

"I made up with Adam," Janey said, unable to keep a straight face while she said it.

AnnaBelle was the one who shrieked this time, launching herself out of her chair and across the room to hug Janey.

They laughed together, and Janey embraced her sister, pure happiness flowing through her.

28

The ten days between when Adam stopped by Janey's drenched, desperate, and determined and his birthday seemed to take a decade to pass. Jess came over every night, and it took every ounce of his willpower to keep the news of his resumed relationship with the boy's mother to himself.

Luckily, Adam had had a lot of patience in the keeping-things-to-himself department.

"So you'll stop by the grocery store tomorrow, right?" Jess asked.

"Yes," Adam said for the fifth time. "All the ingredients for macaroni and cheese. Ribeye steaks. Lots of Diet Coke." He grinned at the boy.

"I'll be here to cook for you," Jess said. "All right?"

Adam sighed, wondering if the boy had noticed anything different about Adam's demeanor the past several days. He'd been sneaking over to see Janey on her days off, and she'd come to his place twice after ten p.m., after Jess had gone to sleep.

The limited contact with her made him grumpy, and he hoped to have his own surprise for Jess tomorrow. Janey had a handmade cookbook for him, a binder she'd put together of all the recipes he'd talked about, with illustrations she'd done herself.

"I haven't been able to read much lately," she'd admitted a couple of nights ago when she'd shown up with the binder in her hands. "Tell me if you think he'll like it."

Adam had marveled at the binder, at Janey's attention to detail, that she knew how much of a choc-o-holic Jess was, as at least half of the recipes in the book were desserts. He'd said, "I have several I can give you that he seems to like."

So he'd copied out all the ones Jess had been using at his house, and Janey said she'd get them added to the binder in time for the birthday dinner the following evening.

Finally, the day arrived. Adam endured bad singing at the station, a delicious birthday cake though it was bought from the grocery store, and a bouquet of black balloons though he wasn't quite forty yet.

"Next year," Sarah said. "This whole place will be draped like the Day of the Dead."

When he pulled into his driveway, Jess had the lights

on inside the house, and the scent of sugar and chocolate greeted him. "Jess?"

"In the kitchen!"

Adam carried the grocery bags in and set them on the clean countertop, taking in scene before him. "Did you make me a birthday cake?" His heart swelled with love for the boy, who stood at the sink, washing his hands.

"It's a surprise," Jess said over his shoulder.

Adam searched for a hint of the surprise, but didn't find even a drop of cake batter or icing anywhere. The pans that had been used lay on the towel next to the sink. Jess turned, wearing a great big smile.

"Happy birthday, Adam." The boy came over and tentatively hugged him.

Surprise bolted through Adam. He grabbed onto Jess and held him tight. "Thanks, Jess." He backed up and held him at arm's length. Looked right into Jess's bright eyes. "I love you, bud. Thanks for bein' here with me on my birthday."

Jess nodded, his chin wobbling and tears splashing his cheeks. "My mom's coming," he blurted. "I'm not supposed to tell you, but I'm really bad at keeping secrets." He sniffed, but the liquids just kept pouring out of every hole in his face.

"I hope you're not mad. She's bringing the ice cream, and she says she loves you too." He swiped madly at his face, still blubbering.

A smile grew on Adam's face, and he started laughing.

Jess managed to get himself under control, and he glared at Adam. "What?"

"Yeah, she told me she loved me a week or so ago when I stopped by her house and begged her to take me back."

Jess blinked, the tears completely gone now. "What?"

"She didn't want to ruin the birthday surprise dinner you two had planned. I went along with it." He started unpacking the groceries. "So are we grilling these steaks tonight?"

"Yes, but...are you saying you guys got back together?"

"Yeah, that's what I'm saying."

"A week or so ago."

"Something like that. It was a Wednesday. I knew she'd be home from work."

"I knew I heard her sneaking out at night!" Jess scoffed. "You guys will never be able to ground me for sneaking out to go see the girl I like."

"Nice try," Adam said. "You leave the house after dark to go see Dixie, and I'll drive around in my cruiser and tell everyone over the loud speaker."

"You wouldn't dare." Jess looked horrified, and he reached for a package of macaroni noodles with a little too much force. "Besides, I'm over Dixie."

Adam laughed and pulled down the salt and pepper shakers so Jess could season the steaks. "Right. Just like I was *totally* over your mom after she broke up with me."

He met Jess's eye and they burst out laughing. "So, I have one more secret...."

Jess shook his head. "No. No way. I can't keep secrets."

"Just for a couple of hours." He reached up to the top of the refrigerator and pulled down a dark blue velvet box. "I may have bought your mom a ring." He cracked the lid and tilted the box toward Jess. "Do you think she'll like it?"

Jess goggled at the ring. "Uh, yeah. I think she's going to like that."

"I was thinking of asking her to marry me tonight, after cake and ice cream. You wanna help with that?"

A devilish glint entered the boy's eyes. "Yeah. I wanna help with that."

A moment later, his doorbell sang and Adam practically jumped out of his skin in his haste to put the ring box back where no one could see it. "Quick plan. Get her out of the room before we do the cake. I'll get the ring in it somehow."

"It's not that kind of cake," Jess hissed.

Adam paused, his eyes flickering to the front door. "What do you mean?"

"I mean, it has to be sliced," Jess said. "How are you going to make sure the ring is in her piece without smashing it?"

The doorbell sounded again, and he yelled, "Just a second!" his mind whirring. "I have no idea how to do this. Maybe I just should answer the door with the diamond in my hand."

Jess shook his head. "Nope. That's lame. Stay here." He shook himself they way Gypsy did when she was trying to get the water off her hair. "Game time."

He strode away, leaving Adam to wonder what was lame about answering the door with a diamond in his hand.

"Mom!" Jess exclaimed in a falsely bright voice. "What are you doing here?"

Adam heard the lighter, more feminine lilt of Janey's voice, and then Jess said in an overly loud voice, "Yes, it is his birthday."

Adam supposed that was his cue to come out and pretend like he and Janey hadn't shared a kiss just last night. He did, the sight of Jess and Janey framed in his doorway one he wanted to hold in his mind's eye for a long time.

"Happy birthday," Janey said, her face radiant with happiness. "But this present is actually for you, Jess." She handed him the beautifully wrapped gift. "It's from both of us."

"It's from your mother," Adam said, lifting his arm and securing Janey against his side. "I told him we got back together a few days ago."

"Oh, you did, huh?"

"He may have blurted out that you were coming over."

He shared a smile with Jess. "Seems like neither one of us are that great at keeping secrets."

She looked back and forth between the two of them. "I'm always going to be the last to know, aren't I?"

Adam shrugged and Jess said, "He has something for you on top of the fridge."

"Hey," Adam said, his heart suddenly fluttering in the back of his throat. "It's my birthday. Doesn't anyone have any gifts for me?"

"You have something for me on top of your fridge?"

"It's for *later*." He said the last word through clenched teeth, glaring at Jess. "Why don't you open yours first, Jess? Then we can start on dinner."

Jess complied, peeling back the blue and gray paper to reveal the binder Adam had seen earlier. He looked at his mom, hope shining in his dark eyes. Adam had seen that look so many times before, usually right before Matt said something funny—or got them both in a heap of mischief.

His heart tugged, and he couldn't believe he was going to get to be this boy's father.

Jess opened the front cover and sucked in a breath. "Mom, did you draw these pictures?"

She moved over to him and put her arm around his shoulders. "I did."

He traced one finger down the page Adam couldn't see. "You said Dad taught you how to draw."

"He did."

Adam didn't know that, and he felt like an intruder in this moment, watching Janey and her son talk about Matt.

"Hey, this is your mom's chocolate pie recipe." He looked up at Adam, his eyes shining with disbelief.

"I told you it was from both of us." Janey beamed at Adam, welcoming him to their moment, to their family. Adam stepped stepped forward, took Janey's hand, and pointed to the SIDES tab.

"Check there."

Jess flipped to that section of the cook book, his eyes travelling past the macaroni and cheese recipe he had memorized. He pulled in a breath and gave a triumphant yell. "The macaroni salad!" He barreled into Adam and hugged him tight.

"All right." Adam cleared his throat. "I'm starving and we haven't even started dinner yet." He gave Jess a look that said, *Not another word about the box on top of the refrigerator.*

They worked together, the three of them, in the kitchen as Jess grilled and Adam put together the mac and cheese. Janey rummaged around in the fridge and came up with a bagged salad to add something green to the meal.

They ate, and laughed, and Adam couldn't believe this could possibly be his reality in the near future. He'd fantasized about it so many times, and those dreams hadn't been close to how wonderful this actually was.

"Time for cake," Jess announced. He jumped from the table and ran onto the back deck.

"You've had the cake out there?" Adam eyed the door as it swung open.

"It's not raining," Jess called. A few moments later he filled the doorway, a gorgeous, three-tiered cake in his hands. "Happy birthday to you...."

Janey joined in, her face a picture of pure delight. Adam hated all the attention, but he grinned through the song, blew out the candles, and stared at the cake. It had rich, chocolate frosting in perfect peaks, with a toy police cruiser right in the middle.

"Jess, this is awesome." He looked up him, those emotions pushing against his composure. "How did you learn how to do this?"

"Internet videos," he said. "Mom, where's that ice cream?"

She jumped to her feet, her face a perfect mask of panic. "I left it in the Jeep." She headed for the front door.

Jess exchanged a glance with Adam and hissed, "I'll stall her. Don't mess up the cake too badly."

Adam waited until the front door clicked closed, and then he sprang into action. He collected the ring from the velvet box and grabbed a sharp knife from the block beside the stove. He sliced a line in the cake near the back of the cruiser and pressed the ring into the space. He re-peaked the frosting and had just wiped the knife when he heard Jess and Janey return.

"I'm sorry, Jess," she said.

Adam rounded the corner, the knife still in his hand. Clearly, he would be cutting and serving the cake. "Melted?" he asked.

"Melted." She set the two containers of ice cream on the counter. "We might be able to get some more solid parts from the middle."

"It's fine, Mom," Jess said. "I'll get the plates." He moved around Adam's house with ease, and Adam cut the first slice—right near the rear of the cruiser. He slipped it onto the plate and nudged it toward Janey. Jess put a fork on the plate, and Janey picked it up.

She waited while Adam cut two more slices, and only when Adam and Jess both had cake did she dip the fork into her piece. Adam worked hard not to stare at her, but she didn't lift her fork to her mouth the way he and Jess did.

"Adam...." She drew his name out, her voice made more of air than anything else.

The scraping of the fork against the plate made him shiver, and he looked at his diamond engagement ring smeared with chocolate frosting.

"What is this?"

"Oh," he said. "That's where that went." He reached for the ring and licked off the frosting. "I was worried I'd lost it."

He looked up and met Janey's eye. Hers were glassy, bright with unshed tears, and Adam swallowed hard.

"So since I love you, and you love me, I was wondering if you wanted to get married?" He twirled the ring in his fingers, finding it a bit sticky. "I want to take care of you and Jess, and I think I'd be pretty good at it." He met Jess's eye. "Did you tell your mom about me?"

His face brightened. "No, I didn't. I kept a secret!" He looked so gleeful that he'd actually kept a secret.

"What secret?" Janey whispered.

"I've been leaving things on your porch for years," Adam said. "Matt asked me to look after you two if anything should happen to him, and well, I took it literally." He shrugged, hoping Janey wouldn't make a big deal about this.

"You're our anonymous angel?" Her eyebrows stretched upward.

"Yes." He held her gaze and lifted the ring. "I still haven't heard a yes from you."

She looked at Jess. She looked at the ring. She looked at Adam.

She opened her mouth, and said, "Yes."

SIX MONTHS LATER

"Mom, come away from the window."

Janey watched as her oldest sister, JoJo, lovingly guided their mother away from the glass through which she'd been staring for a while. JoJo exchanged a glance with AnnaBelle, but neither of them looked at Janey.

Everything had to be perfect for today. Why AnnaBelle had kept saying that, Janey didn't know. She'd already had her big wedding when she'd married Matt. Adam claimed not to care about the grandeur of such things, but AnnaBelle had insisted.

"He's the *Chief* of *Police*. He's been single for thirty-nine years. This is huge for our town."

Janey fiddled with a flower Gretchen had weaved into her hair. She had enjoyed herself as they visited Wedding Row and hired a photographer, who captured Adam in his uniform perfectly. Their engagements included an array of pictures on the beach he loved and then in the downtown park where they'd both spent countless hours as both adults and children.

She'd liked designing the announcements and using police blue, and silver, and gold—their wedding colors. Jess had selected the menu and gone with Adam to the caterer. It seemed that if there was food involved, the two of them wanted to do it together.

She was thrilled they got along so great, and she smiled at herself in the full-length mirror. Behind her, JoJo got their mother seated in an armchair and returned to Maya to finish her makeup.

JoJo lived in Victoria, just across the waterway, and she did permanent makeup, lashes, and eyebrow microblading from a studio in her home. When Janey had called her and asked her to do all the makeup for the bridesmaids, JoJo had screeched in excitement.

Sami, Janey's second-oldest sister, burst into the room. "You should see the park." She leaned against the door, her face aglow with happiness. "I've never seen anything like it. Whoever Sarah is, she deserves a medal. And a raise."

"She's Adam's secretary," Janey said. "And yes, she's a genius." With Janey's mother...not as helpful as she used to be, Janey had consulted with Adam's mom and Sarah about all the wedding preparations. Sarah had worked with Adam for almost two decades, and she wept whenever Janey came into the station. Adam said she'd been crying every time he came to work too.

"Drew just texted," Gretchen announced. "Adam's on his way downstairs now." They'd set up in the storage rooms above her flower shop, because it overlooked the park and provided easy access to parking. Janey had left all the décor to Sarah and Donna, all of the wedding luncheon plans to Adam and Jess. She'd focused on her wedding dress, the announcements, and her bridesmaids.

She turned and found her three sisters and her mother present. So her father wouldn't be able to walk her down the aisle this time. She had Jess instead. Her heart felt too full, and her emotions choked her.

Besides her family, Maya and Gretchen completed her entourage. They'd all been by her side for so long, and she was sure she hadn't properly thanked them. Tears brimmed and JoJo hissed.

"Don't you dare cry before the formal pictures," she said. "And definitely not before kissing him."

Janey's lower lip shook, but she managed to keep the tears contained. She didn't want to create more work for JoJo, who focused on Maya like she'd never get her makeup done properly.

"Adam is in position," Gretchen announced.

"I'm almost done," JoJo said, swiping and swooshing a brush in a circular pattern over Maya's face. "Okay. Finished."

Maya opened her eyes and stood, her silver dress glinting in the sunlight coming in through the window.

Janey had been laced into her wedding gown for a half an hour, and she lifted the skirt to make sure it didn't get too dirty before the I-do's were said. Her heart beat fast in her chest.

"There were no first looks when Matt and I got married," she said as she carefully stepped down the stairs.

"It's easy," Gretchen said. "You stand where Alicia tells you, and you wait for Adam to turn around. She's telling him what to do right now. He's the one doing all the work." She held the back door of the flower shop open so Janey could step into the alley. "You just stand there and look beautiful."

Janey smiled at her and let her gaze wander across the street. Blue balloons in every shade drifted lazily back and forth with the lilt of the air currents. A huge arch had been made of silver, white, and navy blue balloons—their altar.

She couldn't see Adam or Alicia, and her heart *ba-bumped* in a strange cadence.

"This way." Gretchen led the ladies across the street and into the park. Past the fountain and away from where the festivals had their food booths set up. A grove of trees sat just ahead, and Janey finally saw Adam in all his police uniform glory, his brother brushing something from his shoulder.

The Day He Stopped In

Alicia completed the trio, and she was indeed instructing Adam in something.

Drew looked at his phone and then over his shoulder, said something to Alicia, and came toward them. Alicia followed a moment later. Adam remained standing right where he was, tall and broad, with a new haircut.

"Where's Jess?" she asked when Drew got within earshot.

"He's with Joel," Drew said. "They'll be over in a few minutes. Right now, we just need you and Adam." He smiled at her in a soft, brotherly way, and Janey returned the gesture.

"Thanks for taking care of him," she said.

"Yeah, of course." He turned toward Alicia, who started giving directions for how Janey should stand, and where, and if she should have the bouquet or not.

When she was finally ready, she turned back to Adam, who waited only ten paces away. The desire to look into his eyes, kiss his lips, almost overwhelmed Janey, and she couldn't wipe the smile from her face.

"All right, Adam," Alicia called.

Adam turned around and walked slowly toward Janey, drinking her in with every step.

"Smile!" Alicia said, and Adam complied.

Janey giggled, and though Alicia yelled, "Slowly, Adam. Slowly," as her camera went *click, click, click*, Adam practically ran the last few steps and swept her into his arms.

They laughed together, and he set her back onto her feet. "Wow, you're beautiful." He inhaled slowly as he dipped his head toward her.

"Good," Alicia said. "Almost a kiss. Not quite."

He leaned down, his mouth a breath from hers. *Clickety-click*. Janey touched her lips to his, unable to resist.

The kiss only lasted a moment, and he stepped back, holding both of her hands. "Beautiful dress."

"One arm around her," Alicia called. "Pull her right into you, Chief. Yeah, like that. Janey, push that hip out."

She took the picture and lowered her camera. "All right. Best man and maid of honor."

∽

Two hours later, Janey fussed over Jess's bow tie, though it was absolutely perfect.

"Mom." He brushed her hands away. "It's fine."

"I'm so nervous," she said.

"Why?" He looked at her, genuinely confused. "It's *Adam*, Mom."

She glanced from the canopy where she and Jess waited toward the crowd that had gathered for the wedding. Adam had literally invited the whole town. As Chief of Police, he'd felt like he had to. And a lot of people had come. She could barely see his shoulders near the balloon arch, and everything seemed about ready.

"When you get married, you'll understand." She gazed

at her son. "Are you ready for this? Lots of changes ahead."

He shrugged, some of his surly teenage behavior in the movement. "It's fine."

"Your bedroom is bigger." They were moving in with Adam, as his house was bigger, had a better yard for the dogs, and sat closer to the beach he loved so much.

Judge Young, one of Adam's acquaintances on the City Council, emerged from under the balloon arch, and Janey's mouth went dry. "It's time."

Jess linked his arm through hers and smiled at her. "I'm glad you're marrying him, Mom."

"Me too, Jess. Me too."

The wedding march started, piped into the park by the town's amplification system tethered to the street lamps and park lights. A long, black carpet had been laid as an aisle between the rows and rows of chairs.

Janey supposed she should be used to all the people staring at her by now, but the weight of all those eyes still got to her. She hoped she wouldn't trip, and she kept a tight grip on Jess's arm.

He delivered her to Adam, who gave Jess a fist bump before twining his fingers between Janey's. "My love," he whispered before facing the judge.

Janey had never felt so cherished by such simple words. But when Adam said he loved her, Janey knew it was true. Love and joy seeped through her, and the warmth from Adam's body beside hers made everything in the world absolutely right.

When it was her turn to say yes, she said it loud and clear, hoping the person in the very back row would be able to hear her. When Adam said it, his voice caught on the S-sound, and she squeezed his hand.

"You may kiss your wife," Judge Young said, and Adam bent her over, a twinkle of laughter in his eyes.

"I love you," he whispered, his lips only millimeters from hers.

"I love you too."

He kissed her, and Janey didn't care if the time she'd had with him was all she got. Every second had been precious, and while she hoped for many, many more, she felt lucky to have gotten what she already had.

"Mom," Jess hissed, and Adam finally stopped kissing her. He helped her straighten and he lifted their joined hands in the air to thunderous applause.

Hawthorne Harbor
SECOND CHANCE ROMANCE
the end

SNEAK PEEK! THE DAY HE SAID HELLO
CHAPTER ONE

"Hey, Uno." Bennett Patterson took a moment to bend down and pat the Dalmatian that greeted all the firefighters when they came into work. The dog had been a gift from Fire House Two to Fire House One when their previous dog had passed away.

Bennett had spent a fair bit of time training Uno how to jump into the fire truck, where to ride, and what to do on the job.

Not that they had many of those in Hawthorne Harbor. But hey, Bennett and all the other firefighters were prepared, right down to their canine mascot.

He sighed as he straightened, not quite sure if he was ready for his overnight shift. He did like sleeping at the station, because at least then he wasn't home alone.

Not alone, he thought as he went to put his food in the

fridge. Charles was on tonight too, so he'd cook dinner, and Bennett's mouth was already watering.

And he wasn't really alone at home. He had Gemma, the big, black Labrador retriever to keep him company. He'd gotten the dog when she was a puppy, right after his marriage had dissolved.

Bennett pushed away the thoughts and took a deep breath. This, right here. Fire House One. This was where he belonged, and where he wanted to be, even if the possibility of getting a job more interesting than saving a cat from a hot tin roof was slim to none.

Heck, he probably wouldn't even get to save the cat.

Normally, he didn't mind. He'd work out, and read a little to Uno. The Dalmatian didn't care that Bennett took a little longer on some words as he tried to get his dyslexia to cooperate with his brain. He'd maybe call Jason, his best friend, over at the police station and see if they could go out on a patrol. Something.

Somehow, Bennett would find a way to fill the hours.

"There you are." Charles Hiatt appeared in the kitchen too. "You ready for tonight? I brought ribs and brisket."

Bennett grinned at his fellow firefighter. "Totally ready. Did Melinda make any of that potato salad?"

"As a matter of fact." Charles lifted a blue bowl the size of a watermelon, and Bennett grinned.

Charles opened the fridge and started moving things around inside it to make room of the vat of potato salad. "Did you see the note from the Chief?"

"Nope, I just got here." Bennett wasn't going to let Charles know about his internal pep talk, or the fact that he was bored out of his mind in this job.

It was a job, and one Bennett wanted, despite certain drawbacks.

"Inspection by Monday." Charles shoved the bowl inside and closed the fridge in a hurry, grinning like he'd just solved the problem of childhood hunger.

Bennett groaned. "Inspection?" That meant hours of cleaning the station. Not so much as a single dog hair should be found, and wow, Uno lost *a lot* of hair.

"Oh, come on." Charles grinned and clapped one giant hand on Bennett's shoulder. "It'll give us something to do, at least."

Bennett nodded, already mourning the loss of a lazy afternoon ride in the police cruiser, maybe with enough time to stop down at the beach for a snack.

"You didn't bring Gemma?" Charles looked around as if the dog was simply playing hide and seek.

"I let Nelly have her this time." Bennett turned away from Charles and opened the cupboard where the cleaning supplies were kept.

"That kid." Charles chuckled as he took the broom from its spot in the corner. "You're going to spoil her, and then you'll be sorry."

Bennett shrugged, not really caring if he spoiled the cute five-year-old who lived next door. Her parents loved Gemma too, and this way, everyone got to enjoy the dog and only Bennett had to take care of her. Sort of. The Yardley's would certainly care for Gemma for the next two days until Bennett returned home. It was like they'd come to a joint custody arrangement for the black lab. So what if it had all come about because Nelly-the-five-year-old had the biggest blue eyes on the planet? Blue eyes Bennett hadn't been able to say no to. Her parents either, apparently.

As he wiped and scrubbed, dusted and swept, he listened to Charles hum and then sing. Uno followed them everywhere they went, and Bennett's bad mood quickly moved into something more positive.

"Hey, are you still handy with a hammer?" Charles asked after they'd sat down to lunch.

"Sometimes," Bennett said, looking at his friend. Charles seemed made of shades of brown. His eyes were the darkest, just a step or two below his hair. His skin sat a shade above that.

"Melinda wants to expand our back deck. I told her you might be able to do it."

The prospect of another carpentry project brought a tingle of excitement to Bennett's fingertips. He tried to ignore how *a deck* had lifted his blood pressure.

"I can come look," he said casually. "When we get off tomorrow." He really wanted to go right now. If a call came in—he wasn't holding his breath—it would forward to their cell phones.

"Great."

Chief Harvey walked in, sniffing like he was part bloodhound. "Place smells great, guys. You must've gotten my note."

"Yes, sir," Charles said, practically saluting with his barking voice.

Bennett rolled his eyes and took another bite of potato salad, reasoning that he had a job, friends, a dog, and this delicious salad. He didn't need anything else.

But the void he'd felt in his life these past few months simply wouldn't budge, even when he stuffed himself full of potato salad and then, later, ribs.

～

THE WHITE LIGHT WOKE HIM A SPLIT SECOND BEFORE THE shrill ring of the telephone. Bennett sat up, all his senses on high alert as that blinding light continued to flash and the phone got covered with the sound of an alarm.

"Finally," he said, pulling on his pants, then his fire suit and boots. He grabbed his hat and made it into the truck bay four steps ahead of Charles.

"What's the call?" he asked. "Come on, Uno. Load up."

The Dalmatian jumped into the truck and Bennett followed.

Charles read a meaningless address to Bennett, who though he now lived in Hawthorne Harbor had grown up in Bell Hill. Besides, he didn't know every residential address.

"Neighbor reported flames," Charles said, starting the truck, which roared to life and sent vibrations down Bennett's spine.

The alarm sounded one more time, and then quieted. Charles put the siren on, and they picked up speed as they moved down Main Street toward the north end of town.

Hawthorne Harbor wasn't that big, but it took several turns to get to the address. Bennett's hopes fell when they pulled up and found several people standing on the lawn.

There were no flames to be seen.

No fire.

Bennett got out of the truck anyway, his suit suddenly heavy and ridiculous. Charles went first, as he was the lead on duty that night, and Bennett waited with Uno.

"I saw smoke," a woman said. "And then the bright flash of flames. I didn't know if anyone was home. She just moved in."

"Who lives here?" Charles asked.

"I can't remember her name." The woman's hands clawed at themselves. "I don't see her car, and she hasn't come out."

Just then, the front door to the quaint little cottage opened, and a female figure appeared in the rectangle of light.

Charles said, "Thank you," and moved toward the woman, Bennett in tow.

"Ma'am," he called. "Are you okay?"

"I got the fire out," she said, her voice not quite as appreciative as Bennett would've liked.

He also recognized the voice, from somewhere in his far distant past. He couldn't quite place it immediately, and it seemed like she had a spotlight framing her, because he couldn't see her either.

"Well, we need to check it out," Charles said in his best fatherly tone. Not too condescending. Not too demanding. Just like, *Oh, it's not big deal, but we're here so we'll take a look.*

Bennett needed to work on his tone, as most of what he said ended up sounding like a bark.

"Fine." The woman turned, her long hair swishing in the light, and went back in the house without inviting them in.

Another memory stirred inside Bennett's mind. He'd seen hair like that. Touched it....

"Can't be," he muttered to himself. Jennie Zimmerman had left Hawthorne Harbor two decades ago, vowing never to come back.

He followed Charles into the house, which admittedly, didn't seem like it was even remotely on fire.

"Something just sparked in my kiln," she said irritably. "It was nothing. A few flames for a few seconds. I honestly don't know how anyone saw it."

She folded her arms and stood outside of a doorway. "You can't touch anything."

Charles walked right past her, and she turned her face toward Bennett's.

His breath stuck somewhere behind his lungs, making a choking sound gargle from his throat.

It *was* Jennie Zimmerman, and she was just as blonde, just as blue-eyed, and just as beautiful as she'd been in high school.

She glared at him as if they hadn't gone out several times, as if he hadn't taken her to his senior prom, as if he hadn't been her first kiss.

"Hello, Jennie," he managed to say. He wanted to shout, *Do you remember me? Why are you looking at me like that?*

"Bennett?" Her expression didn't soften. If anything, she cinched her arms tighter around herself.

"Bennett," Charles called, and Bennett held her gaze for one more moment before stepping into the art studio.

It looked less like a place someone could create beautiful work and more like a paint bomb had gone off.

Or a plaster bomb. Probably both. Multiple times.

He couldn't glance from surface to surface fast enough, couldn't absorb all the different mediums in the room—or place the smell that hit him like a sucker punch.

"I mean it," Jennie said, squeezing in behind him. "I'm in the middle of four commissioned pieces, and you can't touch anything."

Charles had bent over a huge contraption in the

corner, and Bennett stepped through the chaos of brushes, wire, boxes of clay, paint, and dozens of other supplies to get to him.

His suit was so bulky, he couldn't help touching the tiniest corner of some things, and Jennie sighed heavily behind him.

He wanted to round on her and let her have it. This place was a fire waiting to happen. One spark from the kiln...she was lucky it hadn't ignited some cleaning fluid or any of the dozens of parchments she had stacked on a table.

"This outlet," Charles indicated it, and Bennett immediately saw the black singe marks.

"Shorted," he said.

"Sparked," Charles confirmed. "Ma'am, you'll have to replace this outlet."

Jennie crammed herself into the tight space with Charles and Bennett, her weight pressing against Bennett's side. He told himself not to take a deep breath of her, not to try to find that underlying scent of flowers and fruit she always had. But he did it anyway.

And beneath the scorching smell, and the industrial powder smell of art supplies, he found it.

A sigh passed through his body, and Bennett wondered if maybe he had room for one more thing in his life.

Then Jennie said, "Still bald, I see," and backed up.

Bennett gave Charles a bit more room too, retreating and blinking at Jennie as he tried to make his brain work.

"I don't know how one goes about becoming un-bald," he said. At least it wasn't a bark. He stroked one gloved hand down his very full beard, which he took great pride in as he couldn't seem to get the top of his head to grow hair.

"Still unhappy to be in Hawthorne Harbor, I see." Bennett saw the punch his words carried as Jennie flinched, her face contorting for a moment before she smoothed it back to normal.

She opened her mouth to say something—another insult, no doubt—and burst into tears instead.

SNEAK PEEK! THE DAY HE SAID HELLO
CHAPTER TWO

Jennie Zimmerman was in fact, not happy to be back in Hawthorne Harbor. And to have Bennett Patterson right there in front of her? A witness to her creative madness. Judging how she'd plugged in her appliances.

And now watching her cry like a fool.

She tried to school her emotions but they'd been on a yo-yo for weeks now.

Months, she thought. Six months, to be exact. Six months *today* since her fiancé had not shown up at the altar, leaving Jennie standing at the end of the aisle, her hand clutching her father's arm, desperately hoping he'd come out any moment.

Well, he hadn't. And Jennie hadn't seen him again at all.

"You really can't plug six things into an outlet meant

for two," the older of the two firemen said. Jennie knew his name; she just couldn't think of it.

He held up the surge protector she'd been using. "That kiln is way more than any of these can take. It needs a special outlet with the right voltage." He wore a very serious look, and when Bennett joined him as a united front against her, Jennie finally seized onto her anger enough to ebb the flow of tears.

"Fine," she said.

"Charles," Bennett said, putting his ridiculously huge hand on his partner's.

The two men exchanged a glance and Charles left with the ruined surge protector. Was he going to bag it for evidence?

She'd gotten the fire out herself. Nothing had been too damaged, and there had been no public threat.

"He'll cut the electricity to your studio until you fix the outlet," Bennett said. He seemed sorry. Sort of. Jennie couldn't really tell. He'd always worn his emotions behind a mask, never letting anyone see how he felt.

But Jennie had figured out how to get him to take that mask off. Say all kinds of things. Reveal how he truly felt, what he thought, all of it.

Yeah, she thought, staring at him. *And then you left without even saying goodbye.*

Her biggest regret so far.

"I don't know how to fix it."

"You call an electrician," he said, starting to step past her.

"Wait." She put her hand on his arm, but the fire suit was way too thick. Still, he paused, looking at her hand and then into her face.

A surge of power seemed to jump from him to her. Or her to him. She again wasn't sure. Jennie was unsure of almost everything these days.

"What?" he asked, his voice soft but teeming against his impatience. At least that hadn't changed about him.

Everything else had, though. He'd grown at least three more inches, and firefighting obviously did a body good, because his shoulders filled out his fire suit spectacularly.

She'd always liked that he was bald, and with the thick, black beard he wore with it? Jennie had trouble swallowing, blinking, breathing.

"Are you okay?" He peered closer at her. "I can call an ambulance."

"I don't need an ambulance."

"There isn't a car out front."

"I don't own a car."

"Did you inhale any smoke?"

She shook her head. "I told you, I got the fire out in seconds. The window was open."

He gave one nod and dropped his gaze to her hand, which still sat on his forearm.

"Aren't you an electrician?" she asked.

Those eyes—dark and dreamy and dangerous to her health—turned sharp and hard.

"I never finished," he said. "Excuse me."

Jennie turned and watched him stride out of her art studio, never looking back once.

Everything inside her caved in, and she slumped against the nearest table. What a night this had turned into.

She'd just come into the studio to get her piece into the kiln. Then she'd been planning to maybe do a little bit of the painting Mabel had asked for.

A huge project, the painting was almost a mural, and Mabel wanted it to fill an entire wall in the west wing she was renovating.

Jennie had been grateful for the work. She'd left her studio in San Francisco after the failed wedding, because Kyle the fiancé was the manager of her space.

She simply couldn't come face-to-face with him every day and stay sane. So while she hadn't wanted to return to her hometown, without a studio, or any other job prospects, she hadn't had much choice.

She left her art behind and went back through the house to the front porch, where the firefighters stood talking to one another.

The crowd on the lawn had dispersed, thankfully, and Jennie asked, "So is there anything else I need to do?"

Both men trained their eyes on her, and Jennie wilted

under Charles's and wanted to bask in the heat from Bennett's.

Heat?

She startled at the thought. She was in no position to start another relationship, and certainly not with the high school flame she'd abandoned over twenty years ago.

Nope. Not happening.

"I've cut power to your studio for now," Charles said. "We can give you the names of some great electricians. They'll get you back up and running once everything is in compliance."

Jennie cringed at the last word. She didn't want to be compliant. Not anymore.

Charles walked away, leaving Bennett to stare at her.

"And you might want to clean that place up a little," he said. "Honestly, Jennie, it looks like a crime scene."

She expected him to laugh, but he didn't. She tried to find a tease in the words, but there wasn't one.

"Oh, I forgot," she said, a measure of sarcasm in her voice. "You're Mister Organized."

He shook his head, finally a small smile gracing that powerful mouth. She willed herself not to think about kissing him, but her memories were too huge, too powerful, to hold back.

"One of us had to be, sweetheart." With those as parting words, he left her standing on the front porch. Her heart dangled from a string inside her chest, nowhere near ready to take on another man. Especially one as gorgeous, as stubborn, and as broken as Bennett Patterson.

~

"What do you mean, your studio is shut down?" Pepper Howard slid a cup of tea across the table to Jennie, then set another one in front of an empty seat. So Callie would be coming.

Pepper ran her fingers through her short, mohawked hair before lifting her coffee to her lips. How anyone drank that stuff, Jennie didn't know.

"By order of the fire marshal," she said. "Or something." She actually had no idea what Charles was. All she knew was that he was powerful enough to shut her down. Bennett wasn't a marshal. She didn't have power in her studio, but her house and Internet worked just fine. So she'd spent some time looking him up.

She knew more about him than she probably should, and she was going to keep that to herself during this impromptu breakfast initiated by Pepper.

"What are you going to do about the pieces?"

"I'll get them done." Jennie waved her hand like she could conjure up a new outlet as easily. "So what are we doing here, Pepper? It's barely eight."

The rest of the crowd seemed to swell in and rush right back out, like waves against the shore. People with nine-to-five jobs, something neither she nor Pepper had.

Callie did, though, and as she huffed and sat, she said, "Whew. There is nowhere to park out there." She glanced at Jennie and then Pepper, a smile lighting up her pretty face. "Is this for me?" She wrapped her fingers around the teacup as if it were winter in Hawthorne Harbor and not the height of the hottest time of the year.

"We're here this early, because I have some news." Pepper fiddled with her hair again, prolonging the moment.

Jennie deliberately didn't take another sip of her tea.

"Oh, go on," Callie said. "You're killing us." She nudged Jennie with her elbow and Jennie nodded solemnly.

She couldn't hold the look long, and broke into a grin. "It's about Hunter, right?"

"We went ring shopping on Wedding Row last night!" Pepper practically yelled the last couple of words, drawing the attention of a couple of men wearing suits and gripping coffee cups like their very lives depended on the caffeine inside.

Callie squealed like a stuck pig, and while Jennie congratulated her friend and laughed and smiled and acted interested in the pictures on Pepper's phone, all she could think was, *Good luck getting down the aisle.*

She settled down first, taking another careful sip of her tea though it was already too cool for her taste.

The door behind her opened, and she glanced toward the men that entered. She almost spit out her tea at the sight of Charles and Bennett—*oh, my Bennett*—walking toward the counter to order.

He wore a pair of jeans that disappeared into a heavy-duty pair of work boots and a T-shirt that said *Hawthorne Harbor Fire Department* splashed across the chest.

The arms needed to be taken out, because wow, the man had biceps for days.

"Are you okay?" Callie's question cut through Jennie's stupor, and she hastily reached for the napkin Pepper had extended toward her.

She wiped the drips of tea from her lips, wondering why her heart had started rapid-firing in her chest in such a strange way.

"Is that Bennett Patterson?" Callie asked, pushing her hair over her shoulder.

"He's off-limits," Pepper said quickly, her eyes landing on Jennie's for a moment.

"Oh?" Callie looked away from the two men putting in their order. "Why? We don't like him?"

Pepper nodded toward Jennie. "One of her exes."

Callie hadn't grown up in town, and she'd had no trouble getting a date—at least according to Pepper, who'd been friends with her for a few years.

Jennie was just barely back in town, and it had been hard enough reopening her friendship with Pepper. She hadn't warmed to Callie as easily as she might have if she'd been more functional, but Jennie knew she definitely didn't want Bennett and Callie to go out.

"Oh, was it bad?" Callie's bright blue eyes searched Jennie's.

"She's still interested in him," Pepper said, making Jennie suck in a tight breath. "So he's off-limits until she figures things out."

"I'm not still interested in him," Jennie hissed as he turned, his to-go cup of coffee clutched in one hand while a large slab of banana bread balanced in the other.

"You've never said as much, but you don't date," Pepper said.

Jennie had a reason for that. Just because she hadn't told anyone—not a single soul—in Hawthorne Harbor what it was didn't make it any less valid.

Bennett's eye caught hers, and he lifted the banana bread as if that meant hello.

Jennie's eyebrows shot up, especially when he started navigating through the tables toward her instead of just going toward the exit after Charles.

"Hey," he said, positioning himself next to her. "Did you get that email I sent over?"

"I haven't had time to look," she said coolly, wondering how she could ever truly look him in the face again. After what she'd done all those years ago, and then after bursting into tears last night.

He didn't seem to carry any of the awkwardness with him that he'd had last night, and his gaze flickered to Pepper and then Callie.

"Well, check when you can," he said. "It's got all the

electrician information." His eyes settled on her again, and the weight of them felt like a load of lead.

"Thanks," she said, barely glancing up. Not enough to truly lock her gaze onto his. If she did...everyone in the coffee shop would knew that yes, she was still interested in him.

"See you later. Hey, Pepper."

"Bennett."

The man walked away, and finally Jennie was able to take a decent breath. The lingering scent of his cologne filled her nostrils, and she wished she'd had the willpower to hold out a little longer.

She lifted her teacup to her lips, ignoring Callie when she said, "I see what you mean, Pepper." She cleared her throat and tossed her hair. "So he's off-limits. Who else looks interesting?"

SNEAK PEEK! THE DAY HE SAID HELLO
CHAPTER THREE

Bennett couldn't stop thinking about Jennie Zimmerman. She'd turned up twice in his life in the past twenty-four hours, and he wondered if maybe it was a sign.

Or something.

He didn't really believe in signs. Didn't spend a lot of time in church, or thinking too hard about things.

When Jennie had left town two days after her high school graduation, Bennett had been...upset. That word seemed to fit as well as any others he could think of.

He and Jennie hadn't been terribly serious, though he was a couple of years older than her and had dated her even after he'd left high school and started into some trade professions.

He hadn't finished his electrician training, but he had

become a master carpenter and a firefighter after she'd left town.

He knew she hadn't liked the small town lifestyle, but he'd been hoping some of their last conversations—about marriage and family and a beach house down the lane from her parents—would turn into reality.

His reality had taken him down a completely different road, and it sounded like Jennie didn't know anything about it.

Why he wanted to get together with her and tell her all about it, he couldn't fathom. She hadn't even been nice last night.

But the tears were a dead giveaway of her stress—her *dis*tress. For the Jennie Zimmerman he'd known growing up never cried. Never.

She disliked coffee, and as he followed the chief around as he inspected every shelf and each tiny space for dust or lint, Bennett liked that at least that hadn't changed about Jennie.

Little had, actually. She still had those aquamarine eyes that pulled at him to come closer, hold tighter, kiss longer. That same long, blonde hair that swished around her waistline. Her love of tea. And Pepper Howard at her side.

He hadn't recognized the other woman at the table, but he didn't much care who she was. Bennett seemed to only have eyes for Jennie—again.

"Looks good, boys," Chief Harvey finally said, and

Bennett breathed a sigh of relief. The ribs had been magnificent last night, and then there was the brief fire scare at Jennie's. And with the cleaning, Bennett's long shift for the month had actually gone quickly.

"Someone here for you," Charles said, and the chief turned. "Oh, for Bennett." Charles ducked back out the door toward the front of the firehouse, while Bennett's imagination went nuts.

Maybe it was Jennie, stopping by to profess how she'd never gotten over him, even after all these years.

He shook his head to clear it. He wasn't even looking for a relationship at the moment. In fact, he'd turned down the last three women who'd asked him out. Best thing about a small town? Word had gotten around that he wouldn't say yes, and the girls had stopped asking completely.

He didn't need a girlfriend. He had Gemma. And Uno. And his friends at the station, one of whom happened to be his boss and was staring at him.

"Are you going to go see who it is?" Chief Harvey asked.

"Yes." Bennett sprang toward the door. "Yes, I am." He stepped into the outer lobby to find old Mabel Magleby standing there.

"Mabel?" he asked, glancing around as if Jennie might be hiding behind the petite woman who had to be close to ninety years old.

"There you are," she said with a definite hint of grumpiness in her tone. "Thought you might be napping."

He chuckled and came around the counter where Charles sat filling out some paperwork from last night's adventure.

"Nope, not napping. What can I help you with?"

"You said you'd come help demolish the west wing."

Demolition of a house or project was almost better than rebuilding it. "Of course. Are you ready for that already? I thought you needed to meet with...someone." He couldn't really remember the details. The older woman had stopped him at the Lavender Festival last month to ask him about doing some work on the Mansion she owned and operated.

He'd had his sights set on the winning lavender brownies and had agreed with her quickly so he could slip away before the treat was all gone.

"I'm ready," she said in a sure voice. Her hands shook the slightest bit. "What's your schedule like?"

"I'm off for the next couple of days," he said, shooting a glance at Charles. "Should I come out tomorrow?"

"Tomorrow's fine." Mabel wore a frown but she patted his hand and shuffled toward the door. "Not too early. I'm old these days and need my beauty sleep." She opened the door and stepped into the evening. Once the door snapped closed again, Bennett let his laugh fly free.

"She's a character," he said to Charles, who laughed with him.

"Yeah." He watched the door for a moment. "Wonder what'll happen to Magleby Mansion when she passes."

Bennett fell silent with the sobering thought. "I don't know. I hadn't thought about it."

"She has no kids," Charles said. "Maybe a neice or nephew will take it over."

"Maybe." Bennett went to get his bag and get ready to go home. "I'm taking Uno for a couple of days, remember?"

"Yep. Got it." Charles didn't look up from his work.

Bennett leashed Uno and grabbed his stuff, loading everyone and everything up in his truck. "Want to run today, boy?" He glanced at the dog like he would answer back.

"No? You're young. Gemma will go, and she's starting to go gray around her mouth." He continued his one-sided conversation with Uno as he drove out of town and toward Bell Hill. He didn't live in town anymore, but on the outskirts of Hawthorne Harbor.

The road held six houses, all on the same side of the street, all facing inland with the lush forests of Washington in front of them.

He pulled into his driveway and let Uno out. The dog sniffed around the front yard, took care of his business, and trotted after Bennett as he went next door to collect Gemma.

A booming bark sounded from the back yard, and

Bennett changed his course to go through the gate instead of to the front door.

Splashing and the sweet scent of sugar filled the air as he unlatched the gate and called, "Nelly? It's Bennett."

In the next three seconds, the little girl appeared, soaked from head to toe with a huge smile on her face. "Bennett! Come see Gemma swim."

"Gemma can't—" But Nelly had run off before Bennett could finish. He grinned and chuckled, not overly enthused about his dog being wet the way Nelly was. Uno hovered at Bennett's side, somehow sensing that if he let Nelly too close, he could end up in the pool too.

Because the Yardley's had a huge swimming pool in their backyard—the above ground kind that required Nelly to navigate a ladder to get in and out—and Gemma was currently paddling her way around it, a huge Labrador smile on her face.

"Oh, wow," Bennett said, stepping up to the pool. "Look at you, Gemma. Look at you swimming."

So maybe his voice strayed into a higher octave. So he loved his dog. Big deal.

Gemma swam over to him and lunged at him to lick his face. Bennett laughed but fell back, not needing sixty pounds of muscly dog splashing him with water.

"Do you have to take him?" Nelly asked.

"It's a her," Bennett said for at least the hundredth time. "And yes, you've had her for two whole days." He bent down to look right into Nelly's blue eyes. "I brought

Uno. You can come play with them in the fields, if you want."

Her whole face lit up. "Can I? I'll ask my mom right now!" She turned to race into the house, but Montana Yardley said, "Not today, Nelly. Remember we're going to Nana's?" before she'd taken more than two steps.

Bennett straightened and waved to Montana. "Hey, there," he said. "Thanks for having Gemma."

"Oh, we love her." Montana wore a big smile to go with the statement, but her clothes said she would not be coming down off the deck. She wore a ribbed black sweater with pearls around her neck, and a pair of black slacks. With heels. Apparently visiting Nana was a *very* serious occasion.

Montana extended her hand to Nelly. "Come on, Nels. You need a bath. We have to leave in an hour."

"I'll get—" Before Bennett could finish, Gemma heaved herself out of the pool, bringing at least twenty gallons of water with her—most of it splashing and soaking Bennett's shoes and pants.

He did not want to shower and change for the second time that day, but his only choice was to laugh and say, "Well, that's one way to get out of the pool."

∽

THE FOLLOWING MORNING—NOT TOO EARLY—BENNETT loaded up the dogs and drove toward the beach and

Magleby Mansion. Uno whined, but if Bennett had wanted to run along the sand with the dalmatian, he should've come a lot earlier. The breeze coming off the water probably would've kept him cool enough, but Bennett liked to run before the sun made it's full appearance for the day, craving that feeling of being the only person in Hawthorne Harbor that was awake.

"We'll go tomorrow," he told Uno. He had to be to work for the afternoon shift, so he'd be able to get in his pre-dawn run then.

Uno gave one last whine and put his front paws on the dashboard as Gemma was hogging the passenger window, her whole body almost hanging outside of the truck.

He pulled into the long driveway that led up to the Mansion, his mind automatically flowing back to the time he'd driven this way, his bride-to-be at his side.

He really thought he'd be with Cynthia forever. They got along great, and she laughed at all his corny jokes, and the first couple of years of their marriage had been fantastic.

He pushed the memories away and pulled right up to the front door, which several ancient hawthorn trees shaded.

The stones looked centuries old, with vines climbing them. Every flower and bush grew exactly right, and Bennett wondered how many gardeners Mabel employed.

She used to take care of the grounds herself, he knew

that. He'd visited the Hawthorne Harbor town museum more times than he wanted to admit.

He let the dogs out and said, "Stay," as he indicated the huge gardens and grassy areas surrounding them. Gemma ran off with Uno, and Bennett turned to face the Mansion. A bicycle leaned against the wall behind the stairs, but it almost looked like it belonged there, sort of a vintage piece.

He climbed the steps and tried the door, finding it open. "Hello?" he called, his voice echoing against the stones inside too.

The Mansion stood three stories tall, and Bennett could see all the way up to the top floor from the magnificent stairwell in the middle of the room.

"Mabel," he tried next, and somewhere within the Mansion a door closed.

"Back here." Her voice reached him, and Bennett moved across the stone floor to find her hurrying from an office.

She smiled at him—an actual smile—and Bennett returned it. "I hope it's not too early."

"Oh, pish posh. I've been up for hours."

Of course she had. Bennett simply kept his smile in place and tucked his hands in his pockets while he waited for her to tell him what to do.

"So I'm doing a major renovation on the west wing on the second and third floors." Mabel moved toward the staircase, getting a very firm hold on the banister before she lifted her foot to climb.

Bennett wanted to grab onto her to keep her steady, but he wasn't sure she'd appreciate it. He'd heard her say "I'm old, not dead," to more than one person who'd offered their help during festivals and around town.

So he simply positioned himself behind her so he could catch her should she fall.

Painstaking step by painstaking step, they finally reached the second floor.

Mabel wheezed a bit and said, "So my artist is here, taking some measurements, but she'll be out of the way in no time."

Bennett had enough time to think *Artist?* before Mabel moved through a doorway and into a section of the Mansion that had certainly seen better days.

"This is Jennifer Zimmerman. I'm sure you guys know each other. Her family lives just down the beach a bit." Mabel looked at Bennett expectantly, but he had no idea what she wanted him to do.

Jennie indeed stood in the room, across from the large windows, a measuring tape in her hand. She wore a pair of cutoff shorts that showed her long, tan legs, and Bennett forgot his own name for a moment.

"Of course I know Bennett," Jennie said, a slip of disdain in her voice. None of it showed on her face, which also didn't hold even a hint of makeup. He loved this natural look of hers, as he'd always thought he'd seen the real her when she didn't cover up her imperfections.

"We dated a bit in high school," she said, her gaze skimming past him again. He really didn't like that she hadn't fully looked at him once since she'd been reintroduced into his life.

"You did?" Mabel's acting skills could certainly use some work as well.

Jennie smiled and shook her head, her long hair wisping a bit out of the topknot she'd tied at the back of her skull. Her shirt was the color of bright lemon rinds, and had little lemons all over it, making her seem like the sun illuminated her face.

"I'm almost done," she said, shaking out the tape measure. "I just can't seem to get the length. I'm not sure my tape measure is long enough."

"Bennett can help you," Mabel said, and Bennett sprang into action. He wondered how long he'd been standing there staring, wondering if he could somehow get Jennie to stay while he worked, talk to him the way she used to, and then take her to dinner.

Not going to happen, he told himself. After all, she wouldn't even *look* at him. She wouldn't hang around and chat him up. And going out?

Not going to happen.

But he did hold the end of her tape measure, and move it where she wanted him to, watched her make notes on a clipboard, and let her direct him through a couple more rooms as she took measurements.

"Thanks, Bennett." She bent over a backpack as she slid the clipboard into it. "You really helped speed the process up." She straightened and pushed out her breath, bracing her hands against her back and stretching. Her gaze flicked to his, and he nodded his acknowledgement that she'd thanked him.

"So, what are you doing here?" she asked.

Bennett once again felt like he'd lost an unknown amount of time as he stared at this beautiful woman he thought he'd never see again.

"Oh, Mabel's hired me to do the construction here."

Another woman walked into the room, a tool belt hanging off her hips. Bennett backpedaled quickly. "Well, she's obviously hired Lauren Michaels to do the construction. Hey, Lauren." He practically yelled to the brunette, who smiled and veered toward them.

She was a transplant to Hawthorne Harbor, but she did really fine work, and she'd been the lead general contractor on the new subdivision going in on the northeast edge of town.

Jennie didn't seem like she cared, but she shook Lauren's hand and then finally, *finally*, looked at Bennett.

"So if she's the general contractor, what are you doing here?"

"Demo," he said, wondering where Mabel had gotten to. She'd never said anything about a contract or pay, and he'd need to get those things in line before he just started knocking things down.

"He does a lot more than demo," Lauren said, glancing between the two of them. "He's the best master carpenter in the state."

Pride swelled within Bennett, but he waved his hand at Lauren. "An exaggeration."

Lauren smiled but looked at him evenly. "It's true. My guess is he's here to do the fireplace mantles. All the cabinetry. Anything that Mabel wants crafted from wood." She flipped a few pages on the clipboard she carried. "Yep. She didn't hire me for any of that."

Bennett lifted one shoulder as if to say, *Yep, that's why I'm here.*

Honestly? He hadn't signed or negotiated anything yet. But his fingers practically itched to get working on this beautiful piece of property, and bring new life to it through wood and craft.

"I've been commissioned for five art pieces," Jennie said, and Bennett's smile practically moved into a beam.

"That's great," he said.

Lauren's phone rang and she said, "Excuse me," before moving away and answering it.

Bennett looked at Jennie, glad to find her watching him back. "Carpentry, huh?"

"I guess it's what electrician drop-outs do."

Jennie grinned and shook her head. "And a firefighter. Wow."

He didn't mention the almost-pro baseball career. No need to. No one cared about the almosts in professional sports. "One pays all the bills. The other is just something I really enjoy."

"You always were good with your hands." Jennie gave him a sly smile, and Bennett's heart started jumping around like it had been shocked with electricity.

Was that flirting? Was she *flirting* with him?

"Here's your contract," Mabel said, entering the room, her face slightly flushed. "Wow, there are more stairs here than I remember." She wiped the back of her hand across her forehead and looked at Jennie, who stood there with one hand on her cocked hip.

"Did you get your measurements, dear?"

Jennie startled, tearing her eyes from Bennett. "Yes, ma'am. I'll bring you a sketch of the first piece soon." She started to move away, but Mabel called her back.

"I heard your studio is closed," the older woman said. "Perhaps you'd like to stay and help Bennett with the demolition today. I have a feeling he's going to need all the help he can get."

Bennett may have argued if it was anyone besides Jennie who would be staying. He smiled and looked at Jennie, hoping she'd stay—and thinking he'd somehow gone insane in the past couple of days to even think he had half a chance to try things with her again.

BOOKS IN THE HAWTHORNE HARBOR ROMANCE SERIES

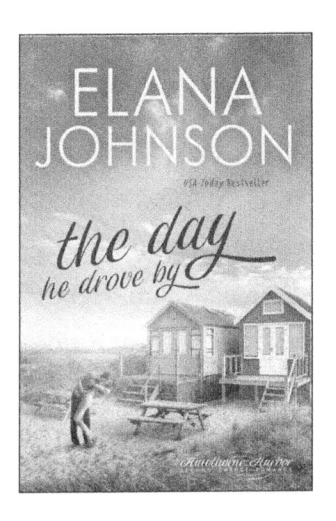

The Day He Drove By (Hawthorne Harbor Second Chance Romance, Book 1): A widowed florist, her ten-year-old daughter, and the paramedic who delivered the girl a decade earlier...

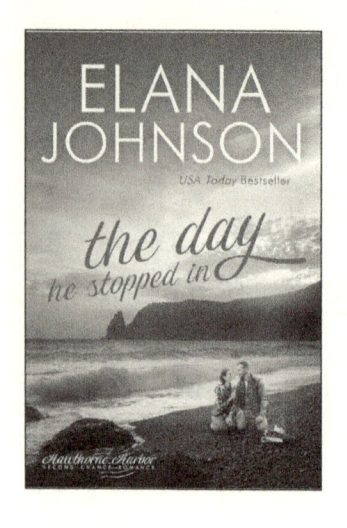

The Day He Stopped In (Hawthorne Harbor Second Chance Romance, Book 2): Janey Germaine is tired of entertaining tourists in Olympic National Park all day and trying to keep her twelve-year-old son occupied at night. When longtime friend and the Chief of Police, Adam Herrin, offers to take the boy on a ride-along one fall evening, Janey starts to see him in a different light. Do they have the courage to take their relationship out of the friend zone?

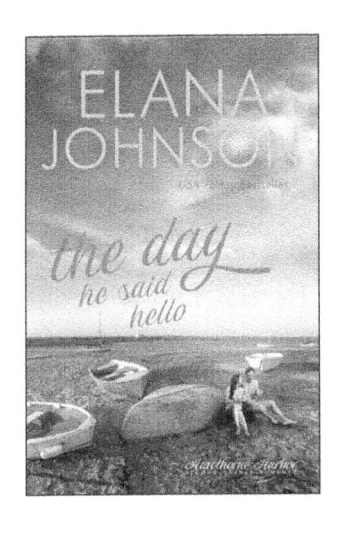

The Day He Said Hello (Hawthorne Harbor Second Chance Romance, Book 3): Bennett Patterson is content with his boring firefighting job and his big great dane...until he comes face-toface with his high school girlfriend, Jennie Zimmerman, who swore she'd never return to Hawthorne Harbor. Can they rekindle their old flame? Or will their opposite personalities keep them apart?

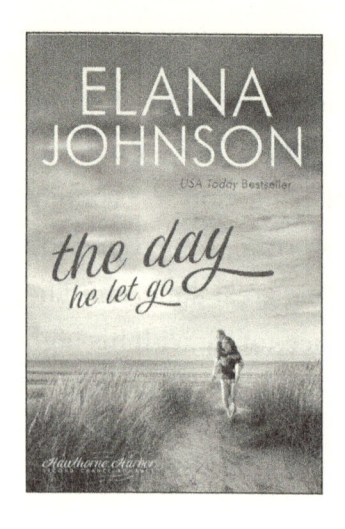

The Day He Let Go (Hawthorne Harbor Second Chance Romance, Book 4): Trent Baker is ready for another relationship, and he's hopeful he can find someone who wants him and to be a mother to his son. Lauren Michaels runs her own general contract company, and she's never thought she has a maternal bone in her body. But when she gets a second chance with the handsome K9 cop who blew her off when she first came to town, she can't say no... Can Trent and Lauren make their differences into strengths and build a family?

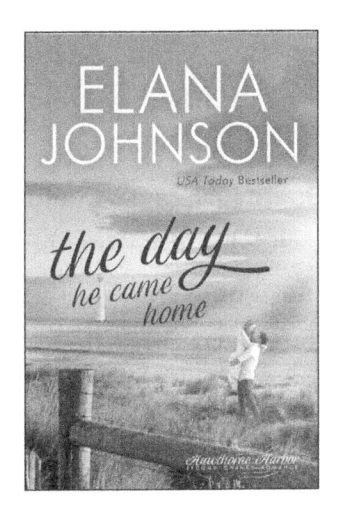

The Day He Came Home (Hawthorne Harbor Second Chance Romance, Book 5): A wounded Marine returns to Hawthorne Harbor years after the woman he was married to for exactly one week before she got an annulment...and then a baby nine months later. Can Hunter and Alice make a family out of past heartache?

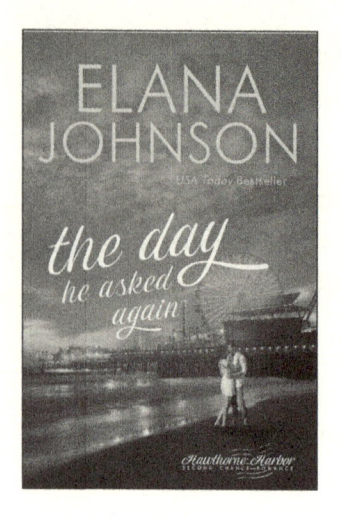

The Day He Asked Again (Hawthorne Harbor Second Chance Romance, Book 6): A Coast Guard captain would rather spend his time on the sea...unless he's with the woman he's been crushing on for months. Can Brooklynn and Dave make their second chance stick?

BOOKS IN THE GETAWAY BAY BILLIONAIRE ROMANCE SERIES

The Billionaire's Enemy (Book 1): A local island B&B owner hates the swanky high-rise hotel down the beach...but not the billionaire who owns it. Can she deal with strange summer weather, tourists, and falling in love?

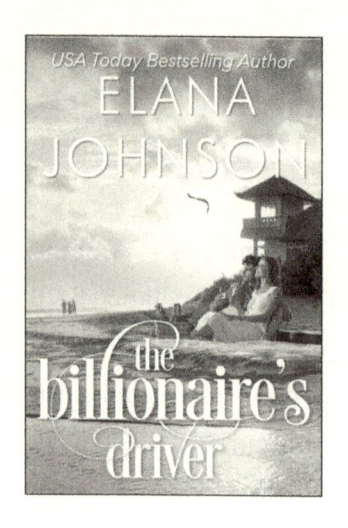

The Billionaire's Driver (Book 2): A car service owner who's been driving the billionaire pineapple plantation owner for years finally gives him a birthday gift that opens his eyes to see her, the woman who's literally been right in front of him all this time. Can he open his heart to the possibility of true love?

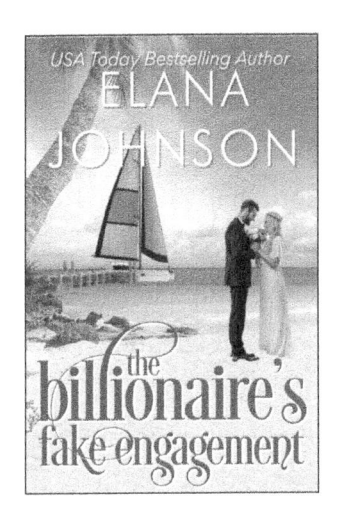

The Billionaire's Fake Engagement (Book 3): A former poker player turned beach bum billionaire needs a date to a hospital gala, so he asks the beach yoga instructor his dog can't seem to stay away from. At the event, they get "engaged" to deter her former boyfriend from pursuing her. Can he move his fake fiancée into a real relationship?

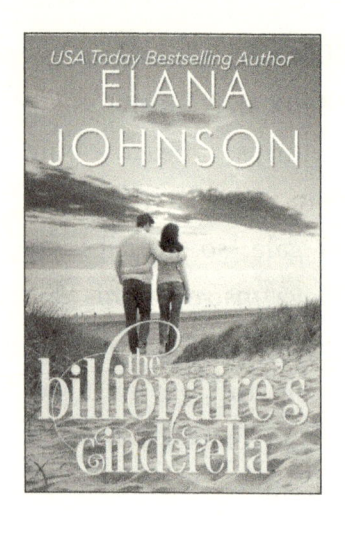

The Billionaire's Cinderella (Book 4): The owner of a beach-side drink stand has taken more bad advice from rich men than humanly possible, which requires her to take a second job cleaning the home of a billionaire and global diamond mine owner. Can she put aside her preconceptions about rich men and make a relationship with him work?

The Billionaire's Bodyguard (Book 5): Women can be rich too...and this female billionaire can usually take care of herself just fine, thank you very much. But she has no defense against her past...or the gorgeous man she hires to protect her from it. He's her bodyguard, not her boyfriend. Will she be able to keep those two B-words separate or will she take her second chance to get her tropical happily-ever-after?

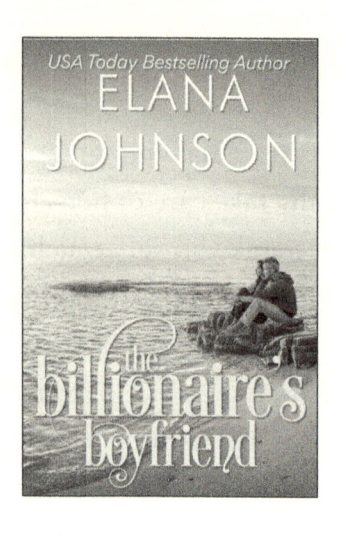

The Billionaire's Boyfriend (Book 6): Can a closet organizer fit herself into a single father's hectic life? Or will this female billionaire choose work over love...again?

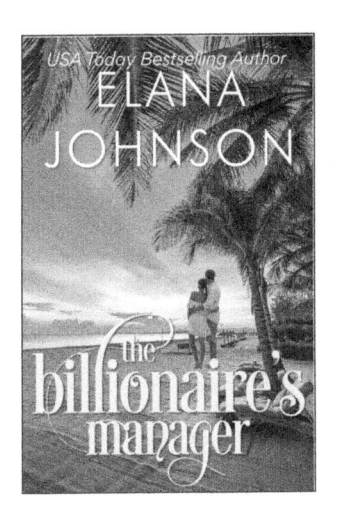

The Billionaire's Manager (Book 7): A billionaire who has a love affair with his job, his new bank manager, and how they bravely navigate the island of Getaway Bay...and their own ideas about each other.

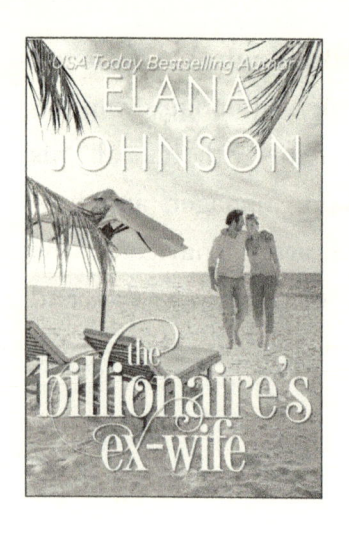

The Billionaire's Ex-Wife (Book 8): A silver fox, a dating app, and the mistaken identity that brings this billionaire faceto-face with his ex-wife...

BOOKS IN THE BRIDES & BEACHES ROMANCE SERIES

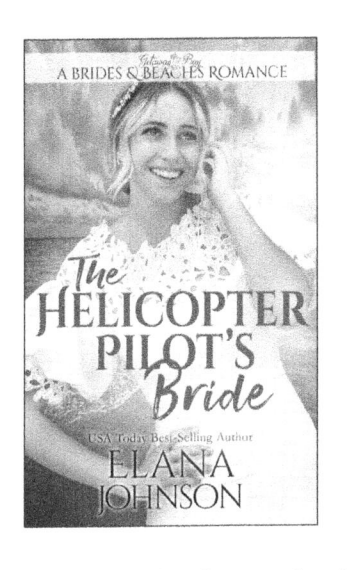

The Helicopter Pilot's Bride (Book 1): Charlotte Madsen's whole world came crashing down six months ago with the words, "I met someone else." Her marriage of eleven years dissolved, and she left one island on the east coast for the island of Getaway Bay. She was not expecting a tall, handsome man to be flat on his back under the kitchen sink when she arrives at the supposedly abandoned house. But former Air Force pilot, Dawson Dane, has a charming devil-may-care personality, and Charlotte could use some happiness in her life.

Can Charlotte navigate the healing process to find love again?

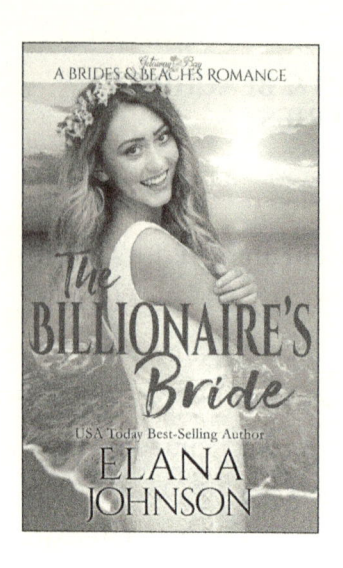

The Billionaire's Bride (Book 2): Two best friends, their hasty agreement, and the fake engagement that has the island of Getaway Bay in a tailspin...

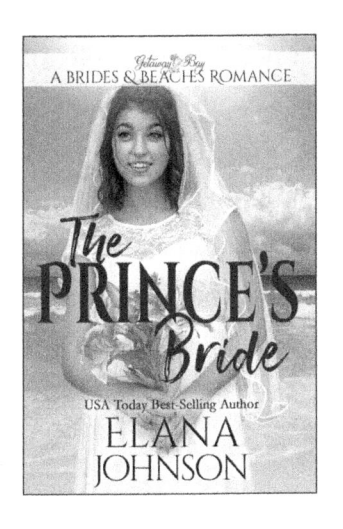

The Prince's Bride (Book 3): She's a synchronized swimmer looking to make some extra cash. He's a prince in hiding. When they meet in the "empty" mansion she's supposed to be housesitting, sparks fly. Can Noah and Zara stop arguing long enough to realize their feelings for each other might be romantic?

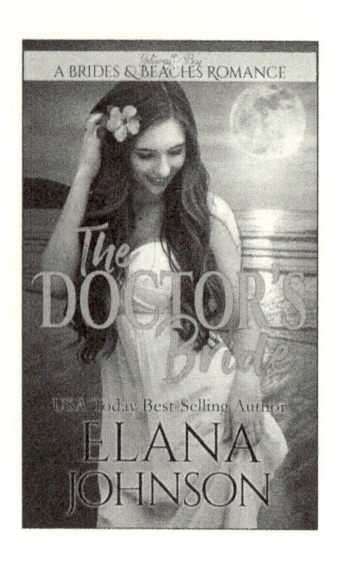

The Doctor's Bride (Book 4): A doctor, a wedding planner, and a flat tire... Can Shannon and Jeremiah make a love connection when they work next door to each other?

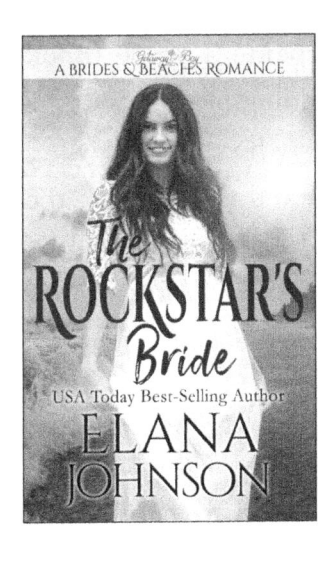

The Rockstar's Bride (Book 5): Riley finds a watch and contacts the owner, only to learn he's the lead singer and guitarist for a hugely popular band. Evan is only on the island of Getaway Bay for a friend's wedding, but he's intrigued by the gorgeous woman who returns his watch. Can they make a relationship work when they're from two different worlds?

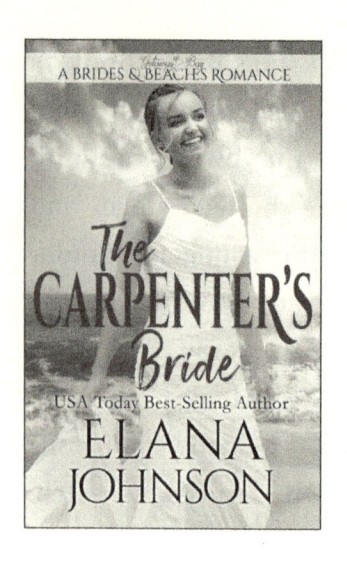

The Carpenter's Bride (Book 6): A wedding planner and the carpenter who's lost his wife... Can Lisa and Cal navigate the mishaps of a relationship in order to find themselves standing at the altar?

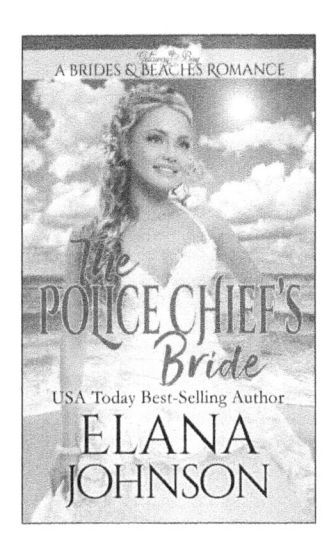

The Police Chief's Bride (Book 7): The Chief of Police and a woman with a restraining order against her... Can Wyatt and Deirdre try for their second chance at love? Or will their pasts keep them apart forever?

BOOKS IN THE STRANDED IN GETAWAY BAY ROMANCE SERIES

Love and Landslides (Book 1): A freak storm has her sliding down the mountain...right into the arms of her ex. As Eden and Holden spend time out in the wilds of Hawaii trying to survive, their old flame is rekindled. But with secrets and old feelings in the way, will Holden be able to take all the broken pieces of his life and put them back together in a way that makes sense? Or will he lose his heart and the reputation of his company because of a single landslide?

Kisses and Killer Whales (Book 2): Friends who ditch her. A pod of killer whales. A limping cruise ship. All reasons Iris finds herself stranded on an deserted island with the handsome Navy SEAL...

Storms and Sentiments (Book 3): He can throw a precision pass, but he's dead in the water in matters of the heart...

Crushes and Cowboys (Book 4): Tired of the dating scene, a cowboy billionaire puts up an Internet ad to find a woman to come out to a deserted island with him to see if they can make a love connection...

BOOKS IN THE CARTER'S COVE ROMANCE SERIES

Boyfriend by Mistake (Book 1): She owns The Heartwood Inn. He needs the land the inn sits on to impress his boss. Neither one of them will give an inch. But will they give each other their hearts?

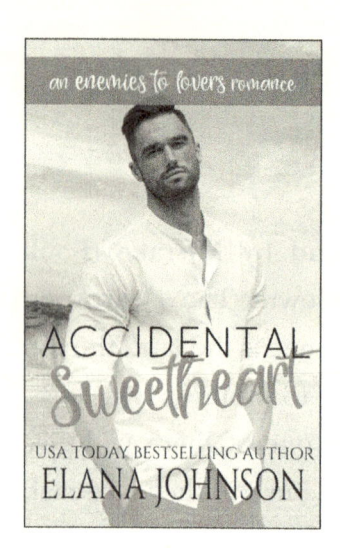

Accidental Sweetheart (Book 2): She's excited to have a neighbor across the hall. He's got secrets he can never tell her. Will Olympia find a way to leave her past where it belongs so she can have a future with Chet?

Bodyguard not Boyfriend (Book 3): She's got a stalker. He's got a loud bark. Can Sheryl tame her bodyguard into a boyfriend?

Not Her Real Fiancé (Book 4): He needs a reason not to go out with a journalist. She'd like a guaranteed date for the summer. They don't get along, so keeping Brad in the not-her-real-fiancé category should be easy for Celeste. Totally easy.

She Loves Him...Not (Book 5): They've been out before, and now they work in the same kitchen at The Heartwood Inn. Gwen isn't interested in getting anything filleted but fish, because Teagan's broken her heart before... Can Teagan and Gwen manage their professional relationship without letting feelings get in the way?

ABOUT ELANA

Elana Johnson is the USA Today bestselling author of dozens of clean and wholesome contemporary romance novels. She lives in Utah, where she mothers two fur babies, taxis her daughter to theater several times a week, and eats a lot of Ferrero Rocher while writing. Find her on her website at elanajohnson.com.

Made in the USA
Las Vegas, NV
11 December 2020